PUT YER ROSARY BEADS AWAY MA

CAHAL DUNNE

Acknowledgements

My sincere thanks to the following for all their helpful
suggestions and encouragement:

Kathleen and Ryan Dunne; Shaun Noon, my step-son; Peter
Dunphy; Sean O Se; Seamus Kennedy; Sarah Breyer; Aimee
Douglas; Diane Byrnes; Don Roos; Kevin Mc Ginty, and
special thanks to my friend Michele Moe.

Cover Design; Shaun Noon, Noon Designs, Pittsburgh
Photo: Archie Carpenter, Pittsburgh

Lover, not just a Wife; Cahal Dunne, Copyright Control
Lucky Child; Cahal Dunne; Warner Brothers Music Sweden
Love is the Answer; Cahal Dunne, Jesse Terry, Copyright
Control
If you could see yourself thru' my eyes; Cahal Dunne, Jesse
Terry , Copyright Control
Peace in my Land; Cahal Dunne, Copyright Control

For a complete listing of all recordings by Cahal Dunne,
please go to: www.cahaldunne.com

cahald@aol.com   Enquiries: Cahal Dunne Music
                 724 449 8821

Anybody who ever played in, or danced to the beat of an Irish showband, has to read this book. Apart from that however, it is a great read in its own right, and should appeal to anyone who likes a story of a young man's dreams and his struggles to make them come true. A universal tale, beautifully chronicled.
Sean O Se, Cork, Ireland

After spending fifty years as a singer/musician in Ireland and the USA, and a radio talk show host on WCWA 1230 AM radio for twenty four years, I can identify with any young person trying to make the big time in music. A musician's life is not all its cracked up to be, and is not as glamorous as it looks. This book is a must read, and a real reality check.
John Connolly, Toledo, Ohio

Put Yer Rosary Beads Away Ma, is a really good story about the ascent of one young man, in his quest for success in music. Many interesting characters, lots of emotion, and a good read! You'll love it!
Diane Byrnes, WEDO Radio
Pittsburgh Pennsylvania

IRISH TERMS AND SLANG
Interpretations, for your reading pleasure

A FIDDLERS'	A damn, couldn't care less
ARSE	Ass
BREAD	Money
BOLLIX	Jerk or idiot. Literally: a bull's testicles
COMPERE	Emcee of a show
COP ON	Figure it out, to 'Wise Up'
CRAIC	Fun
CULCHIE	Condescending name city and town people use to describe country people
DIVIL	Devil, used in a compassionate sense
DIGS	A rented room in a house
DOLE	Unemployment money
DUB	A person born and bred in Dublin
DUNNO'	Don't know
GARDA	A policeman
GOBSHITE	Idiot
GOBSMACKED	Amazed
EEJIT	Idiot
EUROVISION	**Eurovision Song Contest**, televised singing competition; a European/ Middle Eastern predecessor to *American Idol*
FLAT	Apartment
HEAD	Cool name for a musician in the 1970's
HURLEY	An Ash stick similar to a hockey stick

HURLING	The Gaelic game of Hurling is the fastest field game in the world, according to the <u>Guinness Book of Records</u>
IRISH	Gaelic
JANEY	A Dublin term meaning 'Wow!"
JIVE	Irish version of the Jitterbug
KNACKERED	Exhausted
LANGER	Cork term, meaning a jerk
LANGERS	Really drunk
LOSE THE PLOT	Go crazy, Unravel
PUNTERS	Crowd
QUID	A pound in Irish money
RI'	Right
RTE	The National Radio and Television Network, Dublin
"SCA"	Scandal, gossip
SEISIUN	An impromptu gathering of musicians playing traditional music
SLAG	Tease
SLAINTE	Cheers, To Your Health
SUSS IT OUT	Check it out
TENNER	Ten Irish Pounds, money
TOWNIES	People who reside in towns
TRAD. SONGS	Traditional Celtic/Irish music, usually played informally in pubs
UPPEROSITY	Delusions of grandeur
ULSTER	Northern Ireland
YA	You, singular
YEZ, YOUSE	Dublin slang, plural of Ya
WANKER	Irish and English word for a jerk

PROLOGUE

Billy is belting out a Celtic Rock classic at stepson Johnny's wedding. Everybody is having a ball: bridesmaids, groomsmen, aunts, uncles, friends all enjoying the craic [fun] at this very Irish-American wedding. Billy is in rare form, singing with his favorite Celtic Rock band he's hired for the wedding. Even tho' he's in his mid-fifties, he can still belt it out with the best of 'em.

He goes over to the bar and orders a pint. A trio of young men, all friends of his son, see him and join him. Joe screams over the music, "Hey Mr. Golden, how are you?"

"Hiya Joe, how'rya doin'? Are ya finished college yet?"

"One more year to go, this is Josh and Brad, they're friends of Liam. Hey guys, Mr. Golden had a band in Ireland."

Brad shakes his hand, "What sort of stuff did you play?"

Billy points to the band, "That stuff..... BEFORE they called it Paddy Rock, or Celtic Rock or whatever."

"You played that stuff back then? I thought that was new"

"Nah," says Billy proudly, "we were doing it in 1978,…. God it feels like 1878,"….

Billy sees Brad getting a text and smiles, "Yea, way way before texting, cell phones, the internet, credit cards, a long time ago."

"So what brought you to America?" asks Josh.

Billy smiles wistfully…..

Author's note:

The next fifteen pages are a brief history of Ireland. It gives the historical context of the events influencing all parents, teachers and my generation growing up. If you wish to skip this, please go to page 16.

CHAPTER 1

Through the centuries, the land Hibernia, as the Romans called it, was attacked by the Vikings, the Normans [Anglo/French] and of course the English. After a few generations, these invaders, except the English, assimilated into the Irish ways and language, and, 'became more Irish than the Irish themselves.'

In my opinion, Ireland is one of England's greatest colonial mistakes, the Crown always believed Ireland was part of the British Isles, but never really gave the country a fair shake. Apart from Dublin, they never developed the country's infrastructure. Down through the centuries, they just used Ireland as England's breadbasket. Had they developed a few harbors throughout the country, they could have avoided massive deaths during the famine, by developing a fishing industry.

The crime of the famine is astonishing. The Irish population during the early 1840's was approximately nine million. The prevailing opinion among the British landlords was that there were too many people renting tiny tracts of land on their estates, which of course, previously belonged to the Irish. They wanted to clear the Irish off the lands, so they could create huge ranch-like farms.

In the classic American Indian way, the Irish were stripped of their lands, and became second-class citizens in their own country, renting what used to be their land, from their new English landlords.

The arrival of the potato blight destroyed crops. Potatoes were the only food the Irish could afford to grow at the time. It was convenient Providence for the British establishment. The potato crops failed totally for five years. Instead of saving their tenants, the landlords publicly blamed God for the calamity, whilst doing virtually nothing to help on the scale that was needed.

A million people died, and a million left for America and Canada. This massive decline in population was exactly what the British wanted. Sadly, the politics of the times, augmented by landlords who preferred to live in England, and the apathy of the landlords actually living in Ireland combined to seal the fate of those who stayed, or couldn't get out. Poverty abounded; lack of potential employment was rampant; discontent sizzled in the souls of the Irish.

Chapter 2

Finbar Golden was born in Waterford in the late 1920's. He was an academic easy-going, accepting sort of guy. There wasn't much in life that caused Finbar to lose his temper. He should have been a priest as he had all the right qualities to lead his flock: humility, empathy and total faith. In fairness to him, he was comfortable in his own skin. In the future, he would marry into a family that included an Irish athlete/politician of mammoth stature. He never felt overwhelmed by his famous brother-in-law's accomplishments in sports, as Finbar preferred books. In a rare instance of personal reflection, Finbar once explained to one of his sons that his aspirations had been to be a doctor. His mother, however, said industry was the coming thing, and he should study accounting in college, so, like a good son, accounting he did.

During college, Finbar was at a dance one evening and saw a lovely Irish girl. With her jet-black hair, bright blue eyes, and her infectious laugh, he could easily see she was the life of the party, and was immediately smitten. Small in stature, Nora stood barely five feet tall. He did notice that when she was nervous, she quickly
reached for a rosary in her pocket. The smoothness of the beads appeared to calm her inner self. He dared to approach her and appropriately followed all of the courting customs of the day. Eventually,

they decided that marriage was in their future. He asked for her hand in marriage and together they would remain for more than 60 years.

Strangely enough, Finbar was named after the patron saint of Cork, St. Finbar. After marrying Nora, they ironically ended up living in Cork. Throughout the years, he provided a good home for Nora, and what would grow to be their family of five children. He eventually became a principal of the largest school in Cork. The prominence this position brought to the family was always treated with respect, as the Irish do not boast of their accomplishments. Often, an Irishman will nearly demean his position in life rather than crow of its importance.

Finbar was a musician at heart. He was well versed on several instruments. The accordion was his treasured source of entertainment. He inherited his mother's piano when she died, as he was the most musical one of the children. Although it was weather-beaten and old, he cherished the sounds his children would plunk from it as the years progressed.

Chapter 3

Finbar's father, Liam bore witness to the traumatic events of Ireland in the early 1900s, and he imposed on his children an inner pride of their heritage and love of their country that was honest and sincere. He would often remind them of the travails the Irish suffered to achieve their independence. Liam would usually recount the stories in chronological order....

In 1912, the Irish thought they were very close to achieving their freedom from the British throne. Years and years of arguments, battles and negotiations had culminated in the agreement known as Irish Home Rule. A combination of disgruntlement on the part of the British and the ensuing world war delayed the implementation of the agreement. The agreement was ultimately suspended because of World War I.

Concurrently, Irishmen throughout the island were gathering in groups, creating political parties and even organizing troops. Their sights were set upon freedom for the Irish to govern themselves. The Irish Volunteers were quite active in 1913. A secret group within the Volunteers was known as the Irish Republican Brotherhood. The Volunteers would eventually become known as the Irish Republican Army.

In 1916, Patrick Pearse, a young idealistic teacher, poet, and fluent Gaelic speaker, felt it was the perfect time to strike a blow for Irish freedom. The British army was busy fighting WWI. Another leader within the Volunteers, a man called Eamon DeValera, agreed.

DeValera was an unusual character. His heritage was often in question. He was born in the United States to an Irish mother and Cuban/Spanish father. When his father passed away, Eamon was returned to Ireland where he was raised by his Irish uncle, grandmother and extended family.

It was May 3, 1916, Easter weekend. Pearse, the overall leader, expected that if they started a revolt, the whole country would rise up, and finally rid Ireland of British rule. He was wrong. The British simply cruised up the River Liffey, and lobbed shells into the General Post Office. It was here, on O'Connell Street that the Irish made their main stand. Surrenders were made to avoid further bloodshed. All of the Irish leaders, including Pearse and DeValera, were condemned to death. Executions began immediately. The guilty were shot; the British military dragged the executions out to such an extent that the Irish were repulsed and set the determination of the Irish to continue Pearse's dream to break Ireland free from the shackles of England, once and for all.

However, Eamon DeValera's sentence was commuted to Personal Servitude for Life. His life was saved through a combination of four simultaneous facts:

1. He was the last to surrender and was taken to a different prison than the others;
2. The American consulate raised major concerns about the execution of an American citizen; the British did not want to anger the Americans, given that Britain was trying to convince the U.S. to join WWI;
3. His activities with the secret arm of the Volunteers had kept his name from being noticed by the British and MI-6, so government officials felt that he would not be a future threat;
4. His trial had been delayed due to his late surrender and the American intervention compounded by the disgruntled feelings of disgust the British Prime Minister experienced from all of the executions, he wanted no more to occur.

DeValera was released from prison in 1917, under an amnesty agreement reached with the British government. Upon his release, he became very active in the Irish political scene. He was elected president of Sinn Fein, which originally supported a form of 'dual rule' that would give Ireland its freedom, while still retaining association with the

British government. Through the years, it became apparent that this aspiration was not realistic, and Sinn Fein became better known as the political arm of the IRA. Through the years Eamon raised external funds to support his political agenda, at times he visited America and would come home with millions of dollars to support Irish freedom.

Chapter 4

Finbar often recalled the pride with which Liam, his father, would speak of the bravery of Irish figures. The Irish spirit was strongest when fighting for its own freedom. But the Irish never ran from a battle fought in the name of other world needs...

World War I was ending; the world appeared to reach a peace accord. But Ireland was still in turmoil. The Irish Home Rule agreement was still on suspension. The Irish Republican Army were causing havoc throughout the country. British leaders believed that something had to be done. As veteran British soldiers returned from World War I, they found no work available to them in England. In 1920, the British government offered an opportunity to these veterans. They could go to Ireland, where they would be paid fifty shillings a day. There was a severe shortage of uniforms, so they wore khaki shirts and black pants, thus they became known as the Black and Tans. The British Government wasn't too fussy about the quality or character of these men. The goal was to maintain a presence in Ireland, due to the growing unrest.

There were about eight thousand of the Black and Tans sent to Ireland between 1920 and 1922. With little oversight from England, they did as they pleased. Brutal and illegal horrors were committed. These horrible actions brought disastrous results to what few good relations the two countries had at the time. One of their worst atrocities was a cowardly murder one Sunday afternoon in Dublin. The B&Ts drove onto the largest football field in Ireland, Croke Park, in their armored trucks, and opened fire on both players and supporters. Twelve innocent people were killed and dozens were injured. What had precipitated such horrific behavior? The B&Ts felt retaliation was necessary for the killing of some of their soldiers a few days earlier.

Poor farmers in the countryside relied on their cows for milk products; basically a cow meant life or death to these people. Thus, creameries throughout Ireland were destroyed, in retribution for the people's support of the IRA. Just for fun, cows in the fields were shot as the B&Ts drove by in their armored trucks. They raped and pillaged without any official restraint. They lacked all usual military discipline. In 1922, the British authorities realized the B&Ts were a complete disaster and liability, and withdrew them in total ignominy.

Throughout the twentieth century, thousands of Irishmen joined the British army, and fought in both world wars. You would imagine that this fact sounds totally contradictory, when you consider the animosity felt towards England at the time, but it is true. History is not black and white; it's usually a messy gray.

There are hundreds of thousands of Irish people, and millions of British citizens of Irish blood, living happily in England. They fought and died alongside their fellow Englishmen, with great courage. This is evident by the fact that men from Southern Ireland were awarded sixty Victoria Crosses, since their inception by Queen Victoria in 1856. It is the highest military decoration awarded by England for valor, "in the face of the enemy." Since there have been only 1,357 medals awarded, sixty is an astonishing amount of medals awarded to men from the Republic of Ireland.

Chapter 5

As Finbar's children grew, he regaled them with tales of the heroes of the Irish rebellions. The stories, though, also included details of the fights which arose amongst the Irish themselves. For a very long time, the Irish populace maintained hopes and aspirations centered on freedom from England. The journey to their freedom was often less than promising…

One of the junior commanders of the 1916 Easter Rising had been stationed at the Dublin Post Office. He was a charismatic man called Michael Collins. He saw how futile it was to fight the Black and Tans head on, so he devised guerilla tactics, to spread fear and confusion among the British government and military. He had spent time working in England, and had penetrated the highest echelons of British intelligence. Collins was getting daily briefs about what the British were planning. They knew what he was doing, but couldn't figure out how he was so well informed. They also didn't know what he looked like, and everybody knew if they squealed to the British, Collins' men would summarily execute them.

His soldiers assassinated leading security and intelligence men sent over to Ireland, before they even started working, thus scaring off anyone else coming over to Ireland. He was so successful in his military campaign, that in 1921 England was finally forced to talk peace with DeValera. DeValera wouldn't go over to London himself, so he sent a team including Collins. It is said their assignment was 'get as much as you can.'

The British offer was to hand back all of Ireland except six counties which comprised of about one-fifth of the country. These were the counties of Northern Ireland. A majority of people in Northern Ireland stayed loyal to Britain down through the centuries. This was due to the 'Plantation of Ulster.' [Northern Ireland.] Through the centuries people from Northern England, and Southern Scotland were 'planted' in Northern Ireland. Many of the 'in' people of the day received huge tracts of land in Northern Ireland. The king also owed money to soldiers returning from their many foreign wars, payments were made with land instead of cash. This "land grant" procedure was also convenient to get troublemakers and subversives out of the Crown's way, ship them out of the country, and at the same time, have them indebted to England. Unlike previously, these newest arrivals of English and Southern Scottish people stayed true to England, her language, her religion. The majority of the newcomers were historically Protestant. The Irish were Catholic.

Over the years, these new occupiers, destroyed most of the industries in Ireland, North and South.

Catholics weren't allowed to vote, didn't get decent paying jobs, and the English were guilty of all sorts of other discrimination.

During the 1921 peace negotiations with Collins and his team, the British were up to their usual dirty tricks. They wouldn't let the Irish delegation communicate with their leaders in Dublin. They announced bluntly, that if they didn't accept their offer, then and there, they would take it off the table, and squash the rebellion ruthlessly, once and for all.

Collins took their offer, and signed what has become known as The Treaty. He confided to one of his colleagues, that he had probably just signed his own death warrant, knowing the job he would have "selling" the deal. They came back to Dublin, and argued as best they could. He was certain that they could negotiate for more later. All hell broke loose, and two forces emerged: Collins and his men, backing The Treaty, and DeValera and his men totally opposed to the deal. Thus started Ireland's civil war, which was as brutal as any war can be, brother against brother, and cousin against cousin. Collins, known as 'The Big Fella," came back for a meeting in his hometown in West Cork, and was ambushed and killed by anti-treaty forces. He was only thirty-two years old. The civil war fizzled out soon after his death, but it has left bitter scars to this very day.

Some years later DeValera became President of Ireland, and for a couple of decades, Ireland was in a time warp. The newly freed Ireland of the 1920's had left everybody scarred. The Church and State stood lockstep together, and kept Ireland as insular as possible. The Irish populace was totally controlled, similar to General Franco's absolute rule in Spain.

In the '50s, Ireland hardly changed. The Church had a stranglehold on the people, with the tacit approval of the government. Forty years later, the Church would be found guilty of all sorts of physical and sexual abuse of girls and boys. These actions had occurred with the majority of parents kept totally in the dark. Most of the abuse was covered up by the Church authorities. Their mantra was; "protect the Church at all costs." In the early 2000s, their moral authority will be shot in Ireland, and the pews will be almost completely empty of young people as a result.

Chapter 6

Finbar and Nora's first son was of course named Liam, in honor of his grandfather. Hearing the tales of his grandfather, young Liam eventually realized how proud he was to bear the same name. Somehow, this child born with the strawberry-blonde hair, fair skin of the Celts and personality which would not quit, came to be known as Billy, which is Liam in English. Born in the mid 1950's, only thirty years after Ireland achieved its freedom he was shaped by his father's tales of sons and daughters of that bloody and turbulent time, when the Irish suffered desperately under British Rule. Many of the men who fought for Irish freedom were still alive, several of them were Billy's teachers. One was now the President of Ireland, Eamon DeValera.

This is the story of Billy Golden: an Irish dreamer, musician, composer, and all around lover of life.

"Finbar," says Billy's mother, a small but sure-framed woman, to her beloved husband, beaming with pride, "Here's your favorite dinner for you, well done," and hands him a plate of roast stuffed pork steak, roast potatoes, carrots and gravy.
He had just become school principal of one of the largest schools in Cork. "Thanks Nora," as he raises his glass of milk, "Slainte," and their five kids, now teenagers raise their glasses, "Slainte."

Finbar Golden had reached the pinnacle of his profession, and was held in as high esteem as the local parish priest – totally respected, whose authority was rarely, if ever, questioned.

"Fair play to you dad, congratulations."

"Thanks Billy, it's going to be interesting."

"Have ya any new plans for the school?" Billy knew that if he asked his dad a question, he better be prepared to listen for ages to his answer, because that's the way Dad is: intense, thoughtful, and thorough. But this is Finbar's big day, something he's been dreaming of for a long time, so Billy lets his dad fire away.

Finbar sits back in his chair, gets his thoughts together and replies: "Well I'm going to introduce adult education for older people who never got the chance to go very far in their jobs, because of their lack of education. I think there's a real need for this. I'm going to offer night courses for older people, typing, bookkeeping, even planning for retirement courses, that sort of thing. If I can help people climb the ladder in their careers, and be prepared financially and socially, after they retire, I think I'll have done my job."

"Finbar," says Nora all worried, "with all the extra work, will you be able to come home for dinner?" It was impossible for her to imagine not cooking dinner as she has done for the past twenty-two years. Even if she was dying with the flu, there was always a meal on the table for her family.

"Nora," says dad lovingly, "don't go getting your rosary beads out just yet, I'll never miss your dinner, I won't give that up, whatever about anything else."

"Hey Dad," says Noellie, Billy's younger brother, "Ma says we'll be gettin' a new car?"

He laughs, "Well we'll see, I hope we can, 'sure the old Volkswagon is nearly dead, how's your car coming along Billy?"

"It'll be ready tomorrow I hope."

"How's the choir doing?"

"I think we're okay, looks like it might be a nice show."

Billy was the musical director of one of Cork's only pop choirs, The Montfort Singers, following in his dad's footsteps, whose love of music was huge. Finbar had been a member of several of the top choirs in Cork in his time, both mixed and male voice choirs, so Billy, his oldest son, was steeped in music from day one.

Finbar finishes a bite and smiles as he meanders through his Irish recollections... "You know I remember a great story from the old days. The choir I was in was asked to sing for a big American TV special that would be be aired on St. Patrick's Day back in the states. It went out nationally on CBS or NBC or one of those major networks at the time, – big stuff for a choir from Cork. Well we practiced every night for weeks on this one song, *The Banks Of My Own Lovely Lee*, putting just the right emphasis into the feelings of an emigrant looking back on his days walking along the banks of the River Lee as it meanders through Cork city and county.

They recorded us singing in St.Finbar's Cathedral where the acoustics are excellent. Then they took us out to a scenic spot along the river, set up huge lights, put us all up on a mobile stage, and we lip-synched the song over and over for hours.

They promised they would send a copy of the show over to us when it was all finished. Everyone who had cousins in America had been alerted to watch us on TV.

It finally came and we were all gathered in the church hall to watch our big moment. Well, all they showed was about ten seconds of swans floating down the river, and us singing in the background as the credits came up. Ten seconds of bloody swans after all our hard work!!..."

"You know in my time," says Nora, "when the operatic companies came to Cork, the audience knew all the main arias off by heart, and they'd sing them before the opera started."

"How did they know them?" pipes Billy's sister Bernadette.

"They'd learn them off the record player, French, German, Italian, it didn't matter. They didn't know exactly what the words meant, but they captured the mood of it perfectly. They really had great ears. If a soprano, tenor or bass came to town, and didn't perform to the satisfaction of the audience, they would roll a beer bottle or two down the concrete steps from the nose bleed section, right down to the stage. I saw it happen several times, and the singer just completely choked up, the poor old divil."

Towards the end of dinner Finbar asks, "Hey Billy, would you come in tonight to the dinner dance and sing your new record? I think the students would like it, and you can join us for the meal, I know how you like the dinners."

"All right dad, but Sean O Se asked me to play for him in Blackrock Castle, there's a bunch of yanks coming in for a dinner show, so I'll see you as soon as I can, I hope I'll make dinner."

"All right, see you later then."

Billy loved the dinners at these events: huge servings of roast beef or pork with fabulous vegetables, and three, yes three different potatoes: mashed, roasted, and fried. With seven in the family, the portions weren't the biggest, especially when it came to whatever meat Ma had cooked, so the dinner dances were very appealing to Billy, as he was blessed with a very healthy appetite.

After an hour of primping, Billy looks grand—his curled strawberry-blonde hair perfectly in place, a powder blue jacket and ruffled dress shirt trimmed in blue, accent his gleaming blue eyes, a gold pocket kerchief is perfectly adjusted and his dress slacks have just enough flare for the current bell-bottom trend—and he's ready to go! Sean is unusually late so Billy is practicing, waiting to be collected, when finally, the phone rings. "Hello Billy, Sean here, I'm sorry but they cancelled the show last minute, the bus broke down or somethin'."

"Ah no, ...shit, ...I needed the money, my car is broken down."

"Sorry Billy, next time," says Sean and hangs up.

It's now too late to have dinner at the hotel, so he decides to go into town and have a few pints and waste some time, as he hates all the boring speeches everybody will have to sit through, before the dancing starts.

He hops on a bus and goes into his usual bar, the Swan and Cygnet, on Patrick's Street. It's where all the musicians and great characters drink. You get all the scandal, or "sca," as they say in Cork, about all the latest goings on. It's an old rustic intimate sort of pub, with dark oak beams overhead, and a beautiful square mahogany bar, with probably the best pint of Guinness and Murphy's in Cork.

First person he meets is a great old Cork character called Paddy O'Brien, a fantastic bass guitarist who has the biggest hands Billy ever saw, and a fine old beer belly. Billy knows him from conducting the choir in the Opera House. He was a great musical reader, and a terrific improviser when things went wrong on stage. He could play along effortlessly with whatever the musical director played to kill a few minutes, to allow the cast to get their act together, and the audience would think it was all part of the show. That was one of his many talents. Billy was about to find out about another one of his "talents." Strangely enough, Billy never met him in a bar before.

"Hey Billy Boyeeee," in his fine Cork accent, "will ya have a pint? Two pints there Sean." The barman pulls two fantastic looking pints of Guinness and Paddy says "Cheers," and downs almost the whole pint in one gulp. Billy is amazed, and tries to do the same thing so as not to lose face. Just as Billy gets through nearly finishing his pint, Paddy polishes his off with one swallow, and it's Billy's call. "Two more there please Sean."
"Did ya hear about Denis O' Brien the other night?" says Paddy laughing. Denis O' Brien is one of the finest Irish tenors in Cork, no relation to Paddy. Billy had accompanied him at dozens of weddings. He could sing Danny Boy better than anyone Billy had ever heard anywhere. Unfortunately he is an alcoholic, and is banned from almost every pub in Cork for picking fights and generally obnoxious behavior, once the booze kicks in. This was quite a record, considering the number of pubs in Cork.

Denis was a promising Irish athlete, but lost his leg after he fell into a combine harvester when he was only nineteen, and has worn a prosthetic leg ever since. He has a real chip on his shoulder against the whole world, and blames all his misfortunes on losing the leg.

Billy remembers accompanying Denis once in a show a few hours from Cork. He got so drunk after the show, he couldn't drive home, and as Billy wasn't driving yet, they had to spend the night in a hotel. The next morning after breakfast Denis called his wife and said; "Hello Grace, I'm just calling to let ya know I won't be home last night!" Denis O'Brien is a living legend in Cork!

"Oh God," says Billy, "what did he do now?" as he gulps his last swallow down. "Two more there Sean," and within seconds the exact same thing happens, Paddy says "Cheers," and nearly downs another pint in his first swallow, and then proceeds to give Billy the "sca…"

"He got stopped last night, langers [drunk] to the world, and wouldn't let the guard breathalyse him. He was effing and blinding the guard so much, the guard called for backup. A second guard arrived but Denis still wouldn't let them breathalyse him, he just kept shoutin' and roaring, so they brought him down to the police station for a blood sample."

Paddy continues after finishing off yet another pint…"Anyway, when the doctor came to do the blood test, Denis recognized him and went ballistic because the guy was their vet who looked after his dog, and there was no way a vet was going to take blood out of him. The police told them there was no doctor available, and that was the best thing they could do at this time o' night. Denis told them to go screw themselves and started screaming and cursing as only the bould Denis can. Anyway, they told him they could do it the easy way or the hard way, but they were going to take his blood; it was up to him.

Suddenly Denis bent down, rolled up his pants and took his prosthetic leg off, and threw it up on the table. 'Take the blood out o' that you lousy bastards,' he screamed, 'that's the only blood you'll get out o' me tonight.' He's still in jail sobering up…" Paddy lets out a huge belly laugh and downs another pint.

Two fellas are watching nearby. "Hey, d'ya see that eejit trying to keep up with Paddy?" and they both laugh. The other fella says, "Sure Paddy holds the Guinness World record for downing a pint in 2.2 seconds, should we tell him?"

"Nah," says the other fella, "Let's see how many pints he can drink before he pukes, the poor ould bollix."

Billy is valiantly trying to keep up with Paddy, pint for pint 'til he's almost out of money. One of the fellas was counting: "Nine pints in half an hour, jeez he's gonna be langers, the poor ould divil." They laugh as Billy leaves the pub, and heads up to the Metropole Hotel across Patrick's Bridge to sing the song for his dad. The air starts to hit him, and he starts staggering. As he enters the hotel, there's great excitement in the hotel pub, the crowd is spilling out into the foyer. Someone recognizes him, "Hey Billyeee, c'mere boyeee, they're having a reception for Sandy Brown, she's flying out tomorrow to the Eurovision, free booze boyeee, come on."…..

The atmosphere is absolutely electric, nearly everyone is totally plastered, as they get to the counter. "What'll ya have boyeee?" said his new generous friend. At this point Billy couldn't possibly down another pint. "I'll have a brandy and ginger please," slurring every word. He gets the drink and takes a big gulp, so his friend orders another.

Somebody recognizes Billy. "Billyeee hello boyeee, come on over to the piano and sing an ould song will ya," trying his best to make an announcement, "Hey, c'mere," he screams, "noble call now, silence please, Billy Golden is gonna' sing a song all right?" as he pulls him over to the piano, "What are ya havin' boyeee?"

"Brandy and ginger," and he goes over to the bar. The few that were listening push him towards the piano. He sits down and can hardly see the keys, it's all a blur, but he's feeling no pain, in fact he's as high as a kite, life is great.

He starts with the big hit of the day, *McArthur Park*. He gets out a few words, plonking on the piano about someone letting the cake out in the rain, and not having the recipe again. Everybody suddenly recognizes the song, and start screaming at the top of their voices, way way out of tune, and then the climax: ...*AND I'LL NEVER HAVE THAT RECIPE AGAIN, OH NO, OH NO*..., their Cork accents making it even funnier. Everybody is totally plastered, having a ball. Poor old Jimmy Webb, if he only heard them all, murdering his classic song....

Somewhere in his drunken haze Billy remembers about singing his song for his dad, so he staggers out of the bar, and as he's climbing the stairs to the second floor, holding on to the banisters for dear life, he spots a girl staggering down the stairs. She's almost as plastered as Billy, strikingly beautiful, tall and slim, long brown hair, dressed in a beautiful ocean blue deb's ball gown. She's trying with great difficulty to get down the steps in her high heels. She's probably looking for the toilet, totally disorientated, obviously at her high school ball in another function room.

"Dya wanna' go to a party?" Billy mumbles, now totally disheveled, his perfect hair hanging like wild slinkies around the slits of blue eyes, shirt unbuttoned and jacket wrinkled.

"All right," she says, and they stagger up the stairs to the dinner dance.

The first people Billy sees are his parents with the Lord Mayor, wearing his formal gold chain, the Bishop of Cork in all his regalia, and some other important looking people in tuxedos. Billy stumbles over with Mary, totally oblivious to all the big shots. "Hiya Dad, hiya Ma, this is eh…. whassyer name?"

"Mary," she mumbles, hanging on to Billy for support.

"This is Mary, isn't she beauuutiful?" Billy's parents are horrified, totally embarrassed and furious. If looks could kill….

Just then Dick Corbett the organist spots Billy and makes an announcement: "Ladies and Gentlemen, Lord Mayor, Reverend Bishop, Boys and Girls, Mr. Golden's son is a singer, and he's just recorded his first record, so let's have a big hand for Billy Golden." Everybody dutifully applauds.

"…'Scuse me," says Billy drunkenly, as he staggers up to the stage and sits down at the organ which by now, looks like twenty keyboards in front of him. Mary follows right along like a little puppy. Dick pulls the mike stand over, and Billy starts singing. *FELL IN LOVE IN THE WINK OF AN EYE*, he can't remember the next few lines so he goes straight into the chorus: "*BUTTERFLY, MY BUTTERFLY*, everybody come on now let's hear ye, *BUTTERFLY MY BUTTERFLY I'LL COME HOME TO YOU SOMEDAY.*"... There was absolutely no reaction except shock. Billy was oblivious to the fact that nobody knew the song yet, so they couldn't join in.

Dick realizes that Billy's plastered so he quickly pulls the plug and the organ dies. Billy looks up drunkenly at Dick, "What's wrong with yer organ Dick?" as he bashes the keys to try and get some sound out of them.

Dick grabs the mike and says, "Ladies and gentlemen, there's something wrong with the organ, we'll have Billy up again as soon as we fix it."

"Sound as a bell," says Billy, as he almost falls off the stage, straight into the arms of Mary.

Dick plugs the organ back in again and starts with a lively jig, and Billy and Mary fall all over the place trying to dance, shocking all of his dad's students who are on their best behavior. Suddenly Mary stops, has a moment of clarity and says, "You're not Pat."

"No, I'm Billy, who the hell is Pat?" Mary just staggers off mumbling "Pat, Pat"....

Suddenly an older guy pulls Billy aside. "Hey Billyeee, you're making a right ould eejit of yerself boyeeee, you're langers at your father's first dinner dance as school principal. I'm tellin' ya now boyeee, get outta here before you make it any worse all right?"

Billy tries to grasp what he was hearing, and thru' his drunken haze, realizes he's right, and staggers out of the ballroom. He starts to walk down the stairs, but he has to hang onto the banisters, as he's legless. "Shit, I've never been this bad before," he thinks to himself.

He gets to the front door and remembers the nightclub a few doors up. The bouncer recognizes him, and lets him in. He staggers up the stairs to the wine bar. "Give us a cuppa' coffe there will ya." The guy pours him a cup of scalding coffee. Billy takes a big gulp and nearly falls on the floor with the heat of it. Suddenly he gets the hiccups, not your average hiccups, but loud, uncontrollable hiccups.

Everybody ignores him, so he decides to leave and walk home, but soon he realizes he hasn't a hope in hell of making it, he's so scuttered maggoty drunk. His only option was a taxi, so he heads across the bridge, down to the taxi rank,
hanging on to the buildings for dear life as he staggers slowly along.

Finally he makes it and gets into a taxi, "Back Douglas road, opposite Casey's [hiccup] Park.[hiccup] The taxi pulls up to the door.

"Three pounds please," says the driver. He fumbles trying to get his hand into his pocket, but for some reason, it just won't do what he wants. His brain is mush, completely and utterly uncoordinated.

Finally he succeeds, and everything falls on the floor. He sees two pounds, picks them up, and hands them to the driver. He's short a pound. "Wait [hiccup,] here," as he hands the guy the two pounds. He staggers to the front door and drunkenly, keeps knocking loudly until his dad opens the door. "Dad, [hiccup] have ya got a [hiccup] pound for the taxi?" His dad goes out and hands a pound to the driver. Billy goes straight up to the bedroom he shares with his younger brother Noellie, ignoring what would have been the ultimate wrath of his mother in the kitchen.

He tries to take off his shoes, finally gives up, and makes an awful racket climbing into the top bunk bed. Every time he hiccups the springs of the bunk shake and squeak violently and loudly, cutting through the total silence of the night. Hiccups, squeaks and shakes, in full fortissimo, they just won't stop. Everybody is awake and furious, due to the racket in the boy's bedroom.

Suddenly he realizes he's going to throw up, and he's never going to make it to the bathroom. In an attempt to save the carpet, he decides to puke on the wall. He pukes over and over, everything comes up, projectile style. Noellie is horrified in the lower bunk, as he watches the vomit slide slowly down the wall to the floor. "Billyeee, Ma's going to kill ya." Billy didn't hear a thing, he was snoring like a pig.

The early afternoon sunlight shines in through Billy's window, waking him up to the worst hangover in his life. The remnants of last night's wall coating, nearly triggers a repeat performance. Staggering to the bathroom he washes his face, pees like a racehorse, and reluctantly goes down to face the wrath of his mother.

He braces for her roar, but instead the kitchen is silent, other than the clicking of her rosary beads as she holds them in her apron pocket. She should have been an actress, he thinks, man, she's giving some performance pretending I'm not here. "I'm sorry Ma," he squeaks timidly from the kitchen doorway. That's all he needed to say.

Nora stopped drying the dishes, reaches into her apron pocket, removes and solemnly kisses the Crucifix of her rosary, replaces it safely in the pocket of her apron and turns up to look Billy in the eye. Another moment of silence passes, and then she begins her tirade. She definitely made up for her tiny five-foot one little body with the strength of her mouth. "My God Billy Golden, you made a fool of your father last night in front of everybody. How could you do it, in front of the Bishop, the Lord Mayor and all his teachers and students? He's going to kill you when he comes home, how could you be so stupid? We'll be the laughing stock of Cork. ....I can never go outside my door again.... Oh my God Billy Golden, what have you done?"

Her screaming and roaring was killing him, so he goes into the living room for a bit of peace and quiet. After a while, he sees her going out to put the washing on the line in the back garden, so he goes into the pantry, gets a bucket and mop, and with his head still pounding, he slowly drags himself up the stairs to his room and cleans it all up, before his mother sees the mess. Now, he waits for his father to come home in order to apologize. Holy shit, this is going to be rough, his thoughts resonate within his hungover brain.

Finbar finally arrives home and Billy calls him into the drawing room where he's playing the piano. Here goes: "Dad, could I see you a sec?" His dad comes in and they stand face to face. "Dad, I'm so sorry about last night, I made a complete fool of myself and embarrassed the hell out of you. I was never so drunk in all my life. All I can say is I'm sorry."

His dad always took off his jacket and put on his cardigan. This was as much as he ever did to relax. He did this slowly and let Billy sweat for a little while, but then Billy was shocked when he said: "Billy, sure I suppose they'll realize now that I'm human too," as he looks straight into Billy's eyes with obvious disappointment.

Billy couldn't believe his father's reaction, and just wanted to hug him and tell him how much he loved him at just that moment. But you didn't do that sort of thing back then. He just stands there, looking at this fine man, who, if he had been any other father would probably have beaten the daylights out of him, and he definitely would have deserved it. But he was a wise man who knew when and where to pick his battles with his son. He figures this is the perfect time to get Billy to 'cop himself on.' [wise up]

"Billy, I think it's time for you to take the job in the school of music, Miss Duffin won't wait forever for you to make your decision."

Billy shuffles around, "I know dad, but I want to be a musician, not a teacher, you know?"

"You're going nowhere right now Billy, you're drinking and messing around. I think it's time you settled down, get focused on what you want to do. It's a desperate time to be thinking about going out on your own."

"I know dad but."….

His dad keeps hammering away: "Look what happened to Ford's, they just closed it down with a stroke of a pen, then Dunlop's went bang, and it just destroyed Cork, thousands of people out of work just like that. Cork is ruined for years to come. Why don't you take the job and do weddings at the weekends like you're doing now?"

"I want to do more than play weddings dad. I want to be a songwriter and get a record contract, not a wedding singer."

"Billy, I know you, when you want something badly enough you don't give up 'til you've got it, but God Almighty, you couldn't pick a worse time than right now to go for it, and I can't help you with a bit of money, I'm sorry, we just don't have it."

"It's all right dad, I don't want your money, I'll be all right."

His dad keeps pushing, "Just think about it will you Billy. Teaching isn't so bad, and going out on your own is going to be rough. I don't know anyone in Cork right now who's doing music full time, and by the way, if you do go professional, you'd better learn to control that temper of yours. You've never learned how to be a team player; it always has to be your way. That's not how the world works Billy, and the sooner you realize it, the better."

The phone rings, and Nora sticks her head into the room. "It's the school, they say it's something important. "Okay Billy," says his dad, "we'll continue this later."

Billy jumps into his car and races down to Crosshaven village, about ten miles from Cork. It's famous for having the world's oldest yacht club, the Royal Yacht Club of Cork, where the well-heeled people of Cork keep their yachts and indulge in the very posh hobby of competitive yacht racing in one of the world's most beautiful harbors.

Billy goes for a walk around the cliffs looking down on Myrtleville beach, a few miles from Crosshaven. It's always been one of his favorite places to clear his head. Crosshaven was also the home of one of Billy's oldest friends, and college mates Peter Dunphy. Peter was an "old soul" as Billy's mother called him. He was always good for cheering Billy up with his insight and positive advice. Peter was very intense and passionate about everything, especially music. He had mastered the art of living for now, not tomorrow or yesterday, but this very minute.

It starts to rain, so he goes into Bunny's, a great yacht-themed pub looking over the spectacular cliffs and beach of Myrtleville, and waits for Peter.

Peter ambles into the pub, looking and acting like an old absent-minded professor: hair flying wildly, pants two sizes too big for him, and an ancient rumpled sports coat that he probably just grabbed from a pile of clothes on the floor. Fashion and attire simply didn't matter to Peter. "Billy, great to see you, what's up?"

"Hey man, thanks for coming, what are you havin'?"says Billy.

"The usual."

"Two pints please.....You know Peter, I think it's time for me to get outta' here."

Peter's face lights up and replies in his own unique intense way... "Billy, that's the best thing I've heard you say in years. If you stay here and teach for the rest of your life, and play the same shitty old places you're playing now, over and over, you'll end up with a huge beer belly asking yourself: why didn't you go for it you cowardly bollix?"

Billy with all his baggage, and the old Irish self-doubt rearing its ugly head again answers, "I don't know Pete, am I good enough?"

Peter gathers his thoughts, realizing this was a make or break decision for Billy, and knowing Billy's potential better than anyone else, stares right into Billy's eyes. "Look Billy, you won the Castlebar Song Contest last year, and you were telling me about that record fella from New Zealand you met in Tokyo who wanted to bring you over there and promised he'd make you a star, but you said no 'cos it was too far away?"

"Yea but,"…Billy says weakly.

"But nothin' Billy, get outta' here before it's too late, why don't you go to America?"

Billy is shocked at his suggestion. "Peter, are ya mad boyee, I was thinkin' about going up to Dublin."

"Well then go, go yesterday. You know Michael Mortell in RTE. He should be able to help you. It'll be rough for a while, but if you don't go now, you'll never do it." [RTE is Ireland's Radio and Television station]

On his way home, serious thoughts wander through his mind. The concept of change was something

Billy loved, but taking actual movement toward change was very scary. The sixties blew in like a gale-force wind. The Beatles, Stones, and all the Woodstock legends hit the airwaves. Ireland's youth couldn't get enough of it. The cracks were definitely showing. People started adopting their rock hero's fashions, demanding their music be played on the radio, and challenging openly the church's authority for the first time. Here was this amazing liberating rock and roll and folk music, coming through the radio in the early 60's. Billy jumped into this music scene and discovered that he really had a gift and a talent.

Of course, everything Peter said made perfect sense. It was a year since Billy had graduated from college. He had taught part-time in the school of music since poor old Miss O'Leary had died. His mind flashes back to the last time he had seen her in hospital. She had called and asked Billy would he mind coming in to see her.

By then he was in his final year in college, and taking master classes from Ireland's most famous concert pianist at the time, Charles Lynch. He hadn't seen her in years and was shocked at how gaunt and yellow she looked when he entered the room. "Hello Billy, how are you?"

"Fine thanks Ms. O'Leary how are you?"

"Oh, I've been better I'm afraid. Billy, I was wondering would you teach my students until I come out of hospital? It will look good when Professor Lucy hears that you're teaching in the school of music, and it will be some extra money for you."

"Gee, I don't know Ms. O'Leary,…"

"Look Billy, you know my style inside and out, just do what I do and you'll be fine. Now look, here's a pen and paper. I want you to write down a few things about my students." She hands him a paper and pen. Billy could see her up close now and couldn't believe how gaunt she looked, but at 19 he didn't know much about cancer and that she would be dead shortly afterwards.

She was totally involved with her students and gave Billy the lowdown on each one of them: "Now Mary's good but lazy, so don't fall into her trap when she tries to talk her way through her lesson. Brian is hopeless but he really tries his best, so be patient with him," and so on.

She loved and cared deeply for all her students. She was actually Billy's teacher from day one, so he knew how she did things, and after her chat he felt he could do it, especially after the few years teaching the choir. So, he said "yes," and off he went, Billy the music teacher….

Billy remembers his days going for his weekly piano lesson. He absolutely hated the piano pieces he had to learn, until he actually got to know them. Then he enjoyed playing them, but it was a bore learning them, and he really didn't try too hard.

He thinks about this, and decides to take a radically different approach than Ms. O'Leary, as he feels most of the kids are going because their parents are pushing them, and not because they actually want to learn themselves, just like he did in the beginning.

He also looks way cooler than any of the other teachers who are stuffy and a bit condescending. His 'look' for his first day of teaching is definitely cool: long permed hair, wide bell-bottomed jeans, platform shoes, which make him look over six feet tall, and a black double-breasted velvet jacket owned by one of the Bee Gee's, who left it in his hotel room when they toured Ireland. Billy knew the hotel manager, and once the Bee Gees never called about it, he gave it to Billy. He thinks he's hot shit – a big fish in a small pool.

First in is "Hopeless Brian". He's about ten and looks at Billy like a deer in headlamps, not knowing what to say or do. "Hiya Brian, my name is Billy. I'm gonna' be teachin' you 'til Ms. O'Leary comes back, all right? Hey, what's your favorite pop song?"

Brian whispers *Knights in White Satin* by the Moody Blues only to be amazed that Billy knows it and can actually play it. "Would you like to learn it?"

"Yea," says Brian, his eyes lighting up, and relieved when he sees Billy putting his piano books away.

"Well, look just do this"… and he spends the first few lessons teaching all of them their own personal favorite pop song.

Within a few weeks they're playing the song with both hands, albeit a basic version, amazing them and their parents alike when suddenly, even hopeless Brian is playing a song with both hands. When he has them hooked he says, "now look, we have to play your boring scales and classical pieces too, but the faster you learn them, the more time we can have to learn more pop songs okay?"

In a few months his students have broken the backs of their classical pieces, and are actually enjoying playing them, as well as their growing list of pop songs. So much so, that when their parents have parties, and the booze kicks in, poor old Mary and Brian and the other kids are dragged out of bed to play the piano and impress their parents friends with their new little musical genius. Billy enjoys it to a certain extent, but he teaches from three 'til eight, four days a week, and he hates the monotonous routine. He hates any routine, period.

One night as his last student is nearly finished, he can almost taste that first pint of Guinness. He's watching the clock tick off each minute. It makes a loud "click" as it does so. He's watching; 7:58… 7:59…. and then, the bloody thing goes backwards! He knows it has to be an optical illusion, but he would swear under oath that he really saw it, and later in the pub, he takes it as a sign to get the hell out, before he's trapped forever. He really didn't want to become one of *those* teachers. 'Too long a sacrifice makes a stone of a heart.' WB Yates

Billy went to the Presentation Brothers for high school. There were only a few Brothers teaching, as fewer and fewer men were joining up to be priests or brothers. It was mostly secular teachers, who taught, and they were generally excellent teachers. They were, however, allowed to thump, slap, cane, hit, knock, and bully the students, and several of them did exactly that. The best ones didn't. The fear of being hit made most of the boys do their homework. The thought of complaining to your parents never entered your mind. One of their favorite tricks was to thump you in the back, you'd fall out of your desk, and then the teacher would drag you back up painfully by the ear. Teachers had absolute control back then.

Billy could not know that this prevalent threat of physical abuse would virtually stop overnight in the '80s when a teacher hit a student, who told his father, and the dad came into school the next morning, "...to sort it out with the teacher." When the parent went for the teacher, the young man's father had to be held back by some other teachers. As a docker who loaded freight onto ships, he was built like a truck, and would have destroyed the teacher. He instead took the teacher to court, and as he was a very well known sports coach, it made national headlines, and the teacher lost his job. Getting beaten up in school, stopped right there. This is a good thing. Teachers should teach, not bully you, put you down, or put the fear of God in you.

Chapter 7

Billy arrives home just before tea. The whole family is there. Lunch was the main meal in those days, and his mother always had a delicious meal ready when they all came home from school. Evening meal or "tea" as everyone called it, was maybe beans on toast, or a couple of fried eggs, always served with tea and bread and butter, and his mother's delicious tangy homemade marmalade jam.

He breaks the news right there and then, trembling from the inside out, "Listen…Ma…Dad, I've been doing a bit o' thinkin', and I've eh, decided it's time for me to move out."

"Move out?" his mother immediately retrieves her rosary beads, shocked at the thought of losing her oldest son. "Sure where would you go?" In those days boys and girls lived at home right up to their wedding night.

"Dublin Ma,… if I want to go for it, I've gotta' be in Dublin."

"Dublin? And give up the job in the school of music?... Your pension, everything?... Sure what will you do in Dublin, you don't have a job, you don't know anyone up there." In his mother's mind, the world ended a few miles outside of Cork city.

Her panic ebbs with the familiar, worn beads in her hand.

"I'll be all right Ma, I'll find some work. I'll call Michael Mortell in RTE."

Finbar goes into the living room and comes out with his piano accordion. "Here Billy, I'd like you to have this."

"Dad I can't, it's yours."

"Billy, go on take it, sure you passed me out years ago, go on, here, take it." Reluctantly he takes it from his dad's hands, realizing he was giving him his blessing for the move. He knew Billy was determined to go for it.

"Billy," his mother tearfully struggles as she clutches the rosary in her hand, "I thought you were going to take the job in the school of music."

"Ma, I've talked to dad about it. I'm sorry, I've made up my mind, I've gotta' get outa' here."

"Oh Billy, if you go, your job will be gone. Oh My God Billy what are you doing?" her prayers earnestly beseeching the Blessed Mother and her Son to keep Billy safe.

After tea Billy puts his keyboard into the back seat of his car, and goes up to his bedroom to start packing. It didn't take long. His wardrobe, tho' fashionable and cool, included just a limited few outfits. He stuffed his clothes into the old suitcase used for trips abroad when he qualified for all those fabulous song contests. It was covered with all sorts of stickers he had collected from the various countries he had sung in. There were stickers from nearly every country in Europe, and as far away as Tokyo. Then he noticed the sticker from Bulgaria and smiles,…. now there's a funny memory, Bulgaria's song contest:

It was held in a beautiful, tho' run down beach resort called Varna. He and his songwriting buddy bought their usual bottle of his favorite whiskey, Cork's own "Paddy" at Dublin airport. It was around 1973, long before the Iron Curtain fell. They flew to Sofia on a big jet, and then boarded a twin-engined clunker to Varna. The inside of the plane was like a dining car on a train: two seats, a small table, and two Bulgarians seated opposite Billy and his buddy.

The plane moves, its engines straining like crazy making really ominous sounds, that Billy has never heard coming from a plane before. Barely taking off at all, Billy was wondering how much runway was left. Finally, with engines roaring, it thankfully lifts ever so slowly.

Just then one of the Bulgarians facing them said in his very broken English, "this plane,... last year,.... four went," and with his hands flailing and his voice screeching, did a very depressing impression of the plane crashing to the ground. Billy immediately reached for the bottle of Paddy, and the four of them polished it off in no time.

After they had done their first rehearsal with the orchestra, they went to relax on the beach. Within minutes, two local guys approached them wanting to buy their jeans. Huge amounts of local money were offered, but the deal couldn't happen on the beach as they told them that the secret police were probably watching. The Bulgarians looked like okay guys, so the Irishmen arranged a meet in their hotel room later on. In the room they told Billy that they couldn't get jeans, modern shirts, women's tights, anything from the West, but they desperately wanted to look as cool as Billy and his buddy did.

They were yearning for freedom and it gave Billy a huge appreciation of what people had in Western Europe. The run down look was everywhere. It was crumbling from within, it was completely broke and it was obvious that it was only a matter of time before the wall fell.

It was no surprise to Billy after being there, when it all collapsed years later. Even tho' President Reagan, the Pope and the West generally, got all the credit for making it happen, it was the people in Eastern Europe like those guys in the hotel room, standing up for freedom, and yearning for a better future, who eventually brought the wall crashing down.

Billy found out later that they couldn't exchange the money they got from the lads, so he bought two beautiful Bulgarian locally carved timber statues which he hand carried through customs, and includes them in his packing today. With his car full of petrol, he goes to bed early: "Dublin here I come."

Morning dawns beautifully with clear blue skies warming the Irish mist as the green hills of Cork are exposed to the morning's sunshine. After tossing and turning all night, Billy is a bit groggy as he says goodbye to his mother. Gripping her rosary beads tightly, Nora is giving him the "cool" treatment. She is actually trembling with fear of what may happen to her Billy in that unknown world of Dublin. He hugs her tightly, and eagerly heads for Dublin. Billy's trip is a long four-hour journey through every little village and town along the way.

Gawking in awe at the splendor of Dublin's centuries old buildings, the River Liffy running through the center of the city and the hustle and bustle of the streets, Billy realizes he has to find a place to live, and fast. He buys a copy of <u>The</u>

<u>Evening Press</u> and scurries straight to the rentals section to find an interesting ad, or, at least, an interesting price: 'Efficiency for rent, suit one professional person, forty five pounds per month.' He calls and sets up an appointment immediately. The landlady gives him directions and he figures he's about an hour away: "first come, first served," she says.

He hopes he'll be the first to see it, as he manipulates his car through the narrow side streets and approaches the neighborhood. Not sure how to get there, and being brand new to the city, he has to stop several times for directions, which delays him even further.

He pulls up in his car, stuffed with all his worldly belongings, and walks up to a beautiful four story Georgian row house in Monkstown, a posh suburb on the Southside of Dublin. Across the street in all its glory, is Dublin harbor. He knocks and the landlady meets him, not expecting a guy looking like the Bee Gees. "Hello, Billy Golden, I called about the flat."

A dubious once-over is completed by a mid-50's, short as his mother, gray-haired woman. Her piercing blue eyes seem to X-Ray him as she quickly responds "Sheila Ring, nice to meet you, come in."

They proceed down the stairs to the basement flat. It's pretty depressing: one large room with a tiny cooker and sink, no cabinets, a beat up sofa, a table and two old chairs, a bed and a fireplace, wallpaper peeling off the wall in several places, and two tiny windows looking out at the first floor wall. It also felt damp. "You said forty five pounds a month?"

"Yes."
"I'll take it."

"Do you have any references?' Billy, realizing he might be in trouble, tells her the honest truth and hopes she'll give him a chance. "Well no, I'm just up from Cork like, and I lived at home when I was going to college, so this is my first time renting."

"Well I don't know Billy, people usually have references so we can check them out."

Billy plays his last two cards, "Would you mind calling my parents, and eh, I could pay ya for two months in advance as I really like it." Billy writes out his parents name and number and takes out a wad of cash, everything he has. She sees the money and figures he's okay. "Well all right Billy, I'll give you a chance, but I need the money on the first day of each month or you're out, okay?"

"Thanks a million, I'll look after it for ya." He hands her ninety pounds, nearly all of his cash, a fortune to Billy at the time.

Thankfully, he has just avoided the cost of spending his first night in Dublin in a bed and breakfast. She leaves and he brings in all his worldly belongings from the car: a few clothes, a record player, a small collection of his prized long playing records, his keyboard, and his dad's accordion.

He was determined to make a go of it, because his mother said he would be back within a week with his tail between his legs. Just the thing for a budding musician's self esteem, but he knew she was probably saying the rosary every night for her eldest son to be okay.

Chapter 8

Through the 1950s, television was only available to the lucky few, who lived along the east coast of Ireland, and could pick up the BBC.

Finally in 1961, Ireland got its first TV station, RTE. It was a very slow start. People would rent a small black and white television, and watch mostly half-hour American shows like **Green Acres**, **The Fugitive**, **Get Smart**, **I Love Lucy,** etc. Billy was an instant fan.

Some fella' in a bar back then asked his friend: "Hey Pat, what d'ya think of this new television thing?"

"You know Frank," said the other fella', "if ya closed yer eyes, you'd swear you were listenin' to the radio!"

In most Irish homes, there was a picture of Jesus, with a tiny red electric light glowing from his heart. When John F. Kennedy became President, his photo was right up there on the wall next to Jesus, and still is. Everybody was so proud, "that one of our own," a Catholic, whose ancestors had emigrated to America from County Wexford, had made it to the highest office in America. According to news reports, he had done this despite the viral anti-

Catholic bias of the Waspy American elite at the time.

Billy remembers that fantastic summer's day in 1963, when President Kennedy came to Cork. Like thousands of others, Billy was standing on the bridge next to Cork's City Hall, where JFK was given the freedom of the city, and gave a rousing speech. He drove by in his huge limo, or "rolls hardly," as the Irish used to call the big fancy cars back then [they roll along, and hardly turn the corner.] All of Cork witnessed this man with his handsome tanned face, and huge movie-star charisma, which made every woman giddy, like teenage girls swooning over their latest heartthrob.

The bridge was packed, and afterwards, the Cork County Council discovered a major crack in the bridge, due to the weight of so many people crammed onto the bridge at the one time. Apparently, it was a miracle the bridge didn't collapse that day, drowning many, including possibly the President.

Tragically, it was only a few months later that he was assassinated. Suddenly everybody wanted to see his funeral, and in a few days, televisions were installed in nearly all the homes in Ireland that had electricity at the time. Television was truly here to stay.

Soon after, came the **Late Late Show** *with Gay Byrne* as its host. He and his producers were on the cutting edge of their day. He interviewed everybody who was anybody at the time – pop stars, authors, activists, actors, gay, straight and everything in between. The church screamed bloody murder, but fair play to Gay and RTE, they stuck to their guns, and the show became a major force in opening up sheltered Ireland, causing major cracks in the status quo. Everybody was glued to it every Saturday night, and it was all totally analyzed in the pubs the following week.

With the new dawn, Billy can't wait to get started. He calls his friend at the television station, Michael Mortell. Michael is enjoying a very successful career as vice president of music in RTE, the only radio and television station in Ireland at the time. Michael was one of the very few college students who graduated with first class honors in music. Professor Lucy immediately offered him an associate Professorship in Cork University, a huge deal at the time.

Michael ran away and joined the circus instead! He met his lovely wife Muriel and saw the world, well at least Ireland and England anyway…. When he got that out of his system he joined RTE as an orchestral music arranger, and worked his way up to assistant head of music.

Billy got through right away, and Michael invited him to lunch at the station that afternoon. Billy arrives all excited, even tho' he had been there many times with his friend Sean O Se, as his accompanist, when they recorded several TV shows. This is different. He's now living in Dublin and looking for work.

Michael was the original musical director of the choir in Cork, and Billy had taken over from him, teaching the choir many of Michael's arrangements, and as time went by, many of his own.

Billy recalls a funny incident, as he was teaching the choir some years ago. During a break at one of the rehearsals, Eileen the director, approached him, "Billy, we have a new boy who wants to join the choir, so could you give him an audition? We're always looking for more men, his name is Pat."

Billy shakes his hand…. "Okay Pat, can you sing this?" Billy sings a simple little one bar melody, "ah ah ah." Pat tries to sing the melody, but he's a disaster, way way off key. "Okay Pat, do this." He sings two notes, and again, Pat is hopeless. He turns to Eileen who is listening. "Eileen, come on, he's terrible," making sure Pat can't hear him.

Eileen agrees, "Yea Billy, he's not so good all right, but he's an orphan, and the poor fella' has nobody.

This would be great for him. Could you make an exception and let him in…. please?"

How could you say no to that? Billy reluctantly shakes his head, "Well all right Eileen, but God, he can never sing okay?"

Eileen, who by her very nature, would adopt every stray kid in the world if she could, smiled and said, "thanks Billy."

He quietly talks to Pat. "Okay Pat, you can't sing sure you can't?"

"Nah, sorry."

"Look, I'll tell you what, just mime everything okay, never sing... EVER,… okay?"

Pat is thrilled he's in. "All right, thanks a million." Billy can see Pat now "singing" at his first concert with the choir, smiling his ass off, lip-synching the entire show.

At lunch Michael makes Billy an offer he couldn't refuse. "How would you like to be musical director of the Cabinteeley Singers? I'm swamped with work here and you'd be perfect." Billy is stunned. The great Michael Mortell offering him to take over as MD for a popular choir in Dublin, just a few miles from his flat. "They pay ten pounds every

Tuesday night." Billy figured forty pounds a month would pay for his rent so he accepted immediately. He always enjoyed teaching choirs, plus all the craic that went along with it.

"Valerie is their director, she's a terrific lady, you'll like her. They'll audition you, then they vote yes or no – win over fifty percent of them and you're in. I'll call Valerie and put a good word in for you." Billy drives back to the flat elated, tho' a little nervous about tomorrow night's audition. He has to get this job.

Next night he's all dolled up for the job, hair perfect, clothes ironed, shoes polished. He arrives as everybody is coming in. Valerie has to give them the bad news, right there, that Michael has just resigned, and tonight, the choir is going to be directed by Billy Golden. Billy hears them muttering, and shaking their head, obviously upset that Michael is gone.

Everybody knows of course that Billy is being auditioned for the job. Michael was brilliant, so now they're all in a foul mood. They were totally comfortable with him, respected what he did for them, and now they had to get used to someone new, who couldn't possibly be as good as Michael.

She looks at Billy with the 'you're up' look, and gives him the nod. She doesn't give the choir any background at all about Billy, it's literally a case of, 'okay, show us what you can do.'

Suddenly, there's total silence, eyes glare from every direction and Billy feels the hostility in the room. He was younger than all of them, so how could he be any good? Valerie hands him the music. You could hear a pin drop. Billy has a quick look and selects a song he knows well, an Andy Williams number called *Happy Heart*.

He begins the four bar intro on the piano, then the sopranos and altos sing the first four bars in unison. The tenors and basses join in in two-part harmony leading up to the chorus. The choir then breaks into four-part harmony.

Billy hears the basses are way off. He stops playing, shakes his hands in the air, and the choir sort of dies off. "Basses," he says, "ye're a little bit off there, it goes like this," and he proceeds to sing the bass part.

"That's not the way Michael does it," says one smartass with a smirk on his face.

"Well it's my arrangement, and this is the way I want it." Total silence…. Billy is shitting himself inside, but keeps his composure. "Okay basses here's what I want you to sing," acting as casually as he could, and he teaches the basses their line.

"Okay choir, let's try it together now," says Billy, and everybody could hear how much better it sounded. That was it, he's passed the test! He has the job! He also has forty new friends in Dublin.

Over the weeks as everybody gets to know him, and as they realize he's brand new to the area, they are very welcoming and helpful. He offers to teach them how to sight-read, as they were being taught by ear, so it would speed rehearsals up if they got better at reading the music. He also sings all the lines; soprano, alto, tenor and bass, individually onto cassettes, and hands them out each week, so they can learn their parts on their own during the week. This really helps, and they are able to learn way more songs than they had been doing. He offers to teach their kids piano lessons, and several of them take him up on his offer.

Billy knows at this point he's not going back to Cork. He can survive, and once he gets a piano, he can get down to songwriting again. He puts the word out to the choir about it.

He loves jogging down to Dun Laoghaire pier [pronounced Dunleary] and back to his flat. It takes about an hour as he uses his runs to explore the many side streets around the area. He hopes someday to own one of those fine Georgian houses he passes everyday; one big hit would do it.

Naturally the choir introduces him to all the local pubs nearby, and somebody suggests he try Clery's pub, as they have music in the pub Thursday through Sunday morning.

Without pause, he goes right down and meets the manager. Luckily there's a decent upright piano and a very basic sound system, so he does an on the spot audition. He starts with a few big songs of the day, Billy Joel, Elton John etc. Billy Joel was Billy's idol as he wrote such evocative songs, words and music, and what Billy loved about him was he wrote perfect bridges as well as verses and choruses. His words registered big time with Billy, and he envied his craft.

"Okay," said the manager, "I'll give you Thursday nights and Sunday mornings after Mass."

"How much?" asks Billy.

"Twenty pounds," he said.

Billy is thrilled. He was now about to make thirty pounds a week with the choir, the pub, plus the piano lessons. His mother might even begin to put her rosary beads away!

If all went well, he could ease out of the piano lessons as it took up an awful lot of his time driving to the kids homes, teaching them for half an hour, then repeating the process a few more times once the kids got out of school, all for just two pounds every half hour.

On his second Thursday night in Clery's pub, Billy is belting out one of his own songs, *Lover Not Just A Wife*. He wrote this song when a friend's wife was going through a hard time. Billy tried to put himself in his buddy's situation, trying to imagine what he would say to his wife if her friends were putting her down.

LOVER NOT JUST A WIFE

YOU'RE GOIN' THRU' A HARD TIME,
BEIN' TESTED ALL THE WAY
YOU'VE GOTTA' GIVE THEM BACK THEIR BIBLE
AND WE ALL KNOW WHAT THEY CAN SAY
YOU WEAR MY NAME ON YOUR FINGER,
IT'S JUST A DIAMOND STONE
IT'S HARD SOMETIMES, BUT THEY'RE GOD'S LINES
AND YOU ARE MORE, YOU ARE MORE

CHORUS
YOU ARE A LOVER NOT JUST A WIFE
I NEED YOUR LOVE AND ADVICE DAILY,
WHEN I'M DOWN ALL THE DAYS,
YOU KEEP LIFTIN' MY GRAYS
BY BEING THERE, YEA YEA…. YEA YEA YEA

WHEN I WOKE UP THIS MORNIN',
I LOOKED UPON YOUR EYES,
I FELT YOUR WARMTH BESIDE ME,
IT WAS JUST ONE OF THOSE TIMES.

IT'S YOU AND ME THAT MATTER
WHY LET THEM GET YOU DOWN.
YOU ARE MY WIFE, YOU ARE MY LIFE
BUT YOU ARE MORE, YOU ARE MORE

REPEAT CHORUS

He's definitely not setting the place on fire, some are listening, most are ignoring him and chatting and laughing as if he's not there. He takes a break and orders a pint. An older guy approaches Billy, and introduces himself. He's got a strong Dublin accent, about five feet six, stocky build, and a little overweight.

"Hey head," he says, "PJ Tierney."

"Billy Golden," and he shakes PJ's hand.
"You're a culchie?" says PJ. [redneck]
"And you're a Dub?" says Billy. [Dubliner]
"Yea," says PJ, "and proud of it."
"And ya know what a Dub is don't ya?"
"Wha' " says PJ.
"The son of a culchie," says Billy, relishing the quick touché.
PJ laughs, "Good one, I haven't heard that one before."
"Yea, I'm just up from Cork, looking for any work I can get."
PJ doesn't mince his words. "Well you're not going to get too far playing here chief."

"Yea, but it's a start, it helps pay the rent you know," says Billy defensively.

"Look Billy, I was watchin' ya there for a while and you're good. I manage a few bands and we're looking for a lead singer right now, and you playing the piano as well would be a plus. Would ya be interested?"

"What sort of stuff do they do?"

"Ya know, a bit o' rock, all the top 20 stuff, four lads and a girl. You'll get nowhere without a band in Ireland, ya know that don't ya?"

Billy realizes he was right, "Yea, I suppose."

"They're playing in O'Connors tomorrow night in Dalkey. Could ya come along and have a look, I think you'll like them."

Billy is obviously excited at the thought of joining a band. "Yea, all right, I'm teaching until nine, so I'll see you around ten."

"You're a teacher?" PJ is impressed.

"Yea, I got the ould music degree in Cork, I direct a choir here and I teach some of their kids piano."

"Fair play to ya, so I'll see ya tomorrow night then?"

"Okay, hey what do they call themselves?"

The Touch." "I like it," says Billy. "Wow," he thinks, "Dublin really is where it's happening; I'm here two weeks and I might be joining a band. I hope they're good. I wonder what they'll think of a culchie joining them?" [Even tho' he's from Ireland's second biggest city, Dublin people call anyone who doesn't come from Dublin city a culchie.] He finishes his pint and goes back to the piano.

Chapter 9

The following night Billy turns up at O'Connors and the band are playing Fleetwood Mac's *Don't Stop*. They sound pretty good and Billy has a good look at them all:

Helen is a striking blonde in a gaudy sort of way, huge Farrah Fawcett-like hair, lacquered up to the last, gaudy dress, but she manages to pull it off. She's tall with a great figure, nice breasts she pushes up and makes the most of. She's a fine singer and great on harmonies. She was flirting outrageously with all the guys, she knew her way around the stage, and when she introduced songs, she had a throaty laugh that turned on the guys who were actually looking at her, as most of the people were, once again, more or less ignoring them.

Steo, [Steeo] born Stephen, is the lead guitarist and is excellent, and good at back up harmonies. He was the skinniest guy you'd ever meet, and wore very strong geeky-looking glasses.

Robot, the drummer, is pretty good, with a cute smiling face, and long blonde hair.

Jack is the bass player. He's the tallest of them, a good-looking well-built guy, who is a pretty good bass player, and had a sexuality about him when he played, totally immersed, and lost in his music. You got the impression he was making love to his bass guitar when he played.

Mel is the rhythm guitarist. He's also good on back up harmonies. He's average looking, and not as hip as the other lads. Billy learned later that he was a fantastic fiddle player, and his hobby was photography, always taking pictures of where the lads played, and keeping a visual record of the craic along the way. He was ahead of his time in that regard.

Everybody seems a bit shy and are concentrating on just playing, as they know there's some fella' coming to listen to them who might be joining them. PJ probably built Billy up to them, making it sound as if all it took to hit the big time was to join up with this new guy.

Just like Billy's gig last night, nobody was really paying attention except Jacks girlfriend Bridget, who was drooling over him.

After listening to the band for a while, PJ approaches Billy, "Well, what d'ya think?"

"Hi PJ, yea, they're pretty good, but they're getting the same reaction I got last night."

"Yea, but if the two of ye joined together, we could get bigger venues, get a bit of television, that sort o' thing. I know all the Dee Jays and producers…By the way do ya do any writing?"

"Yea, I've written a few songs, got into a few song contests; Tokyo, Bulgaria, most of Europe, won a few here and there. I won the Castlebar Song Contest two years ago."

"Hey that's great, fair play to ya" says PJ, "I'd like to hear them. That's the way we need to go. Nobody will hand us a good song at our stage, so we'll have to write them ourselves to get a deal. Have you tried Eurovision?"

"Every year, nothin' yet," says Billy.

"Well that's THE one. Did ya know that over half a billion people watch it on television every year?"

"Yea, I know it's huge, guaranteed number one in Europe in all their charts, millions."

The band takes a break and PJ introduces everybody. "Hey lads, I'm sure I can get ye better gigs than this if ye join up, ye're not going anywhere right now, so whadd'ya think?"

"An equal split?' says Steo echoing what all the lads are thinkin'.

"Yea," says PJ, "I'll put a bit o' bread in [money] for promotion, pictures, clothes, and you'll need a wagon, so suss it out okay. You can pay me back later, but as Billy will be the lead singer, I think ye need to be called Billy Golden and the Touch. It'll help promote you better."

Jack puts his arm around Bridget's waist, and goes to kiss her. "Hey watch my lipstick," she says bitchily, putting him down in front of everybody. He's just about to touch her hair, "don't touch my hair, Meg just did it." Holy shit what a bitch, Billy thinks to himself. She pulls Jack closer and whispers, "you should be the lead singer Jack, who's this gobshite from Cork anyway?"

"Well PJ says he's good and the band thinks it's a good idea," Jack utters weakly.

"Well it means you've gotta split the money six ways, you realize that don't ya?" Bridget chides.
"Yea, but if we get better gigs?... Jack knows he's fighting a losing battle, whatever Bridget thinks is the way it is.

Just then Robot shakes Billy's hand and says "How'rya Billy, we rehearse every Wednesday in my place, ri'? So can you make it tomorrow at eleven?"

"Yea sure," he says, "where d'ya live?"

"Ballyer," says Robot.

Ballyfermot, is a very close-knit working-class community in Dublin, with a high unemployment rate, and petty crime is commonplace. But if you come from Ballyfermot, you are loyal to your neighbor, and they watch out for you big time....

"509 St. Peter's Road," says Robot.

Upon his arrival, Billy parks a few doors up from Robot's house in his Italian Sports Coupe, a 1970 Lancia Fulvia. Billy loved the car, and had worked his ass off teaching and playing loads of weddings to buy it. It was fire engine red, had twin carburetors, stick shift, and was a mini rocket. He nearly killed himself several times, coming home drunk, flying, or both.

509 St. Peter's Road is a small drab-looking dark red-bricked row house, exactly the same as all the other row houses on the street. The band is packed into a tiny room with a tiny kitchen at the rear. Two steps into the hall on the left, is a steep stairs up to two tiny bedrooms and a bathroom, as basic as you could get. Robot's father meets Billy at the front door. "Hey Billy, Pops Keogh, nice to meet ya, would ya like a cup o' tea?"

Pops is a milkman, and everybody loves him in Ballyfermot. His wife died when Robot was only two, and now he lives for Robot and the band. He's a warm-hearted character, an older version of Robot, and is included completely as one of the lads.

Billy brings in his keyboard, and starts to set up. Mel, Steo, and Helen are sitting on the couch, the only couch. The lads have their amps turned way down, with respect for the neighbors. Jack is half sitting on the kitchen table facing the couch. Robot has only room for his snare drum and high hat in front of the tiny fireplace. The only place for Billy to put his piano is on the kitchen table by the sink facing the lads. The body language is fierce, everybody sizing Billy up, nobody actually looking him in the eye, he's an outsider, a culchie, "let's see what you've got" vibe. The band starts rehearsing, and after a while, takes a break. Billy takes a breather out front as there's no back yard. If you took two steps out the back door, you're in someone else's kitchen! He sees two guys taking the wheels off his car.

"Hey Robot, look what those two bollixes are doing to my car."

Robot shouts down to his friends, "Hey Frank."

"Hey Robot," he replies as he continues to loosen the nuts.

"He's with me all ri'?" "Sorry Robot" they shout back, and start putting the wheels back on and tighten the nuts. "You'll be all right from now on, they know you're with me all ri'?"

"Bloody Hell," says Billy, shaking his head. He never saw crime so close up before.

A few days later the band are getting a promo picture together at a studio. Billy sees an absolute knockout fixing Helen's hair. She's tall, model-like, and has a European look about her, black hair and darker than normal skin. "Who's that?" he asks Mel.

"Jack's sister, Meg."

Billy goes over to her and throws her a line. "Could you spoil me too?"

"Well, let's have a look," she says. She tosses his hair, and applies a little hair spray … there's chemistry, or at least Billy thinks so.

They get into place and the photographer says, "okay lads, big smile please."

Meg sees Steo with his typical pinched look, "Steo, will ya smile for God's sake, you look like someone's trying to steal yer money or somethin'." They all laugh and Billy is immediately turned on by her sense of humor. Steo does his best, but still looks like he's in agony. Meg fusses over Helen's hair, and Billy is impressed that she's giving her time and help, tho' she's getting nothing for it.

The photographer takes a quick burst of shots. "Okay lads, I got it thanks, I'll get 'em to ya tomorrow PJ, all ri'?"

"Thanks Paul," says PJ, "are ye goin' for a jar lads?"

They all jump into their cars and head to the nearest pub. Everybody's having a laugh in the bar. Billy works his way towards Meg little by little, and soon comes face to face with her. "Hi, I'm Billy, that was nice of ya to come along tonight, Meg."

"Well, someone's gotta' look after them, the shower of wankers."

He laughs even tho' she's pretty cold. Billy does his best to break down her wall or whatever it is, there was definitely something. "Are ya a hairdresser?"

"Yea, I work from home 'til my son is a bit older." Billy is deflated. "Are ya married?"

Meg laughs, "God no, one little man in my life is enough right now." That was the first time she smiled and her face just lit up. She looked like butter wouldn't melt in her mouth, totally innocent, as she smiled, and Billy was hooked.

He decided he'd go for it. "Any chance you'd go out with a Corkman?"

"What's so special about a Corkman?"

"I don't know, but we're very good in bed, we hardly ever fall out."

Meg lets out a groaning laugh, "God, is that the best you can do?"

Billy persists, "Well, if you do come out with me, it'll be my first time walking out with a Dublin girl."

Meg seems a little tickled at this quaint country line, not the usual Dublin bravado she hears all the time. "Well I don't know," she smiles teasingly, "it's tough finding a sitter."

Billy goes all in, "Ah go on, I'm off on Friday, we can go for a drink, come on, just a drink." She hesitates..... "Come on," he says, "just a drink."

"Well all right Corkman, if I can find a sitter."

Billy is delighted, but also taken aback. She has a kid, she's way too young to have a kid he thought, but he still finds himself saying, "great, I'll see ya on Friday, hey by the way, what's your son called?"

"Sam," says Meg smiling, and tells him how to get there. Billy is thrilled, his first date with a Dublin girl, and she's gorgeous. He can't wait for Friday night.

He drives the longish distance from the Southside of Dublin right through the city and out to the Northside. It took him almost an hour, but he doesn't mind, it's a new adventure, and he loves to drive his car. As he rings the bungalow's doorbell, he takes in a nice neighborhood, garden perfect, exactly what he would expect of the little he knew of Meg so far. The babysitter opens the door. "Are youse the fella' from Cork?" in her heavy Dublin accent.

"Yea," Billy walks in to Meg doing some old lady's hair in the kitchen.

Glancing at Billy, Meg tells him, "I'll be ready in a few minutes."

"Janey [Wow] Meg, he's a hunk," says the old lady. Meg smiles with a bit of the Irish glint in her eye.

'Tis a nice house, spotless, with a fine big garden out back. He sits down and out comes her six-year-old son Sam, a cute-looking kid with long blonde hair, and definitely, not in the least bit shy... "Hey mister, me mam says you're a singer," in his Dublin accent.

"Yeah, and you must be Sam?"

"Yea, hey mister, my dog can sing."

"Really?" Billy is amused at this little guy, full of personality.

"I betcha' he's a better singer than you."

Meg smiles embarrassingly at Billy, "Sam that's not nice."

"No no that's all right," says Billy, "tell ya what Sam, I'll give you a pound if your dog's a better singer than me."

Sam is only too delighted to show off his dog's talents. "Ri', hey, Seamus you bastard, come 'ere."

Billy looks at Meg, taken aback at Sam's language. "It's a long story," she says, "tell ya later," and goes into her bedroom. Out romps this Maltese Terrier, a little ball of white fluff with two huge black eyes, full of spunk, running full speed ahead straight at Sam. He looks at Sam hoping for a lump of sugar. "Sing Seamus." Seamus just barks. "No Seamus you bastard, sing." Sam does his imitation doggie howl, to get Seamus started, and, sure enough; the dog starts 'singing.'

He starts with a high howl that he brings all the way down without a breath, then starts again, and goes all the way up into high falsetto, and then down again. If he were human, he'd have a career, as he has a three-octave range. He stares at Sam and wags his tail, which you can barely see, hoping for a lump of sugar. Billy gets out a pound and hands it to Sam. Sam is delighted with himself, and gives the dog a lump of sugar.

"You're right Sam," says Billy, "he's a better singer than me." They all enjoy a laugh, even the old lady tries to laugh, but gets a fit of coughing from a lifetime of chain-smoking.

Billy lays on the charm; "you look marvelous my dear."

"Meg's the best, she's been through a lot, you treat her nice now," she says through her coughing.

Meg comes out of her bedroom looking stunning. She was wearing the same baggy sweats doing the ladies hair as she was the first time he saw her. Now she's in a tight skirt and matching blouse and heels, and looks smoking hot. Billy thought he was looking at Miss Ireland herself.

She sees his sports car and is impressed as they leave. "Janey, I thought you were a starving musician like the rest of the lads."

"I am, I worked my balls off for this car."

"Fair play to ya, how fast can it go?" Billy guns it and tears down the road 'til they get to the pub. He parks and blows the horn, an old antique car sound he had installed for the craic blares out. She laughs and they walk into the pub. They sit up at the bar and order.

"That's a great son you've got there."
"Yea, he's a character."
"And his Dad?"
"A right bollix, biggest mistake of me life."
"Yea, but you've got Sam."
"Yea," and she smiles.
"So, tell us, how did the dog get his name?"

"Well when I got pregnant with Sam, we quickly married and it was all right for a while. He gave Sam a lot of attention, more than he gave me,"... as she gazes off into the distance. "Then last year he met some other one and he left, just blurted it out one day and left, just like that. She wasn't the first one either.

Sam the poor little guy cried and cried for his dad, so my dad brought us to a kennel last Christmas and he let Sam pick out a dog. He asked Sam what he was going to call it and he said Seamus. We were bringing him home in the car, and he puked all over the back seat. Me dad screamed 'Seamus you bastard!!!' Sam thought it was hilarious, so it stuck and that's how he got his name."

Billy looked at this gorgeous girl, totally hurt by a jerk who obviously didn't appreciate her. She developed this hard exterior to protect herself. But Billy had just seen her soft side, and felt he was being included in her small group with whom she could be herself. Sipping their drinks, they are oblivious to anyone else in the pub, having a laugh, getting to know each other. After a less speedy drive back to Megs place, he maneuvers a long goodnight kiss. He drives home in seventh heaven.

Chapter 10

Wednesday morning, the band are rehearsing, and getting a little better. Billy's keyboard was a new sound for the lads, and he patiently taught them the right chords when they couldn't figure them out from the record. This impressed the lads, and they were beginning to think it might work out after all, but it was still him and them. He was still an outsider. Pops serves endless cups of tea, and Robot's favorite: thick sliced bread and butter with smashed bananas piled onto the bread, delicious.

PJ arrives towards the end of rehearsal, with his big announcement. "Hello lads, well, you've got yer first gigs this weekend." The excitement is palpable. Steo as always thinking the worst chimes in, "Shit PJ, we're not ready."

"Well then, rehearse tomorrow too."
"We can't rehearse tomorrow," says Steo, "we pick up our dole money."

This whole dole thing was a million miles from Billy's thinking. "You collect the dole?"

"Of course we do," says Steo, "how dy'a think we feckin' well live?" Billy shakes his head. "We're makin' nothin' these days, the odd wedding that's all."

"Well, get ye're arses outta' bed earlier, and get a rehearsal in all ri'?" says PJ.

Billy realizes he could actually collect unemployment dole money himself, as he was being paid in cash only at the time, no official records, but he was doing okay, and his pride got in the way of making some easy money. "I'd rather earn my own money, and holy shit, what would my uncle say if he found out?" he thought.

He could just imagine the phone call from his mother, rosary beads taut between her thumb and forefinger, "Billy, I just got a call from my brother and he was furious. He told me you're getting the dole? The Minister For Social Welfare informed him, that his nephew was sponging off the state. The press will have a field day if they find out. He said you're to stop collecting immediately and get a job."

'Tis true, his Uncle Frank is the Prime Minister of Ireland, and a national sports legend. He won every medal imaginable in Irish sports, and is one of Ireland's most popular politicians. He still has stats from his sporting days that have not been equaled.

Everybody respects him for all his Gaelic sports achievements, and Frank is included in the fantasy "team of the century" in Gaelic hurling. So, you couldn't have achieved much more than that in Irish sports.

Naturally, the expectations for Billy to be a great athlete like his uncle were huge. Unfortunately, Billy was useless. Couldn't kick a ball or hit a hurley to save his life. To make matters worse, he had rheumatic fever and a heart murmur, when he was eleven, so if he chased around a ball like mad, he ended up in bed for a week with joint pains. The doctor warned his parents that he could die, so, they kept him under "house arrest," for one whole summer. As there was no television at the time, Billy just played the piano all summer long. This sports impediment was the turning point for Billy's future musical journey.

Billy is brought back from his daydreaming when PJ makes an exciting announcement. "By the way I've found a roadie for youse, Fran Foley, Doc's brother, so he knows his stuff, and ya know what, he owns Doc's old van, so lads, ye're on ye're way."

Doc Foley was a huge star in Ireland at the time, a fantastic crooner, probably one of the best voices ever to come out of Ireland, good looking with loads of hits, and the girls loved him. He had sung for Ireland in the Eurovision Song Contest, and had even played Vegas.

At the time Eurovision was one of the very few chances of making it in Ireland, and possibly Europe if you won it. The idea of winning this song contest, Europe's American Idol, was always in the back of Billy's mind, and he felt he could do it with a little luck. Billy's dream was to at least win the Irish song contest, whatever about winning Eurovision.

After rehearsal he calls Meg. "How's it goin' like?"

"Hi Billy, great thanks." Billy loves her voice, a soft neutral Dublin accent, sophisticated sounding, but not posh in any way.

He takes a deep breath and says, "Hey, I just bought some pots and pans for the flat, and I'm gonna' try and cook somethin', will ya come over?"

"What can ya cook?"

"I dunno', spaghetti or somethin'."

He actually is a very good cook. When he was in Italy a few years ago, as usual singing in a song contest, he raved so much about a meal to the waitress that the chef came out, and in his broken English, gave Billy the recipe and told him how he cooked it. Sometimes back in Cork, he took over the kitchen and cooked dinner for the family, giving his mother a break.

"I'm half Italian and you're going to cook ME spaghetti?" she teases.

"Then come on over and teach me."

"If I can get a sitter I'll let ya know."

"Ah come on, I wrote a song for you and Sam."

"You're full of surprises aren't ya Corkman?"

"Billy," says Billy….

"Billy," says Meg. He smiles; he's cracking the ice.

After what seems like an eternity for Billy, she arrives at his basement flat. There are two entrances, one from the basement, and one from the first floor. Meg taps on the basement window, and when he sees her again, she takes his breath away. "She hasn't a clue how beautiful she is," he thinks to himself. Man, life is good.

The fireplace is blazing, and he has one of his favorite LP's playing: the brilliant jazz pianist, Oscar Peterson. He thought Oscar had everything: perfect technique, interpretation, and he could improvise better than anyone. Oscar had a full orchestra complementing his style. It was perfect dinner music. He hands her a glass of wine, and her being half Italian, he says, "Salute."

She smiles, "Salute", and looks around. Everything is ancient except for a modern looking piano. "Did the piano come with the flat?" she asks.

"No no, remember I was telling you about the choir I'm directing? One of their mothers died, and she had a piano. Nobody wanted it, and they said I could have it if I hauled it away. Another guy in the choir has a truck, so he and his son and myself dragged it down the steps, and all it cost me was a few pints and a tenner to tune it."

Meg goes over to the stove and tastes the sauce and nods approvingly. "Where did ya learn to cook like that?"

"Ah now," says Billy smiling mysteriously, " sure that's a secret."

"So you give piano lessons here?"

"God no, I'd be too embarrassed to teach here. I go to their homes and teach them for half an hour, then drive to another few kids and do the same thing. I teach the choir every Tuesday night, and I'm playing in Clery's every Thursday night and Sunday morning, you're looking at a millionaire, ...come on, let's eat."

The LP finishes and Billy goes over and puts on another album. "You know, you made that old lady look like a million bucks the other night."

"Thanks, she's a nice person."

"You know Meg, I was thinkin', you should have your own shop in Dublin. You're good enough, and you can small-talk people every bit as good as my mother."

"Yea right," she says dismissively, "and where would I get the money for that?"

"I know someone who might be able to help."

"Is that another of your Cork lines?"

"No no like, I know this guy, Aiden O'Toole is his name. I met him in University and we became friends. He works for the Government giving out grants for small businesses like yours. Meg, you deserve this. You're good enough, and you could employ some other hairdressers; create jobs, that's what they're trying to do. I could call him if you like."

"You're full of surprises aren't ya Corkman." "Call me Billy."

Billy serves dinner and pours her another glass of wine. She doesn't know it, but he had worked four hours for the bottle of wine that afternoon. They are totally relaxed and enjoying themselves. She brings the dishes over to the sink, and rinses them. "So you said you wrote a song?"

"Yea, come on," and he brings her over to the piano, and sharing the bench seat, sings while playing his latest song.

LUCKY CHILD

HOW HE CRIES, HOW HE CRIES IN THE MORNIN'
'COS HE KNOWS THAT YOU'RE NOT VERY FAR
AND YOU BATHE HIM WITH LOVE AND AFFECTION,
FOR HE IS YOUR LUCKY CHILD.

HE IS ALL THAT YOU HAVE IN THE MORNIN'
HE'S ALL THAT YOU'VE GOT IN THIS WORLD
YET YOU KNOW YOUR BOY IS YOUR SALVATION
YES HE IS YOUR LUCKY CHILD.

CHORUS
YOUR MAN HAS LEFT YOU SOME TIME AGO
TO RUN TO THE ARMS OF ANOTHER
AND I KNOW THE STORY AS STORIES GO
IT'S SO HARD WHEN YOU FEEL SO ALONE

HOW HE SMILES LUCKY CHILD IN THE MORNIN'
WHEN YOU LOVE HIM AND HE'S IN YOUR ARMS
AND YE'LL LAUGH AND YE'LL PLAY IN THE
MORNIN'
AND YOU FEEL YOU CAN FACE THE DAY

REPEAT CHORUS

BUT WOMAN, YOU'VE GOT MORE THAN SOME,
YOU'VE GOT YOUR SON
AND WOMAN YOU THINK YOU'RE NOT FREE,
BUT WHAT'S FREEDOM GIVEN ME?

NOW HE SLEEPS HOW HE SLEEPS IN THE EVENIN'

AND YOU FACE THE LONG NIGHT ON YOUR OWN
BUT YOU THINK OF THE FLOWER HE GAVE YOU
AND YOU KNOW HE'S YOUR LUCKY CHILD
AND YE'LL LAUGH AND YE'LL PLAY IN THE
MORNIN'
FOR HE IS YOUR LUCKY CHILD
YES HE IS YOUR LUCKY CHILD

He finishes, and there's a long silence. Here's this Corkman, with his country charm, and lack of the usual Dublin brashness making her feel like a woman for the first time in years, and she likes what she's feeling. She seems genuinely moved by how accurately he describes her situation. A little teary-eyed she says, "That's beautiful Billy."

"You're beautiful Meg." He kisses her, and she responds. He lifts her up and carries her to bed. She stays the night.

Meg wakes up next morning to Billy giving her a gentle shake. "Breakfast," he smiles, "Just a boiled egg, bread and butter, I didn't expect company for breakfast."

She yawns and shakes her head, runs her hands through her hair. "Wow, it's been a long time since I've been served breakfast in bed, thanks." She pulls herself up and straightens the tray.

"Good morning," he says and kisses her gently.
"I must look a mess," she says.

"I've seen worse," he teases. She gives him a dig and laughs.

"Do you serve all the girls breakfast in bed?"

"You're the first."

"Go way outta' that, I don't believe ya for a second, you charmer you."

"Hey," he says, putting his arm around her, "there's nobody I'd rather share a boiled egg with right now than you," and he kisses her again.

They finish breakfast, he takes the tray away, puts on an Eagles LP, and sits on the bed, looks at her and smiles, "t'was a great night."

"T'was," she says, and he kisses her again. She pulls him down to her, "thanks for breakfast," and with *Take it Easy*, and **Joe Walsh's** *Life's Been Good* singing in the background, that very moment in his tiny damp efficiency flat, surpassed any five star hotel, as they cling to each other, and make love again in a lazy Sunday morning sort of way.

Suddenly there's a familiar tap on the window; two quick taps, a short pause, and one more tap. "Oh shit," says Billy, "it's my father, what the hell is he doing up in Dublin?"

"Billy, Billy, it's dad, are you awake?"

Meg frantically grabs her clothes, and puts them on. "I don't want to meet your father like this," laughing nervously.

"Go out the front door, and I'll let him in here all right?" They kiss and smile at each other.....

"Good luck tonight," she says as she's running up the stairs. Billy lets his dad in as she pulls away in her car.

"Hi dad, what're you doing here?" Trying his best to act as if he just woke up alone.

"Hello Billy, I tried to call you but there was no answer."

"Come on in."

His dad has the look of restrained disappointment, when he sees the mess from the previous night. Billy hopes he doesn't cop on to what just went down. "Wow Billy, it's pretty small isn't it?"

"Yea, but I got my own bathroom which is great."

"Well that's good," smiling to himself, remembering the countless times Billy hogged the bathroom back home, dolling himself up for another night on the town.

"Hey Billy, how about lunch? I just drove up for a meeting tonight, and I was hoping to get all the news from you, mum wants to know how you're getting on."

"That sound's great dad, I've about two hours, before I gotta' get ready for tonight. I know a nice place in Dalkey."

Chapter 11

"The Call" is where the band arranges to meet, and then go on to the gig in one van. Depending on where they are going, it's usually at one of the hotels on the outskirts of the city. This is their first time working with Fran, and they haven't met him yet.

"Where the hell is Fran?" says Steo, even tho' he's only five minutes late. Suddenly in he appears in a banged up Toyota Hiace van, radio blasting. The Toyota Hiace was the preferred van for showbands during their heyday. [Think Dodge Caravan today, without all the bells and whistles.]

"How'rya, ye shower of wankers?" was the first thing out of his mouth. This mad colorful guy, who looked like Joe Cocker on a bad day, gives them a crazy smile, turns off the engine, jumps out with a flourish, and throws open the back doors. He's taller than the lads, about six feet one, a little bit pudgy, very light skin and fair hair. "Okay boys, throw your shit in and let's get the hell out of here."

They're heading right across the country towards Galway, packed like sardines in the van, with the gear just barely making it in the back. It's a perfect sunny day in June, and the scenic hills and small villages are postcard perfect. There are no bypasses around the towns, nor are there any decent highways and the intermittent sheep in the middle of road causes anxious nerves to fray. Fran's vocabulary and horn are stretched to their limits with one particular gathering of a ram and four ewes. A stare-down was futile, given the evil glare coming from the ram's hooded, golden-flecked eyes. When the octet determined that the grass was greener on the other side, they slowly meandered across the remainder of the road.

To augment an already anxiety prone trek, today presents an especially interesting challenge. It's fair day in every village and town they encounter; all of the farmers come in to sell their cattle and pigs. They don't park their cars, they abandon them! Add to that all the trailers they have and it's total chaos. Many of the upper windows of the houses and shops have flower boxes, and the flowers are in full bloom. This adds to each town's charm greatly, but the lads could have cared less. Fran does his best to keep the van moving quickly through the countryside, but the entire journey lasts more than four hours.

Their dreams of being on their way to the big time are soon dashed when they arrive at the gig. It's a pretty run-down hotel, and a sort of an inbred looking guy greets them and opens the doors. "Jaysus lads," says Fran, "ye're really startin' at the bottom. Hey," he says to the guy, "where's the dressing room?"

The ballroom guy looks at Fran, his thick glasses making him look even more geeky, "eh, the dressing room?"

"Yea, where the lads can change ya know?"

"Eh," he says, "we don't have any, the toilets are down there, all the bands use them.

"Holy shit, what have I done?" says Fran condescendingly. The last thing the lads needed just then, was being reminded of how big a star his brother was, and who were they to think they had a hope in hell of breaking through anyway?

The showband era started in the late 1950's and lasted through the early 70's. Before them came the big bands modeled after the Glenn Miller and Tommy Dorsey orchestras. These guys could all read music, and knew their instruments. They sat and played all night, except when the odd trumpet, clarinet, or sax player would stand up for his "solo."

More and more people were making a living outside of the farm, and were doing better than their farming parents ever did. Suddenly they had cars, and were able to go dancing in the next county, and meet their future wives.

In 1955 a band called the **Clipper Carlton** from Northern Ireland made the scene. They were an excellent bunch of musicians, who could both read music, and play by ear. Their make up was: trumpet sax and trombone, lead and bass guitar, organ, drums and a lead singer, maybe two. This would become the classic showband formula, for the next twenty years or so in Ireland.

The Clippers came on stage in flashy suits, and actually stood up all night, instead of the staid old-fashioned big bands who sat down, even doing some dance steps in unison, a la Buddy Holly. They also did some "show features:" carefully rehearsed comedy pieces in the style of Laurel and Hardy etc. and they brought the house down. This was new. This was exciting. They played to a thousand to two thousand people every night. People got in line hours before the dance, to make sure they got in to hear their new music heroes.

Shortly thereafter, came **Brendan Bowyer and the Royal Showband**. They were a sensation, and deservedly, dominated the scene for years. Brendan could swivel his hips every bit as good as Elvis, and then after driving the girls crazy, sing a hymn or a rebel song better than anyone else at the time. They made fortunes, and with very shrewd management, had a very successful run in some of the top lounges in Vegas.

There were a few top bands, but there were hundreds of mediocre bands travelling the Irish roads, in the glory years of the showband era. Anyone who could play three chords on a guitar joined a band, and started to make "easy" money.

One great thing the showbands did was level the playing field for country people. People from big and small towns, "townies," as they're called, sometimes looked down on culchies. If you had any rhythm at all, and the Irish do, if you could waltz and jive, and owned your own car, man, you had it made, no matter where you came from, city, town or country.

You could listen to your heroes on stage, dance the night away, and look forward to a "ration of passion," later on in your car, if you got lucky. Dancehalls were known as "ballrooms of romance," and many a marriage in the fifties', sixties', and seventies', started there.

Even though there were hundreds of bands, only a few broke through to become big international stars. This was because they just covered the current hits of the day, very rarely playing their own music.

Nobody gave a damn about the new kids on the block. It's the late 70's, the waning days of the showband era, and times and tastes were changing. The dancehall and hotel owners were milking the last of the dance scene. Most of them never modernized their venues through the glory years. The new nightclubs and discos were way more comfortable, and they had a full liquor license. The days of a thousand to three thousand people at a dance hall were well and truly over.

The dancehall owner very reluctantly hired someone local to serve the bands tea and ham sandwiches. The ham was so thin you could see yourself through it, and it was placed between thin slices of white bread and butter. It was appreciated, but it was a bore getting the same 'showband sandwiches' as they were called, everywhere they went. Pubs at that time never had any food for sale. So, most bands were treated like crap, except for the very few. Some larger ballroom owners served a good meal to the bands, but Billy and the lads were light years away from playing in those dancehalls.

Billy's admiration for those showband guys, thousands of them in the glory days, regardless of how good or bad they were, was sky high. They crisscrossed the country six nights a week, in shitty wagons, terrible roads and mostly crummy welcomes from dance hall owners, not to mention the freezing dancehalls.

That they put on a good "show" was a testament to all of them. If they didn't, their managers quickly replaced them. Some of those same band managers owned the ballrooms as well, so they controlled everything. They made fortunes when the taxman wasn't as clued in back then to the huge cash cow that the whole showband scene was in the 60's and early 70's.

There wasn't much loyalty either among the bands in those days, especially if the band was "manufactured" by a ballroom or multi-ballroom owner. They had no qualms about poaching a better musician or lead singer from another band.

It was all about the money, rarely about the music. The mission of showbands in the 60's and 70's was: play all the latest Top 20 hits as close to the records as possible, throw in a few old time waltzes, a couple of jives, then good night, pay me, back into the wagon, and if you were lucky, drive home and sleep in your own bed.

In these glory days there were as many as five hundred bands criss-crossing the country, seven or eight in each band, usually packed into a worn out van, all hustling for bookings.

The managers created all sorts of gimmicks to create publicity for their bands. They lied to all the national papers that their latest single was racing up the charts, while they bought hundreds of their own records themselves.

Marriages crumbled, many of the musicians became alcoholics, as the money was there, and they had to kill so many long nights in hotels after the dances. The pay at the time was at least five times what their friends made holding down a day job. This of course was the main attraction, easy money, or so it seemed to the outsider looking in. Some of the bands were the cream of the crop, genuinely good and had huge followings.

Some of these highly paid guys bought houses, rented them, and are now sitting pretty, but unfortunately, the very few smart, and really talented ones, were the exceptions.

The halls are always freezing until the heat is put on, if they actually do, and then it only comes on an hour before the crowd comes in. It's rough on Helen who is trying to change and get ready in the cold, much less that she has very little privacy. There are no mirrors of any kind anywhere, except what she brings with her.

At tonight's run-down hotel, **The Touch** brings in the gear to set up, and have a sound check. Fran is at the back of the hall mixing the sound, no lights, just the ordinary lights that are on the stage. The crowd slowly comes in, a very small crowd as **Billy and the Touch** were totally unknown.

About an hour or so into the dance they're playing away, a little nervous, doing their best, when suddenly a fight breaks out in the middle of the hall between a few of the punters.[crowd] The lads have never seen anything like this, so they stop playing.

Suddenly everybody looks up at the stage. With that the hotel owner runs up the hall. "You bloody idiots, what the hell are ye doing, keep playing for f***'s sake." This is the first time they've seen or heard the hotel owner! They start again and go through the motions, not a great start, but a start.

At the end of the night, Billy visits the small ticket kiosk where the owner is counting the money while the lads tear down their equipment. "Very bad crowd tonight, very small," says the owner, "only a hundred and two." Billy and the lads are on a 50/50 split, and he is stunned when he says one hundred and two, as he's positive there was closer to two hundred people there.

This was another famous tactic the ballroom owners used, and they knew if you questioned their numbers, that's the last time you played in their dancehall. Once again, the "bigger draws", the better known bands who had a loyal following, could put a band member into the ticket kiosk as people were coming in. If the manager gave them any crap, they would simply play in another nearby dancehall.

Billy despised him and swore he would be treated fairly someday. He counts out the money, "three hundred and twenty pounds," and even then, reluctantly hands Billy the money. "Tell PJ to give me a call," which means he thought they were okay, and of course he could rip them off again.

PJ gets his twenty percent right off the top, which is nearly double what the lads get, just for making a phone call. The lads cover all the expenses; gas, hotels, van insurance, clothes, instruments and truck repairs. When they complain to PJ, he quickly retorts: "When you make it, you get to call the shots okay."

As well as PJ's take, the lads learn of "the backhander." This is a bribe, usually fifty pounds; this again is more than any of the lads are paid. Sometimes the dancehall owner was either too busy or too lazy to actually be there, so he had a manager in charge. He had total power about who got booked and who didn't. One bad word and you were out, so everybody paid him off. Usually he was a real slimeball reveling in his Godlike position. Any band that didn't play along got some concocted complaint, total lies, but the owner never booked that band again. As Johnny Cash lamented… "the lads walked the line."

The following night, **The Touch** are playing in Donegal, to a larger crowd. It's going well and once again a fight breaks out. This one is more intense than last night's, totally a result of the "craic": the booze, the girls, the raging hormones, feuds over some guy who might feel his girlfriend left him for no apparent reason, and he'd show her latest fella' he could take him on. Their buddies would join in and fists would fly. Thankfully, most of them were plastered, so they usually missed by a mile.

The crowd moves like a wave right up to the stage; individuals within the crowd are kicking and punching wildly. The lads push lightly on the backs' of the punters to protect the stage area, and to insure the safety their equipment. They assume that the mob will turn on the band, but are very relieved when a punter shouts up, "sorry, sorry…" The band had nothing to do with the fight, and the mob respect the lads trying to protect their equipment. They didn't mind the gentle push, and went right back to punching each other out.

Finally exhausted, the punters start dancing again like nothing ever happened. This was more of a country than a city thing, but the lads were doing mostly country gigs, so after a while they hardly noticed, they just kept playing.

During the 70's and 80's, hotel and dancehall owners provided chicken suppers for everybody attending. This was a way to get a bar extension in the hotel dancehalls: serve food, keep the booze flowing for another two hours. Unfortunately, without any doubt, it was the most tasteless burned to a cinder chicken you ever tasted, with equally dried-out chips.

By the time the poor old cremated chicken reached the diners, the chicken bones were as hard as rocks. For the craic, the punters threw the chicken bones at the band. The overall intention was to throw the band off the beat. An amazing success was celebrated if the bone hit the drummer's cymbals. Needless to say, the bands all dreaded chicken suppertime. They had to avoid the bones, flailed at them like in a torrent, while they focused on playing the right chords. Bouncers at dance halls were a pretty rare sight. Unless things got really out of control, the dance hall owners didn't intervene, and firing chicken bones at the bands was considered acceptable.

The Touch is singing their least favorite but most requested slow dance song, *Feelings*, when a culchie fires a chicken bone, and it gets stuck like a dart right between the strings of Steo's guitar. He doesn't see it and plays the crappiest out of tune chords ever. Everybody bursts out laughing, except Steo of course – 'easy money', yea right.

At the end of the night, they're wrapping up the wires and packing the van. Suddenly Mel comes in with a bloody lip. "Some punks jumped me outside." Billy had just unscrewed the four legs off his Fender Rhodes piano, and for some reason he could never figure out, runs out first. There were eight of them. Billy puts his fists up, thinking it's boxing rules, but immediately gets a kick in the balls and goes straight down, writhing in agony. These guys were street fighters, dirty street fighters at that.

Just as they are coming in to kick the hell out of him, the lads arrive like the cavalry with the piano legs, whacking indiscriminately. Steo whacks one guy in the head, and he goes straight down unconscious. Another guy gets an almighty smack from Mel's piano leg in the back, and goes down. Fran is stabbing another guy in the stomach, over and over with a mike stand. Jack is banging another guy's head into the ground. The lads can see Jack's hand in the guy's mouth - "open yer mouth ya bollix ya," he screams, but it was obvious the guy had lock-jaw and couldn't open it to save his life. Fran comes over and pries open his mouth. He just lay groaning on the ground. The other guys run away.

Their band was born that night. No more 'him and us' crap. They are now one tight band of brothers. They took care of each other. Even tho' Billy was useless, he was the first one out, and didn't back off even tho' there was eight of them. That was good enough for the lads. They walk back to the dancehall. Staring from the window are the faces of the owner and his bouncers. "Shite, we'll never get a gig here again," says Mel.

The boys are stunned when the owner says, "Jeez lads, ye're tough men," in his strong Donegal accent, "even my bouncers were afraid of those bastards." He gives a withering look at his bouncers. "Those guys have been giving me trouble for the last two years, and you skinny pricks took care of them for me. I'm going to call PJ tomorrow and book ye again next month, will ye have a drink before ye go lads?"

They go in and down a few with their new best friend, and he gives them a few bottles of Guinness for the road. They all drink except for Fran. They're all impressed when he explains; "Doc was in a bad accident due to the roadie being hammered a few years ago, so no drink for me thanks." Fair play to him, he took care of the lads, even tho' he looked like he could drink them all under the table, except for maybe Helen. She was in a league all of her own, when it came to holding her drink.

They're all delighted with themselves on the way home until Steo says "Shite, they'll probably come back and kill us next month."

"No problem," says Robot, "I'll bring some o' the lads."

Jack gets into the back of the van and in seconds he's comatose. The head drops, bang, gone, out like a light. Nothing, and I mean nothing woke him up.

Driving home, Fran starts speaking in a language nobody had ever heard before. "Legads, yegou wegere gregeat tego negight."

"What did ya say?" says Billy thinkin' he was going deaf or somethin'.

"It's the bege, the ben, the showband lingo."

"The what?" says Helen.

"It's a language all the bands speak, when we don't want any of the punters to understand what we're saying."

Helen is intrigued, "So how does it work?"

"Well ye just put an eg [aig] before any vowel like "egi legike yegou," looking at Helen. "Eg –I, legike – like, – yegou – you, get it?" They all start practicing.

Looking at Steo Fran said: "Egi thegink yegou egare ega pregick."

"You think I'm a prick?" says Steo.

"Yeges" They laugh and keep practicing, except for Jack, comatose in the back.

Tiredly, gazing out the van window, they are amazed when they pass a showband truck on the side of the road, and all the lads are mooning them – pants down to their ankles - hilarious. It's the funniest thing they've ever seen. Fran explains, "All the lads do that for a bit o' craic." He blows the horn in appreciation.

Once back in Dublin Jack wakes up fresh as a daisy and jumps out of the van. Everybody is jealous and amazed that he could sleep thru' all the roaring that went on.

Chapter 12

Sound asleep and still groggy from last night's excitement, Billy's woken up by the sound of the phone ringing in the upstairs hall. He drags himself up the stairs. It's Meg all excited: "hey Corkman, you made a call for me."

"Yea I did. Did Aiden call ya?"
"Yea, and he thinks he can help me."
"Wow Meg, that's fantastic."
"I can't believe you'd do that for me Billy."

"Hey I told ya you're the best hairdresser in Dublin, and you're not a bad kisser either."

"You're not too bad yerself boyeee," taking off his Cork accent. "Hey c'mere girl," he teases, "it took me twenty years to develop this fine Cork accent, so don't even try all right. So, what's next?"

"Well, I'm in town right now lookin' around. Any chance you could pick up Sam from school?"
"Yea I can, what time?"
"Half two at the Mercy Convent down the road from me, dy'a know it?"
"Yea, I'll be there, and I'll look after dinner tonight."
"Spaghetti?" teases Meg.
"It'll be a surprise ... for all of us."

Billy is actually on time, outside the school, and sees Sam coming out. He honks his obnoxious horn. Sam skips over, looking cute in his school uniform of dark grey long pants, white shirt, blue tie, and grey sweater.

All Irish school kids wear uniforms. The poorer kids aren't put at a disadvantage when their parents can't afford to dress their children in the latest fashion. It levels the playing field for every kid.

"Where's me mam?"
"She's in town, she asked me to pick you up."

It's a sunny day, so they drive along the beach road. Sam sees someone driving on the beach. "Hey Billy, can I drive yer car on the beach?"

"What? You're a bit young to be driving a car aren't ya?"
"I wanna' be a racing driver when I grow up, can I Billy please.... please?"

"Okay okay," says Billy, so they drive onto the beach, stop, and Sam climbs onto Billy's lap, and starts steering the car slowly. "Faster Billy, go faster".... Billy speeds up, "faster, faster".... he guns it, and they're flying along the water's edge, wipers flapping wildly, whooshing the spray away, Sam screaming with joy.

Finally at the end of the beach, Billy slows down. "That was great Billy, can we do it again?"

"Hey, maybe another time all right? You know what Sam, I think you could be a racing champion all right…. Don't say a word to your mother about this or she'll kill me, our secret okay?"

"Okay Billy," looking up at him, and hoping he might be his new dad.

"C'mon, let's get an ice cream."

As she comes in that night, Meg smells pork chops grilling, and sees a tin of baked beans in a pot warming up. "Thanks Billy, I'm starvin' so I am."

"Well, did you find anything?"

"Janey, the rents are so expensive, I'd never make any money. I saw one place that was closed for years. T'was filthy so it was, and t'would probably cost a fortune to fix it up. But the price was all right, and it's in a great location, just off Grafton Street."

Billy has an idea. "Hey, we could fix it up for you."

She laughs and shakes her head at the very thought of it. "What do you know about fixing things up? You said you can't hammer a nail into a wall for God's sake."

"Yea, you're right, but Steo says he's an electrician, and Mel says he works for a carpenter every now and then, and sure we could clean it up for you. Look, call Aiden and tell him you've found a place, get the grant money to fix and stock the place, sign the lease and off ya go, Meg the millionaire."

"And what about customers, where will I find them?" Billy's on a roll. "Call everybody in your book, tell 'em to spread the word. I'll tell everybody in the choir how good you are. Hey, I just got a great idea, we could ask Doc to open the place, get your picture in the paper together. We can put an ad in the paper inviting everybody. They'll all want to see Doc, and get their picture taken with him. Give 'em some deal if they'll make an appointment on the spot, some sort of discount or somethin'."
Meg isn't convinced. "I dunno', whad'ya think Sam?" Sam is all in. "Go on Ma, Billy is right, you can do it."
"Well,"..… She lights up, "all right, I'll do it."
Billy and Sam beam at each other, "Yea."

That same evening, Bridget and Jack are on a date in their local bar. "So," she says, "whad'ya think of the gobshite from Cork?" Bridget's immediate put down of Billy, no getting to know him - guilty on all counts.

"He's all right for a culchie, he knows his music all ri', I think PJ has the right idea puttin' us together."

"Well, I think you should be the lead singer, you're the best lookin' fella' in the band, that's what the girls go for, not a bleedin' piano player."
She sees a good-looking girl giving Jack "the look", and Jack isn't turning away. She explodes. "Do you want to shag her?"

"Ehhhhhhh, noooooooo".... He says unconvincingly.

"Ya do ya bollix ya, ya do, you can play with yer own feckin' willie from now on....Jaysus..."

"Bridget," says Jack weakly, "calm down will ya, I was only lookin'."

She screams at him: "...your mother said I was the best thing that ever happened to you. She said you need someone with a bit o' common sense. You're mine all ri', an' don't you bleedin' forget it."

Sometimes he figures; "what the hell am I doing with a bitch like her? The lads are right." But she was sort of like a bad habit, and with the band getting more work, it would be an awful lot of extra time and expense to meet someone new, plus all the hard work of dating again. That's how he saw it, so Bridget it was. She was there.

Chapter 13

With the van again loaded to the hilt the lads are approaching their next gig in a very small village. The place is literally in the middle of nowhere.

Fran pulls into the site identified for the show, flabbergasted to see a huge run-down tent with a stage, known as a Marquee, set-up in a field. Of course it's lashing rain to dampen any excitement the lads have for the gig.

"Shite look at this place, it's a dump, PJ ya bollix ya," says Steo. The ground is so soggy from the rain, the van immediately sinks in the mud with all their weight. They get out and look inside. The organizers had erected a shaky looking stage: a very amateurish job, with a dirty looking canvass tarp covering the big hole from the stage to the ground. Of course, it's at the other end of the tent, so the lads have to get out and push the van through the muck, right around to the back. There were a couple of Christmas lights hanging over the stage, and as usual, it was freezing as they set up.

The lads head back to the village to find a pub, a pint and a good turf fire to warm their shivering selves before the show. Within minutes, Helen is flirting outrageously with a local culchie.

Billy relaxes, while a two-piece band with an awful drum machine is playing country and western tunes, Irish style with loads of jives. [jitterbugs] Several girls are jiving together perfectly on the dance floor, as the local lads at the bar eye up the 'talent' for later on at the dance. Billy is always amazed at the their terrific rhythm, and how they flow perfectly, never missing a beat. He never learned this dance, as it's truly a country thing, almost instinctive in country people. The boys were also very capable of jiving, when they needed to, as all their mothers would have taught them growing up.

Robot is holding court at the pub counter with Jack, Steo, and a couple of new friends. Of course, he comes up with another hilarious joke… "Mary and Charlie were married forever. They were mad about each other, but Charlie died young and she was heartbroken. The local undertakers knew how much they loved each other, and they were wondering if there was anything o' Charlie they could leave her. Rigor Mortis had set in, and Charlie's willie was standing up, nice and proud. They thought for a while, and one of them said, "I'm sure Mary would like it just to remember the good old days with Charlie, ya know."

So 'swish' they cut it off, put it into a vacuum-sealed glass jar, and they gave it to Mary. She was delighted, and she put it on the mantelpiece over the fireplace. So every night before she went to bed, she touched the glass tenderly and said, "good night Charlie, good night."

Well years went by 'til one day, she was having the house painted, and didn't one of the lads turn his ladder around and hit the bleedin' jar and it fell to the ground, smashing into smithereens. Charlie's willie lost its eh, its old glory, and shrunk to almost nothin'.

"Oh shite," said one of the painters, "she's going to be one pissed off old lady, and she won't pay us."

The other fella' started thinkin' and he said, "Hang on, I have an idea." He went out to the van, and brought in a spring, stuck it inside Charlie's willie and 'whoosh,' it sprung right back to its former glory. He put it in a jar and put it back on the mantelpiece. She never noticed the difference. Every night before she went to bed, she kept saying "good night Charlie good night."

Well one day she was dustin', and didn't she knock the vase. It fell on the bleedin' floor, the ould jar smashed, and Charlie went bouncing all over the place. She pulled up her skirt, and started chasin' it, and jumping up and down she said, "Over here Charlie, over here," as Robot acted out the old lady jumping around the room chasing Charlie's willie. They were all on the floor.

With great reluctance, Fran gathers the lads, as they have to get back to the Marquee in spite of the lashing rain and gale force winds. People are streaming into the tent which shakes wildly. It's 11:55, the band is about to go on, and there's no Helen. "Where the hell is she?" says Fran.

"I saw her leaving the pub with some culchie ," says Jack.

Billy walks around the tent looking for her. He checks the van - no Helen. He comes back up to the front of the stage, looks down the hall, and suddenly hears all sorts of moaning coming from under the stage. He lifts the tarp and there's Helen on her back, her stage dress pulled up, with said culchie from the pub on top of her....

He calls the lads down from the stage, and they all stare in disbelief. It's like a scene from the "Three Stooges" in the movies: five heads looking under the tarp, wide-eyed, mouths open, in total shock at the spectacle.

"Helen," shouts Fran. She looks up in shock, hair all messed up, mascara all over her face, dress ruined in all the muck. "You're fired."

"And we want the dress back, we bleedin' well paid for it," says Steo as he drops the tarp leaving her speechless. The show goes on without Helen, as she pouts in the van.

As usual, a fight breaks out, with about half the crowd having a go, coming right up to the stage blasting away. The priest who booked them comes up and asks them to stop playing. "Lads, come on now," he pleads, "there's no need for this, come on now lads cut it out, come on." Just then the wind picks up, and the stage shakes violently. The priest loses his balance, and falls right into the fighting crowd, microphone and all, and totally disappears.

After a while the fight dies down, and the disheveled priest re-appears, straightens his collar, and gives them the thumbs up to play again, which they do. The leaky tent is no match for the lashing rain, so the lads have to keep moving their equipment to a shrinking amount of dry stage, to avoid the cup-fulls of water falling down from above, and possibly electrocuting them. It starts to really freeze as the lads are putting the gear back into the van.

As they're driving home later on, drinking the usual bottles of Guinness, they bought in the pub before the dance, Mel pipes up: "hey Fran, I'm bursting for a piss."

"Me too," says Billy. Fran reluctantly pulls over. Mel is in front with the briefcase full of the weekend's take. They all do their thing and drive on, except Jack of course.

About a half an hour later Mel screams "Oh shite, the briefcase, I left it on the road when we had a piss."

The band groans, "Ah Jaysus Mel."
"I'm sorry all ri, I'm sorry," he says.
"Shite," says Steo, I have to pay me car payment tomorrow."
"I have to pay my rent," says Billy, "let's go back all right?"
"It's bleedin' well gone, you know that," says Steo, always the optimistic one.
"It's worth a try all right," says Billy.
"Why does he have to keep the bleedin' money anyway," says Steo. Robot is in the back seat, stares into his face, and crushes him with his perfect answer: "do you own a bleedin' briefcase?"

Meanwhile, Helen is in a really shitty diva-like mood, pouting, in the back seat. "You'll have me back, ye can't do without me, ye shower of wankers," as she raises her head in proud defiance and looks out the window.

Billy screams at her, "Hey, I don't want to hear any of your old bullshit. You just screwed up big time, ya let us down. Ya never come to rehearsals, and now this, what the hell d'ya expect?" Helen shakes her head in disgust.

"Well I wanna' be paid for the last three nights, you better pay me."
"How much did that culchie pay ya?" Everybody bursts out laughing at Robot's razor sharp quip.
"Piss off Robot," says Helen, and in fairness she laughs too.

It's about twenty minutes back and it's getting bright. There's the odd car coming up the road. "Shite lads, we're screwed," says Steo. Fran is tearing along as fast as the van can go. He turns a corner and hits some black ice on a long straight stretch sheltered by two steep hills. The van skidded all the way to the other side of the road. Amazingly he's able to keep it from hitting the ditch, and the van swerves right over to the other side again. He does this about ten times doing a slow swan lake type slide, gaining a little more control each time he swerves. Luckily, no one was coming the other way. Finally, he straightens the van out and immediately pulls over and stops. His shoulders slump, and he gives a shiver, "f***." Everybody cheers his amazing skill and luck, except Jack of course, who as usual, slept through the whole thing.

Just then another car passes them, honks, and the driver gives Fran the thumbs up for his brilliant driving. Fran takes off again, turns a corner, and sees the same guy picking up the briefcase. Fran pulls right up to him, rolls down the window and says, "That's ours boss okay?" He sees four other determined angry-looking men getting out of the van, and gets the message.

"Yea sure," and hands over the briefcase.

Mel checks it. "It's all here, thank you God."

The lads see the five frozen wet spots and drive slowly home, all lost in their own thoughts but probably wondering the same thing - "What the hell am I doing?... There's gotta' be more than this".....

Chapter 14

Mel and Billy share a love of traditional music. Mel always brought his fiddle along, and Billy had his dad's accordion. Once they had all the gear set up, if there wasn't a pub nearby to kill a few hours, they'd have a jam on stage, before the dance started at midnight.

They played jigs and reels at breakneck speed. Sometimes Steo and Robot would be bored, so they joined in and added a rock beat and distorted guitar, Jack would fly up and down on his bass guitar, doing the craziest free sounds he never did doing the top twenty covers, and it sounded pretty good.

"You know this is good shit," says Billy, I'd love to play some of this sometime."

"Forget it man," says Mel, "they'd boo us off the stage. All they want to hear is the top 20, but it did sound good didn't it?"

"Yea, it's a bitch, there's no market for it." Says Billy.
"Yea," says Mel, "maybe someday.".…

Tonight, the band is playing in Dingle, one of Mel and Billy's favorite places. It's not because of the Co. Kerry dancehalls or dancers. Rather, when their gear is set up they head over to a "seisuin," an informal pub-gathering of traditional musicians in Flaherty's pub. It is the first pub you see coming into Dingle town, owned by a terrific Irish musician called Fergus O'Flaherty.

Flaherty's is a bar that looks the same as the day it opened many moons ago. It has a beautiful natural stone exterior, and the inside never got a lick of paint in decades. It still has the original "snug," where women in the 1950's and 60's were, very reluctantly mind you, allowed to drink. It's a tiny closet-sized room next to the bar where women could drink and not be seen, and certainly couldn't mix with the men - Taliban, Irish style. When a woman needed a drink, she tapped on a confession-like window. The bar owner opened it, gave her her drink, and then slammed it shut again, nearly taking the nose off her.

When Ireland got its freedom in 1923, except for Northern Ireland, the new Irish government did their best to revive the Irish language, and subsidized the people who lived in those poorer regions where the land wasn't the best, so there wasn't much to pillage or plunder, consequently the Irish language and the old ways survived.
This allowed many of them to stay on their farms continuing everything Irish rather than having to emigrate. They still do so to this day.

Due to Ireland's history of British rule, most Irish people grew up speaking English as their first language, as did Billy and the lads. In most parts of Ireland, the English did their best to squelch everything Irish, especially the language, but thankfully, they didn't succeed. All school children had to learn Irish at school, and Billy was good at it. When he was twelve, he spoke to a man in Irish who visited the school. It transpired that the man was an Irish inspector, who awarded Billy and a few of his buddies a scholarship to live with the local native Irish speakers. Thus, Billy spent three months in Kerry learning the true Irish language.

"You know," says Billy, "when I was twelve I got a scholarship to learn Irish a few miles from here."
"Really?" says Mel.

Billy shares his recollections: "Yea, about seven miles from here, in a tiny little village called Ballydavid. My parents abandoned me there for three months," he laughs. "I cried my eyes out when I saw where I was going to stay for what seemed like an eternity back then. T'was a two-story house with no electricity, no toilets, nothin'. The kitchen had a black stone floor, and I can still picture a big heavy black pot of boiling water hanging over the simmering turf fire for the tea.

There were only about twenty houses, and two pubs, in the village back then. I stayed with this old overweight woman in a big black shawl. I never saw her in anything but that black shawl, and a long black dirty dress that was always dragging along the floor …"

"Wow," says Mel.

"…Yea, she had a son and a daughter living with her, two classic middle-aged Irish spinsters who farmed their small farm. Her other eleven children were in America.

I remember she used to sit in her chair in the kitchen, rocking away for hours, her rosary beads in her hands, back and forth in a steady rhythm, trancelike, looking at the turf fire, saying nothing, probably missing her children. The living room was locked. It was only opened when the parish priest came, or when one of her children came to visit from the States, which never happened while I was there. I used to fantasize about what was in that room. In my mind, I pictured all sorts of treasures in loads of huge mysterious trunks. If it was locked, there had to be something valuable in there.

I remember the priest came to say the stations once, and when it was opened for the first time, there was nothing in it except a table and a few chairs. It was a huge anti-climax for a kid with an over-imaginative brain.

When mum and dad drove away, that first day, I walked down past the front of the house, straight down to the harbor, the smell of cow manure hanging in the air, a whole new smell to a city slicker like me, and saw this amazing sunset. I felt all on my own down by the stonewall, and cried my eyes out. But ya know, I knew I was leaving someplace really special three months later. It truly is a magical place. I've seen some of the world, and Dingle is one of the nicest places I've ever seen. I still love that smell of turf burning in the fireplace, ….. man, I even miss the smell of that cow manure.

I learned how to milk a cow, save the hay, bring the cows to the bull. Mind you, the cows seemed to know their way fine without me. Dingle's where I learned all the Ceili dances and sets. I loved it.

Every Sunday, people had a roasted chicken for dinner. I went to school with a fella' called Tommy Johnston, and it was our job to pick the two unfortunate chickens. We'd chase them around like crazy, and pick one from each farm. Then we'd chop their heads off with a hatchet and line them up in a race to see how many steps the headless chickens would take before dropping.

Mel laughs, "And that's where you learned all the Trad. songs?"

"Yea, how about you?"

"Well, my dad comes from Clare where traditional music is huge. His dad taught him all the songs from the area, hundreds of them, and he passed them on to me. Ya know, what we did last night after the soundcheck was bleedin' great. I wish we could try it and see what reaction we'd get."

"Hey, they'd think because it's Irish, it can't be any good, it's a bitch." Billy looks over at a guy standing at the bar. "See that guy over there? I think he's one of the pricks who made my life miserable when we were at school every day."

"Whad'ya mean?"

"Yerra', they thought it was great craic to catch us guys down from the big cities to learn Irish, hold us, and put their hands down our pants and feel us up."

"You're jokin' me."

"No, really they did. T'was a bitch, these guys just kept repeating sixth class until they could leave school legally at sixteen, not the sharpest knives in the drawer ya know, huge bastards, but they never caught me."

"How come?"

"Well whenever I saw them gettin' ready to pounce, I'd mosey over to the school wall that separated the girls and boys playgrounds, and when they made a run for me, I'd jump over the wall into the girls yard. It meant getting a slap from the teacher, but I didn't give a fiddler's about that, they never got me."

Mel and Billy join in with the other traditional players. The people in the pub, the very few people, really listen with great respect and admiration for the musicians playing the very complex trad. songs. Once the music starts, a slow air, a lively jig, everyone is immediately transported to another world. The music carries them all to another magical place for a few beautiful moments, casting its spell on everyone present: no gimmicks, no crazy light show, just the Irish music of the centuries, their music. Once the music stops, the spell is broken, and they become human again. Their thoughts return to their lives of milking the cows, cutting the turf, saving the hay, surviving the Ireland of the West.

Billy was always torn, when he had to play just covers in Ireland at the dances. He needed to pay his rent, but was transported to another world when he was lucky enough to join in with these Irish musicians. The Guinness was always flowing, so it was as close to heaven as you could get, as they totally lost themselves in the music.

Your gigs were judged back then, not on originality, but on how closely you could sound like the original record. **Billy and The Touch** did not realize it just yet, but they were going down a musical road that would be a hit for them later on.

Chapter 15

At rehearsal the following Wednesday, PJ makes an exciting announcement: "lads, I gotta' bit o' good news, I got a gig for youse in Sweden."

"Sweden, holy shit," says Robot, "Did ya hear that dad, we're going to Sweden."

"An' I'm going with youse, ye'll need someone to look after ye, ya shower of sex maniacs," says Pops.

"What's the bread like?" says Steo, as always, thinking about money.

"About the same as now, but they'll feed ye, and pay for travelling expenses, and give youse an apartment just around from the pub."

"Pub?" says Steo dismissively.

"Yea, it's a pub gig, the most famous one in Stockholm, but you can play what you like, no shite like now. Mel, you play some Irish stuff on your fiddle and drive them crazy all ri'? It's for a month, and if they like ye, they'll book ye twice a year, but there's one thing I want youse to do when you're there. I want youse to write a song for the national song contest. The scene is getting worse and worse. The smaller dance halls are closing up, bands are quitting left and right, so you gotta' get some publicity, and the Eurovision is it, all ri'?"

Steo knocks it immediately as usual, "Well we haven't written it yet, then we have to get into, and win the national song contest, then win Eurovision, Jaysus, PJ, that's a lot ya know."

"You can do it," says PJ "I'd like a freebie to Israel wouldn't youse. I can just see Steo riding a camel." They all laugh except Steo of course, who for once can't come back with a stinging reply.

PJ gives them the bottom line: "I think Ireland is finished lads. I'm trying to get ye out of Ireland, but ye need Eurovision or a hit or both ya know?"

"What d'ya think," says Mel, "a rock song?"
"Nah," says PJ, "they seem to go for the big ballads, so come home with a winner all ri'?"
"I've been workin' on somethin'," says Billy.
"A ballad?" asks PJ.
"Yea PJ, Billy's in love," says Robot.
"Oh yea?"
"Yea with Meg." says Mel.
"Nice one! All right lads, good luck, just do the month here and off youse all go to Sweden."

PJ leaves, and the band rehearse the latest number one hit record: another pop song that will be forgotten in a few months. Billy is bored with its three chord trick formula, and suddenly has an idea. "What d'ya think lads, how about doing the stuff Mel and I have been jamming with all along in Sweden? I don't know about you, but I'm sick to death of doing covers over and over every night. We've a lot of them done already, we just need a bit of tightening up that's all. It sounded fantastic when you came in with guitars and drums when we were messing around after the sound checks, so whad'ya think?

Robot likes the idea, "I say yea, let's try it, it should be a bit o' craic in the pub, what d'ya think Jack?"

"Yea I suppose," says Jack, sounding like he's half asleep as usual.

By now, Billy and Mel had quite a few traditional tunes rehearsed together. They enjoyed playing the Irish tunes in perfect unison, as fast as they could, so at this point they were pretty tight. It was easy enough to add guitars to what they were doing. As they rehearsed, Mel and Billy starting together, then bringing in the drums and guitars, they discovered how suitable and adaptable the old Trad. songs were to rock and reggae tempos. They had absolutely no idea how successful it would be. Billy starts to write some new songs for Sweden, and starts to really think about that love song he was writing, daydreaming about actually winning the national song contest, and all the publicity, and opportunities that would go along with it.

Billy hears the phone ringing one floor up in the public hallway. Nobody knew if it was for them or not, and if it was for someone else, they would run up or down the stairs and knock on the door to see if that person was in. They only wrote messages if it was an emergency, and pinned them on the person's door, totally primitive by todays standards. Billy runs up and answers.

It's Meg, all excited like a little kid. "I got it Billy, I got the grant money, and I'm signing the lease today."
"Fair play to ya Meg, when can you move in?"
"Immediately."
"That's fantastic, I'm thrilled for ya. All right, we'll be there on Monday, I'll tell the lads tonight."
"Are ya sure?" she says.
"Hey, you'll be great, I'll see ya tomorrow night."
"All right, thanks for everything Billy."
"Well done Meg," says Billy trying to be cool, but delighted Aiden came through, and Meg obviously passed their test.

That afternoon, the band is heading back to the hall where they had the fight in Donegal. They all drive to the "Call" as usual, everybody is there except Robot. "Hi there," says Billy to the lads, "Are ye ready for Donegal lads? I just hope those bastards don't show up."

"Yea, holy shite, I don't wanna' go through that again." says Steo all worried, even tho' he came out swingin' that night, and probably saved Billy's life.

Just then Robot drives up and suddenly five of the toughest looking guys get out of the car, Skinheads, Mohawks, Hippies, everything your girlfriend's father would hate to turn up at his door. They all look at Robot. "Reinforcements," he says, "we'll be ready for 'em if they show up." He gives his unique laugh, a kind of a high-pitched "puh," and they all cram into the van. "D'ye feel better now lads?" proud as punch of his buddies, his own private cavalry.

Two Skinheads are crammed into the front seat, smelling as badly as they looked. Fran turns to them with contempt. "Have any of you wankers ever been to Donegal?"
One of them said "I've never been outta' Dublin."
"I wanna' see what Donegal women are like," said another.
"Not much," says Steo.
"Ah piss off," says Mel, "just because you can't get one."

"Bullshit," says Steo, "you couldn't pull a girl out of a burning building even if ya tried, she'd wait for the bleedin' fire brigade," as he looks out the window, reveling in knocking Mel.

They're on their way, and one of the skinheads lets go an almighty fart. After a few seconds, the smell is absolutely revolting. "Jaysus," screams Fran, "what have ya got up yer arse, a dead rat or somethin'?"

"What the hell d'ya eat?' says Steo.

The Skinhead couldn't care less, and just smiles proudly. Fran quickly rolls down the window gasping for breath. Up 'til then, Fran had the worst killer farts, but this guy was in a league all of his own.

After five excruciating hours, literally stuck together, they finally arrive in Donegal. Billy says to Robot's cavalry, "Okay lads, ye can go to the dance if ye leave everything in the truck."

"Wha'?" they all chime in.

"If the pricks come back they're right there all right? Robot, come on man, we don't want a fight unless they come back okay?"

Robot realizes he's right, knowing the lads would love to take on a culchie or two, for the tiniest reason. "Yea, Billy's right lads, put 'em in." He puts his bass drum box in front of them, and they reluctantly drop an unbelievable load of weapons into it: knives, hammers, chains, everything except guns. If they were available in Ireland at the time, they'd have them too.

The dance goes well, no fights, and Robot's gang have a ball trying to pick up the Donegal girls. "Well lads," he says, did ye enjoy yerselves, an' ye didn't have to do anythin', the bastards never showed up?"

"Yea Robot, bleedin' great it was, can we come with youse again?"

About an hour down the road, Fran sees car lights behind them. "Okay lads, it's time for your initiation, there's a band behind us."

"How d'ya know it's a band?" says Billy.

"Sure who else would be crazy enough to be drivin' around in the middle of nowhere at this time o' night except a bunch of idiots like ourselves. C'mon', it's time to christen yer arses." He speeds up to gain some ground from the other band, and he pulls over further up the road. They all get out and quickly pull their pants down to their ankles, just like the other band did last week.

Robot, of course has to bring it to a whole new level. He and his mates jump up onto the top of the van, take all their clothes off, push their willies back between their legs, and as the other band passes, they see four bare-assed guys mooning them road side, and six tough looking guys on top of the van doing the full Monty, minus willies, screaming and roaring as they give the band the finger.

The band blare their horn in approval all the way down the road, 'til they turn the corner. That was a first, and the talk spread all over the country about the mighty craic that band had coming home from Donegal, courtesy of **Billy and the Touch.**

In the 1950's, Sean Lemass became Ireland's Prime Minister, succeeding Eamon DeValera, and was successful in attracting industries to Ireland, and thus slowing down the curse of emigration somewhat, and opening Ireland up to the outside world.

For decades, the pub was the main social outlet at night, mostly for men only of course. For as long as anyone can remember, country pubs always had "after hour" drinking. The owner would officially shout, "time gentlemen please," when it came time to obey the official closing time. Some people would leave, but most stayed on drinking. There was no hurry home, and usually the craic was only starting at the "official" closing time.

If the guards made a raid, they would strongly hint to the owner, that they might be making a call on his pub next Friday night. After all, they had to keep up their friendship with the local publican. Where else would they drink on their nights off? They would very nicely knock on the door, and there would be a scarper out the back, or, if the pub was attached to the house, everybody would hide in the owner's house. The guards would make a quick "cover your ass," inspection and leave. It wasn't unusual for the owner's kids to be awakened by the noise and be told, "Mary, go back to sleep, 'tis only Pat and Dinny Murphy under the bed!"

It wasn't always fun and games for the bands. Coming home from Donegal and other Northern areas took two hours off their journey back to Dublin by cutting through the North, but they did it very reluctantly. The roads were better at the time as England subsidized the North to the tune of billions every year, so it saved the wear and tear on the wagons.

However, it meant being stopped at the border by British soldiers pointing machine guns at you, and if they wanted to, ordering the lads out of the van to inspect their equipment, to make sure they weren't smuggling anything into the north, or bringing contraband back into the south....

During 'The Troubles,' as they were called, in the 1960's through the 1990's, the British Government, through their intelligence services and soldiers, were guilty of all sorts of military collusion, assassinations, blackmail, and every other dirty trick in the book, working hand in hand with the extreme elements of the Protestant militias. This has been well documented, and is accepted as fact internationally.

Going through the border checkpoint wasn't too bad in daylight on the way up, but coming back at four in the morning, it was pretty spooky: total silence, the high lookout towers, the barbed wire, armed soldiers, and knowing there were other soldiers hidden in the ditches with machine guns at the ready. They were only doing their job, but the lads resented British soldiers doing this in Ireland, even tho' that's not how the soldiers saw it.

There was always tension in the van until they got through the British security checkpoint, and were back in the "Free State'" as the people from Northern Ireland call the Republic of Ireland.

PJ usually booked them into Catholic areas where they were expected to play *Ireland's National Anthem* and not *God Save the Queen* at the end of the dance. This was the punters way to peacefully protest England's rule in Northern Ireland who banned the *Irish National Anthem*. Thus, in Catholic areas, this was one of the night's most anticipated songs. Bands from the south were expected to play it.

You could hear a pin drop, and sense the tension, the pride, and the loyalty to Ireland as they began to sing. The lads actually sang it in Irish, making it even more patriotic, and added three-part harmony, so the crowd especially loved their version, as most bands just played it instrumentally. They always gave the band a huge applause at the end of the night, signaling that they considered themselves Irish, even tho' they were technically British citizens.

One night PJ booked them into an area where both Protestants and Catholics attended. Music thankfully, was one of the few neutralizing forces at the time, except for the extremists on both sides, who were blind to everything unfortunately. PJ probably didn't know it was a mixed area, and the dance-hall owner forgot to tell them not to sing either anthem.

The boys do their usual Irish anthem, and you could see people scarpering out the door. Just as they finish, the lads hear the sound of breaking glass outside. The owner comes running up to the stage and screams, "Get outta' here as fast as ye can! Get lost for a few hours. When ye come back I'll let ye in to pack up yer gear. Ye'd better move now or ye'll be beaten up or worse." When they go out they see the van's windscreen smashed to pieces, and an angry mob hanging around.

The owner had a few buddies, Catholics, the lads assumed, escort them to their van, and they sped off into the night, trying not to sit on the broken glass. They drive for twenty minutes into the middle of nowhere, and with no front window, sit frozen in the van, scared shitless.

As they wait there, they remember what happened to another band from Dublin in 1975, just a few years ago. A top Irish Band called **The Miami**, had a huge following all over Ireland, north and south. Their lead singer was an up and coming singer/songwriter called Fran O' Toole. He was Irelands' Davy Jones, at the time, and the girls loved him.

They were playing up in Northern Ireland, and were heading back to Dublin after the dance. They were stopped by what they thought were British soldiers, who were actually manning a bogus military checkpoint. They were a Protestant paramilitary organization called the UVF, the Ulster Volunteer Force. Four of the soldiers were actually full time members of the regular British army in Northern Ireland, but that night they were on an entirely illegal mission.

1975 was one of the bloodiest years of the entire troubles. The Protestant extremists got word that the British Government had been conducting secret talks with the IRA to try and resolve the situation. They took this as a total betrayal, and they figured they'd soon be forced into some sort of union with the Free State.

Some of them saw this as a great opportunity to send a strong message to the Irish to stop coming north, stop interfering in Ulster, as they called it. There was no way they were going to be pushed into any agreement with the Free State, no matter what. Ironically, the lads in the Miami showband were both Catholic and Protestant, and some of them actually came from Northern Ireland.

The bogus soldiers ordered the lads out of their minibus to 'check' for anything unusual, and lined them up at gunpoint. Apparently, what they were actually doing was hiding a time bomb amongst the band's gear.

While two men hid the bomb, it exploded prematurely, and they were blown to bits. In the panic, the other men opened fire on the lads as they made a run for it. Three of the band members were killed, including Fran O'Toole and two other band members were severely injured. It was probably meant to explode in the van further down the road, but the senseless killings stunned Ireland.

Two UDR soldiers and one former soldier were found guilty of murder, and received life sentences. It was described in a 1999 report as, "one of the worst atrocities in the 30 year history of The Troubles." The Irish Times diarist Frank McNally summed up the massacre as "an incident that encapsulated all the madness of the time."

The collusion between the British security forces and the Protestant militias was proven beyond any doubt, over and over, so it was a very scary time in Northern Ireland.

Shaking with fright with these recollections, **Billy and The Touch** wait in the pouring rain for an hour. Thankfully nobody bothers them, and they drive back to the dancehall. They literally throw their gear into the van faster than they ever had, and get the hell outta' there. The boys are especially happy once they get back into Southern Ireland that night. "That could have been us," they thought. Every band in the country thought the same.

As promised, all the lads turn up at Meg's newly rented space on Monday morning. The place is a complete disaster, a damp and shabby 40 x 20 feet area, with broken windows, filthy toilets and floors, garbage everywhere, bare bulbs, and wallpaper pealing from the walls. Meg had made a few calls to have the electricity turned on. There was one light working near the front, so they could see what they had to do: Mission Impossible....

Steo chimes in in his usual crappy way, "Jaysus lads, we've got ten days to fix this place up, plus gigs this weekend, we'll never get it done."

Fran in fairness turns up, even tho' he wasn't connected to Meg in any way, but after the fight in Donegal, they were like the three musketeers: all for one, and one for all. "Ah shut up ya wanker," he says. "My brother, Doc, is doing the opening for nothin', so move yer arse Steo, and get all the lights working. I told Doc it was nearly finished. If he saw this shite he'd never do it."

Meg and the lads get down to it. They start throwing out all the garbage, so other people can start installing shelves, lights and counters. The toilet is completely blocked, and it's disgusting what they take out of it. After a few days, it's ready for a paint job, and they leave every day exhausted, with paint all over them. Billy sees Meg isn't afraid of hard work, as she gets down and dirty every bit as much as the lads. It turns him on big-time as he sees the sweat pouring off her. He can't stand it any longer. He sneaks up behind her, pulls her into the toilet, and they have a "quickie," as the lads are hammering away right outside the door, their screaming and roaring creating the perfect romantic ambience! Robot suddenly becomes the gay hairdresser, sits Fran down in one of the new fancy high chairs, and pretends to cut his hair in a "way over the top" diva performance. Pops as always, serves endless cups of tea, enjoying all the carry on, and probably wishing he was twenty again. The craic in the bar next door each night is mighty, 'til finally the sign comes and they proudly hang it up outside......

MEG'S HAIR STATION

The designer did a bang-up job. It's a large oblong-shaped 10 x 4 foot timber sign, painted in a black matt color, with gold trim all around the sides, and Meg's Hair Station done in a clever 3D standout type also printed in gold. It really catches your eye as you pass the shop.

Ten days out, but Thursday quickly comes; opening day, and they just about make it. There are people all over the place, mostly ladies wanting to see Doc, who lays on the charm real thick. Robot is in his element acting as master of ceremonies. "Okay ladies and gentlemen, thanks for comin' on this great day for Meg, c'mere Meg." Meg shyly comes forward." Isn't she great everybody, havin' the balls, eh sorry, the courage, to open her own business in the center o' Dublin, let's give her a round of applause, all ri'? She needs all yer support now, all ri'? Hey Sam, c'mon over here and take a bow." Sam joins Meg. Everybody is charmed at how cute he looks. "She's a hard workin' single mother, so she needs yer support now all ri'? So, without further eh," he smiles embarrassingly, he can't think of the word "ado," "Ye know de word I mean, ri'? We'd like Meg and Doc Foley to officially cut the ribbon. Let's hear it for Meg and Doc Foley." The crowd cheers, Meg and Doc cut the ribbon, and everybody goes inside for the free champagne.

The Dublin Moore Street women are all there, and at their Dublin best. Many of these women would have been selling flowers in their outdoor stalls all their lives, surviving all sorts of weather, eking out a living, tough because they have to be. But they have huge hearts, and are always up for a laugh. "Ah Janey Doc, you're a grand man," says one of them, "will youse sing us a song?" Doc smiles as cameras flash. He signs free photos for all the ladies. Sam is having a ball serving champagne. Meg gives out loads of coupons, the sun shines, a good day all in all. As they crawl towards their beds that night exhausted, Meg is ecstatic. "That was great, bleedin' great."

"Yea," says Billy, "and Sam, you did a great job with the champagne."

"Yea," he says, "some ould one gave me a pound." They all enjoy a good laugh.

"Well Meg," says Billy, "you're on your way."

"Yea, I'm scared to bits….. But it's great"….. She turns to Billy, "nobody ever believed in me like you Billy, thanks."

"C'mon Seamus," says Sam, "Good night ma, good night Billy." She gives him a hug and turns to Billy. "Good night luv," and kisses him gratefully as they get into bed.

"Wow," says Billy, "I suppose a blow job is out of the question?"

Meg smiles, "Golden, I'm knackered, see ya tomorrow."

Chapter 16

A few weeks later they board the ferry to England, a five-hour hop across the Irish sea, the first leg of their journey to Sweden. They're all out on deck, excited about getting to Stockholm, watching Dublin harbor slowly disappear. It's natural beauty glowing in the sunshine, the impressive church spires of Dun Laoghaire, and the horseshoe shape of the harbor with its fine Georgian houses descending right down to the coastline, creating a spectacular visual image for all the passengers.

They go inside, check out the small bar in the ferry, and kill a few hours there as they know they'll have a whole days drive across Wales to the east coast of England to catch the ferry to Sweden.

They disembark from the ferry, and begin their marathon journey. After the longest drive of their lives, they finally see a sign for the ferry to Sweden five miles up the road. Suddenly Fran sees the red and blue lights of a police car flashing behind them, and pulls over. "Ah shite, what does he want?" says Fran. He pulls in behind them, gets out and inspects their van, literally a piece of crap.

"You know you got four bald tires there mate?" he says to Fran in his clipped English accent.

"No officer," says Fran. "Where are you going?"

"To the ferry sir, we'll fix 'em as soon as we get paid."

"You know, I should arrest you lot, but as you're getting on the ferry, and my father's Irish, I'll let you go, get the hell out of here all right?"

"Thank you officer." says Fran, and drives off. "Jaysus lads, we've really gotta' buy a few tires, all ri'?"

They drive onto the ferry, and are delighted to find that it's much more sophisticated and upscale than the Irish one, and they party all night in the disco bar. There are loads of gorgeous Swedish girls on the ferry heading home from their holidays in England. "Hey lads,' says Fran, as he looks out admiringly onto the dance floor, "If this is any indication, I might be movin' to Sweden." None of them have the courage to ask any of them to dance.

The excitement grows as they arrive in Sweden, and start driving on the right side of the road for the first time ever. It's made all the more difficult as the steering wheel is on the right side of the van. It feels like the cars are skimming by them, missing them by inches. After a few hours they approach Stockholm, and are impressed by its natural beauty. The huge scenic harbor protects hundreds of tiny islands, many of them with beautiful summer homes, with their distinctive red roofs and white frames.

They arrive in the Old Town, Gamla Stan, just down the road from the King's palace. It looks exactly like what you would imagine an old medieval European town should look like, thankfully unspoiled by any modern building. It's full of quaint narrow streets, with charming little colorful town squares everywhere. Wherever they look there are incredibly beautiful old architectural buildings with all manner of eclectic stores. There are chic cafes with street-dining everywhere.

They make a left turn off a big square, and there it is: Engelen Pubben, or the Angel Pub in English. Fran parks the van, and they all go in for their first look. They're disappointed at how small the place actually is. There's room for maybe two hundred people max. There's a small stage up front, and a long bar all the way down the room, almost to the front window. At the end of the bar, a small corridor leads into a narrow intimate dining room. They look at the cost of beer, and were floored: t'was nearly three times the cost of a pint back home.

The manager, who seems like an okay guy, greets them. "Welcome to Stockholm," he says in perfect English, but with a heavy Swedish accent going up and down like the Swedish chef in the Muppets.

He reviews their work schedules along with when and what they can eat. "You work every Monday 'til Saturday, starting at nine o' clock. Sunday, you are free, but you must take your equipment off the stage because we have jazz every Sunday. You can come to the restaurant before you play and we will feed you. You can eat anything you want on the menu, except steak. You play four forty-five minutes sets, and you can have two free pints of strong beer every night."

"Jaysus Billy, they speak like you," says Robot at his teasing best.

"Piss off," says Billy laughing, but he was right on. They do go up and down, just like the Cork accent.

The lads learned later to their delight that one of the most popular discos in Stockholm was right underneath them. It was owned by the same people, so they could go down after their show and dance the night away free, including beer of course.

Even tho' the manager told them their limit was two beers a night, they abused that big time. The first thing you do in a new place is get to know the barmen, so **Billy and The Touch** made sure to make those acquaintances quickly. The crowd tipped the more they enjoyed the music and they went wild for them, so the barmen made out like bandits for the month, so it was free beer, as much as they wanted, no charge. Even the manager turned a blind eye, as the place was crammed every night after the word got out, so everyone was happy. Every time the barmen got a decent tip, they would ring a bell, which looked and sounded just like a bell in a firehall. The bell got quite a workout that month.

There's magic immediately, and thankfully, the first night's a huge success in so many ways, even tho' the place is only half full. They click straight away when they hit those first mad frantic notes of a Celtic rock tune. The Swedes never heard anything like it before, and they love it. They teach the crowd the proper clapping to *The Wild Rover*, and they enjoy the drill. The lads do a faster version than usual, with Mel doing some great licks with the fiddle. Billy and Mel literally tear the place apart that first night with their new, wild and sexy Irish sound. Steo, skinny as ever, with strong looking geeky glasses, adds terrific distorted guitar sounds, great solo licks, and of course Robot lets it all hang out, his long blonde hair, flying all over the place as he lets it rip on the drums.

They are totally into it for the first time, creating something absolutely new, no limits, no copying anybody, doing their own thing for the very first time. As the night goes on, together with the audience's fantastic reaction, they're beginning to realize they really have something fresh and new with this Celtic rock sound.

Jack becomes a star in that little pub in Sweden with his version of **Thin Lizzy's** *The Boys Are back In Town*. As he plays, he goes into another world, just him and his beloved guitar, totally into it. He looks like he's literally making love to his bass guitar, and it's a huge turn on for the girls. Here was this handsome man, exuding a carefree sexuality, doing what he was born to do, and playing with an abandon, he never displayed before.

Thin Lizzy were his heroes. They were all brilliant musicians, and the one and only Phil Lynnott, was a Dub of course. He was also a bass player like Jack. As he played his hero's songs, it looked as if he was channeling Phil back to life. Phil died at the peak of his career from a drug overdose. In years to come a statue will be placed, in his honor, in the center of Dublin.

Jack gets really carried away, and suddenly jumps from the stage onto the bar, and slides down the counter on his knees. The Swedes frantically grab their expensive beers before he knocks them down, all the while playing the hell out of his bass guitar. It was absolutely intoxicating, and the crowd laps it up.
Of course Jack's counter routine becomes a staple during the month's gig. The band loves the music

they're playing, getting better and better as the month went by. The crowd are going wild every night, and the lads learn some basic Swedish, "thank you, we love you," etc.

Their bit of Irish comes in handy as well as they could say to each other in Irish: "Hey, I fancy the one on the right, you take the one on the left all ri'?" They assume the girls are doing the same thing in Swedish.

Their new showband language, "the ben" comes in handy also, as the Swedes could hear them speaking English, but obviously can't understand a word. They assume the lads aren't being ignorant by speaking in Irish, it's just that they can't understand them, because of their lack of English, and of course the lads heavy accents. By then, the lads were so good at the "ben," they were able to speak whole sentences backwards using the "ben," so no one could possibly understand what they were saying.

The crowd shouts up, *Streets of London*, Ralph McTell's iconic song about loneliness. Luckily Billy knows it and they discover that his brilliant song about the forgotten and shunned in London is huge in Sweden. The audience knows every line about real down and out homelessness.

The contrast to their standard of living compared to people living on the streets really clicked with the Swedes, who are way ahead of every other country- offering asylum to refugees from all over the world who need a new and safe home. Sweden offers free intensive language courses for these refugees, so they can assimilate as quickly as possible.

The Swedes pay outrageous taxes, sometimes over 90% of what they earn. Yet despite the obvious drain on the economy, there isn't the animosity towards the new immigrants that you would expect.

Billy asks a girl about this, and she explains, "Yes, we pay a lot of taxes, but we get a lot in return: free education, great standard of living, and we're taken care of wery well when we get older. We believe in helping other people not as fortunate as we are. There are wery few countries that have what we have." The lads try not to giggle when the Swedes don't pronounce their v's.

Yet despite all of the good stuff, Billy could sense a deep feeling of loneliness, and lack of a strong identity and self esteem among many of the younger people he met. He could understand why a song like the *Streets of London* resonates so deeply with the Swedes he meets in the pub, who were mostly middle-to-poorer working-class people.

Many of the girls are single mothers, who live with the father of their child for a while, then move on. With many of them already coming from broken relationships, there was definitely a sense of sadness and loneliness. Not one of the lads parents are separated, so the contrast is pretty dramatic to them all. They may not have the standard of living that the Swedes have, but they have a strong family unit, which they begin to appreciate for the first time.

On the other hand, the owner of the pub told Billy that "it's a sin" to be successful in Sweden, and he was actually looking for ways to get money out of Sweden. When he got to know Billy, he offered Billy the chance to open a hotel in a place called Portlaoise. It's about an hour's drive south of Dublin. Its biggest industry is a huge prison, which housed a lot of IRA prisoners in the 70's. All roads leading into and out of Dublin from Cork, Limerick, Kerry, and Waterford, have to go through Portlaoise.

A few months ago, the lads got a flat tire there one morning around four a.m., coming home from a dance. Billy couldn't believe how many trucks passed by, heading in and out of Dublin, as they were changing the tire.

The lights went on for Billy: "An all-night diner would be perfect right here," he thought, especially now as the band scene was coming to a crashing halt. This could be a winner, beats teaching anyway, he thought. People heading out of Dublin could have a guaranteed breakfast there, thus avoiding the early morning Dublin traffic, and people would have a convenient spot to eat at any time, before heading in or out of the busy city, day or night.

At the time, there was only one all night restaurant in Ireland, and that was right in the middle of Dublin city, and it was expensive. A few days later PJ and himself came down, had a look around, and talked to a farmer about possibly selling them a few acres. When they got back from Sweden, he would follow up on it.

He was telling the owner about his plans for an all-night diner, and suddenly he turned around and offered Billy a 51/49 deal. "Build a hotel and have your twenty four hour restaurant in it, as well as another better restaurant with a function room," was the offer. It was an amazing opportunity for Billy. All he had to do was get all the planning completed. He was confident he could do this, as Ireland needed all the investment it could get at the time.

The money would come from Sweden. Billy would have a 51% stake in it from day one. He would have to give up music and devote all his time to this new venture. This would be a really tough pill for Billy to swallow. It was very tempting as the recession got worse and worse, and the music venues were drying up big time. He seriously thought about it, but things changed dramatically a few months later for the lads, so he never followed up on it. The bottom line was: all he wanted to be was a musician.

Back at the pub, Billy could see how much the crowd wanted to join in, especially as the strong beer began to hit them, and the frantic Celtic music drove them crazy. He got the idea to hand out the words of many of the songs they sang, so by the end of the month, it was one big party every night.

The owner of the pub hired a photographer to take publicity shots of the band on stage. Billy posted a few to PJ to get some publicity back home. The crowd was going wild that first night, especially when Jack jumped onto the counter on his knees, making love to his beloved guitar…. Snap!!! ….. What a shot!!! Jack on the bar counter in all his glory, girls screaming, trying to get their hands all over him. A few days later Bridget's mother shows the picture of "her" Jack on the daily paper in all his glory with the heading:

GIRLS GO WILD FOR **THE TOUCH** IN SWEDEN….

"Shit, shit, shiiiiit," she screams, and runs up to her room and slams her door.

Next day, the lads explore Stockholm's old town on foot, down around the King's Palace. They watch the changing of the guard, and are all typical wide-eyed tourists in this, one of the most beautiful cities in Europe. They're all on a huge high from last night, knowing it's all going to be good for a month: all of them really looking forward to playing each night, and not doing it just for the money like back home, not to mention the girls. They felt like the Beatles that first time in Hamburg. Perhaps this new music could be what they need for Europe and the big time, and as PJ said, maybe even America?

They get to a traffic light and it's red. It goes green and it clicks rapidly. They were impressed, realizing it's for blind people to let them know when it's safe to cross. There was nothing in Ireland like that at the time.

Next light they see a blind man waiting for the clicks to cross. Robot couldn't resist. He gets out his drumsticks, and taps rapidly on the pole imitating the sound. The blind man walks straight out onto the oncoming traffic, and nearly gets creamed. The poor man is all confused, and finally gets across the street, bringing the traffic to a complete stop amidst all the angry people blowing their horns. The lads think it's great craic altogether.

Later on, they stumble upon a sex shop. "C'mon lads, let's go in," says Fran. The lads are reluctant. "Ah for f***'s sake lads, we're in Sweden, who's going to know?" They all go in. They look around, and are amazed at all the paraphernalia: dildos everywhere, magazines, oils and sexy lingerie. [It was such a long time ago, porn videos were a thing of the future!]

The lads stock up on condoms, buying loads of extra packs for their friends back home, as they were banned in Ireland. They all come out of there laughing nervously like kids who've gotten away with something naughty.

Billy walks out with a long narrow box. "What's that?' asks Fran. "It's for Meg."

"Look what I got," says Robot. He takes out a small white cylinder that looks like a throat spray.

"What's that?" asks Mel. "It's eh,…. delay spray for men."

"What?" says everybody laughing….only Robot… He shuffles around shyly as he explains: "eh, whenever I'm, eh, with a girl for the first time ya know, as soon as she touches my willie I come all ri'? It's very embarrassing all ri'." They all laugh. It was just the way he said it, not trying to be funny at all, made it even funnier than usual, Robot, being totally honest.

"So how does it work?" inquires Fran.

Robot looks at it trying to find directions and says, "Ah shite, it says 'see leaflet for instructions,' we've gotta' go back."

They all troop back, and the guy at the counter is your stereotypical Indian guy with that unmistakable accent.

"Eh, excuse me," says Robot, "eh, how does this work, ya know?"

"One moment please," he says with a big smile, and turns around and grabs a massive black dildo off the shelf. He places it right in front of Robot's face. It's so big, it's bobbing all over the place, just like a slinky. "You spray around here," he says, pointing the spray can around the head of the dildo. "Wait three minutes before you go in, very very important, three minutes."

"Will it work?" Robot asks.

The Indian guy answers a mile a minute. "Yes yes, very good, very good, she will be very pleased indeed, very pleased, I promise." They all walk out, and the Indian guy follows them out the door.

"Remember, wait three minutes, three minutes before you go in, very important, very important" The lads are on the floor.

That night they leave the apartment, walk over to the pub, and see a line outside waiting to get in. "Holy shit lads, look at that," says Fran. They are all amazed and excited. They are lucky enough to experience the high so very few musicians are ever privileged to feel: people wanting to hear you and your music, and willing to line up and pay for that pleasure.

They walk onto the stage, and the vibe is electric. Jack lets fly with *Whiskey In the Jar*, a la **Thin Lizzy**, but faster, Steo does the electric guitar solos, and Mel matches him note for note on the guitar in perfect harmony. Jack jumps down onto the counter again, and the place goes wild.

Fran is squashed into a corner by the front door, mixing the sound, and a beautiful Swedish blond comes over and asks, "who is dat?" looking at Jack.

"Ah that's just Jack."

"He is fine," she says.
"Yea, and he's a virgin," says Fran, stirring the shit.
"Nay, he can't be," she says in total disbelief.
Fran keeps it up, "I swear, his girlfriend won't do it until they're married."

She's amazed, and starts chatting away in Swedish to her friends, and it spreads around the room, everybody telling their friends, laughing as each of them mutter away in Swedish: "He can't be a virgin, he's in a band." … "He's too good looking to be a virgin."… "I want him."… "He's too old to be a virgin."… "He is perfect, how can he be a virgin?"… "I never had a virgin."….

At the break, the girl approaches Jack. "Hi, my name is Pia, you are a very good musician. This is my friend Kerstin."

"Hi," says Jack very shyly, not looking straight at her,….
"Eh,.. Jack," and he shakes her hand, "this is Mel and Robot."
"Robot?" says Pia, as she flashes a huge perfect smile.
"Yea, a car went over his head when he was young, and he just got up and walked away," says Jack.
Robot was instantly in lust as he stared at Kerstin.
"We are going to a party tonight, would you like to come?" asks Pia.
Robot is beyond smitten, "Sure, can we bring the lads?"
"Ya, you are all welcome," she says.
"Great," says Robot smiling at Kerstin, she smiles back, and sparks begin to fly between them.

After the show, the lads hurriedly stow their gear, clear the stage and they all jump into a taxi. They are excited and curious as they head off to their first Swedish party. Pia and Jack are getting to know each other in a corner, and he's beginning to see the obvious differences between bitchy demanding Bridget, and warm and open Pia, no pressure, and oh so gorgeous. He was really enjoying being with her, and starts to come out of himself a bit, plus he's on a terrific high after the reaction to the band tonight.

A Swedish guy comes over to the lads and with a big smile on his face says: "we like you Irishmen, you play good music, please, …. have a drink." He pours them a shot of vodka. He does this for everybody there. Suddenly he stands up and sings a sort of a rugby song that they all know. It sounds like a rousing war song they would sing just before going into battle. They all stand up and join in in full gusto. It lasts about thirty seconds, then he says "Skol," they all say "Skol," and down goes the vodka in one gulp. The lads, standing in amazement, do the same.

Another Swedish guy fills all the glasses again, and a few minutes later, he jumps up, raises his glass, and starts singing another rousing song. They all stand up, sing along, and when they finish, they shout "Skol," and down the shot in one gulp. The lads are having a blast.

Meanwhile Robot and Kerstin disappear into a bedroom. He gives the lads a wink. Their passionate kissing quickly moves to clothes being ripped and thrown off their bodies. They fling themselves onto the bed, locked in sweaty arm and lip embraces. With all systems go, Robot suddenly surfaces for air and mumbles, "Eh, I must go to the toilet all ri'?" He doesn't want to dress again, as that would give her the wrong impression, like he's chickening out or something, so he grabs a girl's red robe hanging on the door. He quickly rummages through his pants pocket and finds the Delay Spray, and scurries into the bathroom.

He's rock hard at this point, and he sprays his willie as instructed by the Indian guy. Thinking one quick spray could never work, he sprays it again. "Ah shite," he says and proceeds to spray and spray 'til the can's all gone.

As he re-enters the room, he basks in the glow that she is totally naked. He remembers the Indian's guy's directions: "Wait three minutes before you go in, three minutes, very important," so he buys time with deep, passionate kisses. She is melting around him, he's in heaven. Suddenly she goes down on him. "Shite." he thinks, "what'll I do now?" But it feels good, so he says nothing.

After a while she says, "What have you got on down dere?" in her heavy Swedish accent.

"Wha?" says Robot, trying to act all innocent, and, at the same time, totally unprepared for this situation.

"What have you got on down dere, I can't feel anything," as she comes up patting her cheeks and checking her jaw, all worried, doing all sorts of crazy contortions with her mouth.

Although he got great mileage out of this later on, he looks at her, and realizes he has to fess up. "Look, I like ya, and I wanted to give ya a good time all ri', so I bought this stuff," and he shows her the can of Delay Spray. "I'm sorry."

"Thank you for telling me," she says, "don't ewer do that again, all right?"

"Ri'," he says, noticing that she said 'again.'
They heartily and eagerly return to their hot, sweaty attempt at lovemaking; he goes in, and after a few thrusts realizes he should have come by now. He thrusts harder and faster, no come. He's delighted with himself, and gives what he thinks is the performance of his life. The only thing that bothers him is he never came, and starts to think that he's done some serious damage to his willie.

Eventually, they collect their decorum and exit the bedroom. The lads see her, opening and closing her mouth, and still tapping her cheeks. They realize what probably just happened, and without a doubt, it was one of the greatest laughs they ever had together. Once again, it could only happen to Robot.

On the way back in the taxi Fran asks him, "Well, did it work?"

"Yea, t'was great, best ride of me life, but I think I f***ed up my willie."

Fran bursts out laughing, "Don't worry Robot, it's just like goin' to the dentist, it'll wear off soon."
"I hope you're ri'," says Robot.
"Fair play to ya Robot," says Fran, "you're the first one to score."

The following night, the pub is packed again with an atmosphere of pure madness. The crowd loved the Celtic rock tunes, doing their best to learn the words, as Billy had printed them out for them. They went straight into a reggae version of the *Rare Ould Mountain Dew*, and the crowd valiantly tried their best to get the *Didlee Eyes* right in the chorus.

They were way ahead of the Irish at the time in their musical tastes. They knew every word that Bruce Springsteen ever wrote. They screamed the chorus of Elton John's classic *Goodbye Yellow Brick Road*, lighting up their cigarette lighters and swaying along – total magic. The boys felt like rock stars.

Just before the lads last set, Jack gets a call from Pia. "Would you like to come back to my apartment tonight?"

"Eh,… yea,…. how do I get there?"

"There's a bus outside the pub, it's number 78. It comes every half hour on the hour. Go four stops and get off. I'm in the white building across the street. You can't miss it. Go up three floors to number 325."

"Hey lads, that was Pia. I'm goin' back to her apartment tonight."
"Poor ould Bridget," says Steo sarcasticly.
"Yea." …. Jack's conscience hits him and he hesitates, "Yea, I dunno' should I go?"
"For feck's sake Jack," says Mel, "she's got you by the balls. Pia is gorgeous man, Jaysus, if you don't do it, I'm gonna' have a go."
"Screw you," says Jack.

Robot chimes in, and seals the deal as always. "Mel's right Jack, Bridget is a bitch, 'Jack don't touch my hair, Jack you can't go to rehearsal today, you can't do this, you can't do that," taking her off perfectly, "come on man, you're getting old, you're 25."

"Well,"… says Jack almost convinced.

"Look," says Fran, "nobody's gonna' say anything when we get home, okay?"

"All ri'," he says. "Good," says Fran, I'm goin' down to the disco, are ye comin'lads?"

Jack is ultra careful about his beloved bass guitar, so he decides to bring it back to the apartment before he catches the bus, rather than trust it with the lads. He looks at his watch: twenty minutes 'til the next bus, so he sits down, and instantly conks out, comatose as usual.

The lads come back from the disco, and find him stretched out on the sofa. Fran can't believe what he see's. "Jaysus lads, would ya look at him, he's getting laid for the first time in his life, and he falls asleep, holy shite, I'm goin' to bed,…. I'm way behind in me wankin." The boys can't believe it, and leave him there as they go to sleep.

He gets an almighty slagging next morning from the boys, merciless. "I suppose the ould sex drive isn't as good as it was when you were young Jack wha'?" says Robot.

"I fell asleep all ri, an' I don't have her phone number. I hope she'll come in again."

"I doubt it," says Steo, Mr. Positive, as always.

To Jack's complete amazement and pleasure, she comes in again the following night with Kerstin just as the lads are taking their first break. Fran shouts into Jack's ear above all the noise, "Jack, look at her, …. she's gorgeous, will ya go over there and apologize, it's now or never."

"Yea Jack," says Robot, "but bring her back to the apartment, no bleedin' busses all ri'."

Jack skulks to Pia, hat in hand as they say. He struggles to explain his ability to fall asleep at the drop of said hat. His description of the care he renders to his guitar and its safety actually touches her heart. When he culminated with the fact that he had simply intended to rest for a few minutes until the bus arrived, only to be rudely awakened by the band members in the early morning, she was truly impressed with his sincerity. He asks her to give him one more chance to spend some time with her and he promises that he will not fall asleep this time. To be certain, Pia tells him that it would be best to go directly to his apartment after the show. He agrees wholeheartedly.

They aren't even in the door and she's all over him, and he loves it. He doubted if Bridget could ever be as natural as Pia was in bed. Pia explains that she must head home and leaves around two or so. Jack is in ecstasy.

At about four a.m., there's a knock on Billy's door, it's Robot's Dad. "There's somethin' wrong with Jack's willie."

"Wha,… whaddy'a mean?" says Billy, still drunk and half asleep. "It's the size of a cucumber, come on, I think we've gotta' bring him to hospital." Billy goes into Jack's bedroom, and there's Jack moaning in agony, holding his not so wee willie.

"Look," says Pops. Jack shows it to Billy, who can't believe it; it's bulging exactly like the size of a thick cucumber, massive except for the head which looks tiny compared to the massive shaft, ready to explode at any moment from all the pressure.

"I think it's going to blow lads," says Robot, and everybody laughs only to suffer from immediate guilt about laughing.

"Get me up ye shower of wankers, I gotta' go to the hospital. Shite, me first bleedin' ride"… The lads begin to realize he was really in agony. His face was pale, he couldn't move without support on both sides; they were afraid that he might faint.

"What happened?' says Billy. "I dunno', we did it, and oooh she left, and I started oooh to feel guilty about Bridget, oooh and then it started to swell up." Tears were running down his face, he looked like he might be a goner. They lift him out of the bed, and he continues to moan in agony with every step. The lads help him down the stairs, and across the square to the taxi stand. "Hospital quick," says Pops taking charge.

The taxi squeals off like a rocket, and within minutes, they get to the emergency entrance at the hospital. They shoulder-carry him in slowly, register and sit down. After a few minutes, a doctor comes over and introduces himself, and brings them into a room.

Jack tries to tell him what happened, and he takes one look and is stunned. He starts muttering away in Swedish. He goes to the door and he calls all the doctors and nurses in to have a look. They're all trying to keep a serious face chatting away to each other in Swedish .... "I've never seen anything like this, the poor bastard must be in agony." A nurse said, "Just when you think you've seen everything."....

The lads watch as the doctor gets a big syringe-like thing with a long thick needle on top, about the size of a turkey baster. Using his arm to represent Jack's willie, he explains to Pops and the lads, "We'll have to cut here, the foreskin, so we can relieve the pressure, then we have to use this to suck out all the puss and blood. He will have to stay here at least two nights."

It would be funny in his up and down Swedish accent at any other time, but the boys winced. "God the poor bastard," says Billy as he shudders at the thought.

"Don't worry," said the doctor, "he won't feel a thing, we will give him drugs that will make him wery wery happy."

"But we need him on stage tomorrow night," says Steo.
"Steo," says Fran throwing a withering look at him.

"You will have to find someone else to take his place," said the doctor, "I've never seen anything like this, I think it's a wirus, but I'm not sure. You have to go now, come back tomorrow." With that the boys give Jack the thumbs up, even tho' they were thinkin' how screwed he was, and went back to the apartment.

They all troop back to the hospital next morning. They see Jack's willie all bandaged up with a couple of huge ice packs around it to help with the swelling. "How'rya?" says Fran.

"Fanntastic, let me tellll ye llladzz," as he slurs his words from the drugs, "you shhould askk the docctor to give you whatttevver he gavve meee, it'z fantassstic sttuff whateverr it iz." Jack is so drugged up he's all smiles, not a care in the world, totally unlike his usual shy self.

"So what happened to ya?" asks Mel.

"Thhe docttor told mme it wazz a fluke, he thinkz an ovvernighttt viruzz, butt I think itt wazz me conscienze."

"What was she like?" asks nosey Steo.

"IINNncredible, until thizz shiiite. Whhat'rye ggoin' to do tooniight?"

"They found a bass player for us, we're goin' back to rehearse right now," says Mel.
"I'm zzorry ladzz, I'll bee alll rright tommorroww."

"We'll be all right for a night," says Robot, "hey Jack, if only Mel had taken a photo of your willie last night, you'd have been a bleedin' legend" .... "Whaat'll ya telll Piiia iif shhe comes in?" They all laugh, even Steo. Jack, true to form, is already sound asleep, and they leave.

The substitute bass player arrives and after the rehearsal manages to keep up with them. They were all thinking about Jack and his dilemma, yet they were able to focus on the music. They were just getting into the second set, when who should walk in – of all people – Bridget! She was the last person anyone would have ever thought would walk into that pub in Sweden. The lads don't see her in the crowd, but if they did, they would have thought she was a ghost. Bridget in Sweden? She got on a plane to London, then caught a plane to Stockholm, then found the pub in downtown Gamla Stan, unbelievable.

She looks up, expecting to find "her" Jack only to find he's not on stage. "Where the f*** is Jack?" she says to Fran. No 'how'rya, kiss my ass,' nothin'. She catches Fran totally off guard, literally stunned, that she was actually here in SWEDEN for God's sake!

He stutters and stumbles, "Eh, he's in hospital, what the hell are youse doin' here?"

"Hospital?...Is he all right?"

"Eh, he's all right ya know, just a little accident, nothin' to worry about, he'll be out tomorrow."

"Accident? Whadd'ya mean accident, is he hurt?"

"Ah Jaysus no Bridget, well his pride might be hurt a little," as he sniggers to himself.

"Which hospital?"

"How the hell do I know, I didn't drive the bleedin' ambulance. The lads at the bar probably know." She storms over to the bar, gets the name of the hospital, and races out the door, into a taxi.

She tears into the hospital, and there's Jack still all drugged up, as happy as can be. She sees his bandaged up willie, with the ice packs all around it, thankfully for Jack, almost all back to normal.

"Jack love," she says when she sees him, "Are youse all right?"

Jack, convinced the drugs are playing tricks on him mumbles, "Jayzzuzz Bridget, whatt are youze dooin' herre?"

"What happened love?" all concerned about "her" Jack.

He begins to tell her exactly what happened, still high as a kite, the tale takes a bit of time. It's as if he's on a truth drug or somethin', incapable of telling a lie, he blurts it all out. "Welll, a very funny thing happened Briddgget, wait 'til I telll ya. I lost my virginnnity last night. Youu wouldn't do it, and if ya saw Piiia, you'd understand, I….I couldn't say no ya know. She's gorgeous Bridget, bleeedin' gorrrgeous….. We were makin' love and afterwards me willie swellled up like a cuucumber, you should'a seen it Bridget, huge it was. I was in agony Bridget, pure bleeedin' agony, worse pain o' me life, an' I ended up in here."

Suddenly Bridget lets loose a right hook straight into Jack's eye. "F*** you!" she says and storms out the door. She did not return to the pub nor the apartment. She took a taxi directly to the airport, purchased return tickets and retraced her steps to Ireland. She was a terribly unhappy, frustrated virgin indeed.

Chapter 17

The pub is rocking and roaring, the lads are belting out another crazy night, with a wall-to-wall crowd going gaga. The lads are in hysterics when they see Pia coming in. She looks to the stage, her face drops to immediate disappointment, as there was no Jack.

"Where's Jack?" she asks Fran.

"Hospital," trying to keep from laughing.

"Hospital? What is wrong with him?" Fran whispers the news into Pia's ear. She's stunned. "I will go see him right now."

"Ah janey I wouldn't do that now Pia," as he grabs her by the arm gently, "he's sort of embarrassed ya know, I'll tell him you came in. He'll be back tomorrow night." Fran could just picture the two girls fighting it out in the hospital ward. Pia sits down all worried...

The doctor felt comfortable releasing Jack from the hospital in the morning. Rest was recommended, and a nice supply of pain meds were included with his discharge papers. He felt well enough to perform with the band that night and was even more elated when Pia and Kerstin arrived at the first break. Pia rushed to Jack, confused to see him proudly sporting a really dark shiner.

"Hey Jack, I'm sorry."

"It's all right, it wasn't your fault," he says nobly.

"I feel really bad, are you okay? What happened to your eye?"

"Eh,… 'tis a long story, ya know." says Jack.

"Can I see you again?" she asks.

Jack's left hand subconsciously starts fiddling through his hair. He always does this when he's shy or embarrassed. "Yea, I'd like that."

"Can we show you a little bit of Stockholm on Sunday?"

"Yea, that would be great, can I bring the lads?"

Not the answer she was looking for, but she was equally noble. "Ya, we'll meet you here at twelve."

"All ri'," says Jack, and goes back up on stage for their final set.

Chapter 18

After Bridget's surprise appearance in the pub, the band gathers in the morning to start work on their song for the national contest. Billy shares sheet music with the chords of his draft of the song. The first time through it, they like the sound and they think it's pretty good. "That's as far as I got, just the verse. I think it needs somethin' really different for the chorus to make it happen. I tried everything but I'm stuck, any ideas?"

Steo is the most creative among the other lads. He plays around for a few minutes, totally focused, trying all sorts of chords and then he gets the muse. The light goes on. "How about trying minor chords in the chorus?" He starts playing a few different chord combinations.

Whatever Steo lacks in social graces, he makes up for in his music, as he could pull some amazing ideas out of his head. He takes the minor key the verse was in and reverses the chord progression of the verse exactly; it works. Billy is impressed, and they all get into the act.

The song was going around in all of their heads, each adding a little, sometimes good, sometimes not so good. After a couple of hours, they've nearly got it. "Let's leave it for a few days, and if ye come up with any better ideas, let me know before I figure out the words okay?""""

Billy's approach to songwriting was music first, then the words. When he had time he'd doodle on the piano for hours. He'd try and work out a melody with chords that weren't used in that way before, which is like Mission Impossible. But every now and then he sort of stumbled onto a few chords that made sense, and sounded good. Then he'd try and create a melody.

Usually, he came up with the chorus first, and then struggled with the verse. Somewhere around this point, lyrics started to come to him, and he would throw pages and pages of lyrics away 'til he had one reasonably finished set of lyrics. He always wished he had the self-confidence to approach the best lyric writers in Ireland at the time, lyrics not being his strong point. But his Irish doubt and lack of self-confidence kept him from doing so.

Billy envied the genius of Elton John. The hottest lyric writers of the day would hand him their lyrics, literally in the recording studio, with a band right there, ready to record. Elton would create a perfect melody for those lyrics in a few hours, and shortly thereafter, another classic was born. He wrote the music for the Lion King in two weeks, much to the consternation of other Broadway writers who would take years to do the same thing, and possibly not come up with as good a result.

Billy remembers the time his band opened for Harry Chapin at the RDS Stadium in Dublin. In the 70's, the RDS was one of the biggest venues in Ireland. He didn't know much about Chapin at the time, so when he met him backstage he wasn't in the least bit intimidated. "How many songs a year do you write?" Billy asked him.

"365"
"Wow," said Billy, amazed.
"How many do you write?" asked Harry.
"Oh about twelve or so."

"Oh that won't do at all. I write one a day, and I record them onto my cassette player. Then at the end of each month, I go over all thirty songs, pick out the best bits of them all, a verse here, a chorus there, maybe even just a title. I'm usually in the same state of mind each month, so they are usually pretty similar. I work on just those bits for a while, and I get one good song from it all. At the end of the year, I have twelve new songs for my next album."

Billy swore to try and find more time to compose, but it was hard composing songs, when you're trying to survive. Harry would tour for a certain time, then go home for months, with loads of money, and have plenty of quality time to write, and perfect all the bits he'd written along the road on his bus.

When Harry took to the stage, Billy was blown away. He went straight out the next day and bought Harry's record, and learned *The Cat's in the Cradle*, and *Taxi*. Billy thought…now there's a real songwriter, as he listened to the lyrics. Billy learned more about Harry Chapin's contribution to the fight against hunger in America, which Harry's brother still leads today. When Harry died a few years after visiting Ireland in a car crash, Billy read the news with sadness. The world had just lost a great talent, and a humble human being.

On Sunday, the girls take the lads for a boat-ride around Stockholm's Archipelago. Its majestic scenery of about 30,000 big and small islands impresses them all, with holiday cottages dotted along their coastlines, and sailboats big and small, everywhere.

"In the winter," says Pia, "ice skaters skate on this wery place." It was hard for the boys to imagine such an ice buildup when they rarely got snow back home. "It stays bright in the summer months 'til elewen, and I have seen many fantastic sunsets sailing out around here with my parents, they own a summer cottage on one of the islands, like so many people here in Stockholm. The sunsets are unforgettable," she says with pride. "Before WWII, fishermen lived on the islands. It was a hard life, but after the war, the younger people on the islands didn't want to work as hard as their parents, so they went to the city for work, and fishing around here has almost died out."

Robot is delighted with himself, clinging to Kerstin. It's a glorious day, so they visit a beautiful park with fountains and gorgeous gardens. The lads think they are in heaven: nearly all the girls in the park are topless, a veritable Swedish smorgasbord, a feast for their Irish eyes. So, for a few unforgettable hours, six pasty skinned guys, lie on their bellies and lunge back and forth on the grass, as the girls parade by: a perfect day.

Kerstin, in her lovely up and down Swedish accent says, "Robot, would you like to come to my parent's summer home next Sunday?"

"Eh, just you and me?" thinkin' he had just won the lottery.

The possibilities are soon dashed when she says, "No, my parents will be there also, and would like to meet you, they have been to Ireland."

He hesitates, "Eh,... I dunno', I'd be sort a' like embarrassed, ya know."

"Robot, it's all right, they are looking forward to meeting you, please come, I think you will enjoy the country."

"Well all ri'," he says even tho' he's never done anything like this before, and he won't have the lads for backup.

At breakfast, around midday Monday morning, Billy has an exciting announcement: "Lads, I've finished the song, and I've hired a studio for nine o' clock on Wednesday morning, so we need to run over it all right?"

"Yea yea, shite I hate gettin' up in the morning," says Steo, "and then playin' all night. What's the studio like dy'a know?"

"State of the art, 16 tracks."

The musical side of Steo starts to get excited when he hears 16 tracks. "Wow, I'll be able to do a few overdubs."

In Ireland at the time, there were very few recording studios, and even then, the best studios had only eight tracks to record everything. Billy didn't know, but in the future, there would be no limits to how many tracks were available.

"I've been thinkin' about that minor part," says Billy, "and I think a girl would be perfect. I asked the studio if they knew anyone, and they said they knew a good female singer. It's gonna' cost us about two hundred quid, [pounds] but I think it'll be worth it. So, whad'ye think?"

"Yea,…. I can hear that," says Steo, "where the hell is Helen when ya need her?"
"I wonder how she's doin'?" says Mel.
"I wonder who she's doin'?" says Robot.

Upon their arrival at the studio, the boys are trying to look cool, but they are awed at the size and sophistication of it all. It's the first time any of them have been in a studio except for Billy, and that was an antique compared to this one, absolutely state of the art.
Robot is doing a sound check, amazed at the incredible sound of the studio drums coming through his headphones. He's tickled pink when he hears how good he sounds when he does a drum-fill on the top-of-the line studio drums. Steo and Mel are doing acoustic guitar licks. With the reverb the engineer gives them, they've never heard themselves sound so good.

The singer comes in and the engineer introduces them. She's a beautiful looking Swedish singer, a little older than the lads, who has an air of confidence about her, like she's seen and done it all.

Billy runs over her part on the piano, and they quickly hear that she has "it," well worth the two hundred pounds. They run over the song to allow the engineer get a good balance in all their headphones. When everyone is happy he says, "Okay tape rolling, *Love Is The Answer*, take one."

Billy starts the haunting piano intro, which sounds great on the studios magnificent Steinway grand piano. He quietly sings the melody to give him the proper feel. If he sings too loudly, his voice will bleed into the piano mikes and mess up the final mix.

Steo and Mel come in after eight bars with matching acoustic guitars, and it's beginning to sound like a song. Jack spots a fretless bass guitar in the studio, and decides to record with this instead of his bass guitar. It sounds way sexier, as he can bend the bass notes much more than he could with his guitar. The song is beginning to take shape. Robot eventually comes in with a fabulous drum-fill straight into the chorus. They go into the control room, listen to what they have just put on tape, and are happy so far. They add another run of acoustic guitars, in the two chorus's doing something slightly different, which keeps the song building dramatically. Then Steo changes over to his electric guitar, and does another run. Billy adds some string-like synthesizers to give it an orchestral feel, building all the while, and finally he and the girl singer do the vocals. She nails it first time, the lads add harmony they've been practicing, and then double track the same thing, and finally, they start mixing it.

This whole process is what really turns Billy on more than anything else. Having a grain of an idea, working on it, and finally recording it. It was as much of a turn on as great sex. They all wish they had more tracks and money of course, to add even further to the song. Fran is impressed: "I think ye could win with this one lads, I'll send it over to PJ tomorrow, ye have to have it in by Friday."

Billy marveled at the Beatles, the Beach Boys, Queen, and so many other great bands, who were able to get seemingly impossible results with just eight tracks. They would record huge chunks of a song, using all eight tracks, mix it and then mix it down to one track, hearing in their heads what the final sound should be, and hoping like hell that they got the right mix as the process took forever, so they had to be right when they mixed it down to one track.. Then they'd record another huge block of other instruments, possibly in another studio, mix it down to one track, again hoping they got this mix right. Then they would add even more, burn that down to one track, do it a few more times, and then mix the eight tracks, which sounded like a million tracks when they were all finished, and came up with classics like *Hey Jude*, *Good Vibrations*, and

Bohemian Rhapsody all of which are truly amazing achievements for their time.

Saturday is another magical, standing-room only night in the pub. After the show, Kerstin drives Robot out to her parent's house. It's totally dark, so he can't see too much, but he can hear the ripple of the lake water, and is just about to go to bed with his precious Kerstin: life is good, no parents in sight....

He wakes up to a spectacular scene: a lakeside cottage with the water almost lapping up to the house. There's even a little sandy beach. It feels like a million miles from where he comes from, in so many ways. He's a nervous wreck coming down for breakfast, as he's very conscious that her parents know he's sleeping with their only daughter, and couldn't possibly imagine a similar scenario back home.

Thankfully, he is soon put at ease with the warm welcome he receives from Kerstin's father. "Welcome to our home, my name is Hasse," and shakes Robot's hand. "This is my wife Eva," in perfect English, "Eva doesn't have too much English."

She's a beautiful looking lady, high cheekbones, blonde hair, tall and blue eyes: the classic Scandinavian look. "Eh, hello,... Robot," as he shakes their hands nervously. "I can see where Kerstin gets her good looks from," as he shyly looks at Eva.

Kerstin immediately translates, Eva smiles and says "thank you" in English.

The ice is broken, and Robot relaxes a bit, even tho' they're way more formal than what he's used to. Hasse points to a huge helping of bacon and eggs, and some fishy stuff he doesn't like the look of. "You are wery welcome," says Hasse, "We have been to your country, and we like it wery much, please, have some breakfast." He devours it, and later they take out a canoe from the shed and enjoy messing about on the lake. They have a swim, enjoy some skinny dipping, totally free, and he has the time of his life. "If the lads in Ballyer could see me now," he smiles to himself.

As they enjoy a simple, yet elegant meal, Hasse says, "after dinner we would like you to join us in a Scandinavian tradition."

"Oh yea?"

"Yes, a Swedish sauna," says Hasse. Robot looks uncomfortably at Kerstin, and she holds his hand underneath the table knowing how he's feeling. "And then we run into the lake, or jump whichever you like," says Hasse trying to be funny.

After dinner they go to their room, and Kerstin comes out of the bathroom wearing a long towel, and hands one to Robot. "Take your clothes off and we go to sauna."

"Ah shite Kerstin, are your mother and father going to be naked in the sauna too?"

"Don't worry, you won't see a thing in the sauna with all the steam." She laughs at Robot's shyness, despite all his bluster.

So he undresses, and they walk over to the sauna in their towels. They go in, and, as Kerstin said, he can barely see a thing. He sits down, and begins to enjoy the heat, a first once again for Robot.

"We like to come here at weekends, especially in the winter," says Hasse.
"You run out of here and jump into the lake in the winter?" asks Robot incredulously.
"Yes, thru' the snow into the ice cold water, they say it's very good for the heart."
"Sounds like bleedin' torture to me."

"Well," says Hasse, "we have a little drink before we run into the lake, it's called Glogg. It's a hot-spiced wine. It warms us up for the cold water. Eva made some for us, so you can try it."

"Before we jump into the flippin' lake?"

Robot hesitates, Kerstin holds his hand and says, "It's good fun, I promise you will enjoy it."

"Well all ri'," not wanting to spoil the party, but thinkin' of himself running naked along with his girlfriend's parents into a lake….. "Holy shite, wait 'til the lads hear about this"….

They sit back and relax, until for divilment, Kerstin's hand slides over to Robot's willie, and it immediately stands to attention. Just then Hasse says," Okay, we go run into the lake now." They all leave the sauna, towels wrapped around them, and have a shot of Glogg. Robot likes it despite his reservations. Hasse says "Skol," and Eva, himself and Kerstin take off into the night, dropping the towels just before getting into the water's edge, with Robot following, his right hand holding the towel, and his left hand slamming his erect willie against his stomach screaming, "go down ya bollix ya."

Well the cold water soon took care of that problem, and he enjoys himself immensely. They repeat the process a few times, and between the Glogg and the steam and the dark night, he loses any inhibitions he had, and has a ball.

During the second week of their Swedish adventures, Mel met a lovely Norwegian girl, with a terrific personality. Together with his new rock status playing his fiddle, and Anna looking up adoringly at him almost every night, he loses all his hang-ups about his average looks, and preferring Irish music to pop music. It is now their meal ticket to the future, thanks in great part to his fiddling ability.

Steo, fair play to him, met a great girl who, after a while, brings him out to a store and dresses him up big time. She takes him to an eye place and he gets a pretty cool pair of glasses, which does wonders for his usual grumpy personality. He gets into the new groove and swagger they have on stage every night, and the boys have the greatest time of their lives, that unforgettable month in Stockholm.

Sooner than they could believe, their time in Sweden was at an end. They are all on a high as they go in for their last night in the pub. All of their ladies are in the crowd, cheering for **Billy and The Touch**. The place is bursting to the rafters, champagne is flowing, and the atmosphere is electric. Billy has written out the chorus of one of his songs:

85 HIGH IN KILLARNEY

WE'VE GOT COSTA DEL KERRY
WHERE IT NEVER RAINS
LASH ON THE SUNSCREEN
'SURE WHO NEEDS SPAIN?
THE PARTY'S ON AT GRANNY'S
NEW BOYFRIEND'S POOL
WE GOT PINA COLADA AND SUNNY WEEKENDS
PARADISE, TOO HOT TO WORK,
'COS IT'S 85 HIGH IN KILLARNEY
AND THE GIRLS ARE GOING TOPLESS IN CORK

As the crowd learns the words, the lads are pleasantly stunned to see the occasional girl flash the lads. As the weeks went by, virtually half the girls gave them a flash. Tonight, the flashes were as fast and glorious as a strobe light. At the end of the song the lads said, "tack tack, vi alskar dig." (Thank you, thank you, we love you.)

As they close out their final song, the owner comes out on stage. He is a very famous comedian in Sweden, apparently he's the Bob Hope of Sweden, and the crowd love him. "Would you like them back?" he says in Swedish. The crowd screams, "Ya." He smiles at the lads, and says, "Okay, we will have them back soon." The crowd screams: "en gang til, en gang til, [one more time] accompanied by a slow hand clap, which in Sweden, is a sign of appreciation.

The lads are behind the bar loving all of this, and they come on stage for one last song. They blast out another frantic Celtic rock song, and the crowd just goes bananas. The boys really felt like rock stars, and are all wishing that they didn't have to go back to the grind of the showband scene after all the unforgettable nights they've just had in Sweden.

Of course there's one last piss-up in the apartment that night with all the girls and a few new friends. Since most of the lads had met some Swedish girls, it was a very bittersweet night for them, with all the goodbyes, and thoughts of home.

They rise early, pack their gear in the van, and head back to the ferry. Fran proudly says, "Look what I bought, a radar detector," and plugs it in. The cops were beginning to use them in Ireland, but they were very rare. "None of the lads have them yet, so I'll be one up on the boys."

"Shite lads," says Steo, "tis going to be a bollix doing the same old scene again after this," bringing them all back to reality sooner than they would have liked, but he was right.

Billy tries to lighten things up. "Ya know, I have a good feeling about this song, and sure we'll be back in Sweden again in six months.

Jack was still actually awake and says, "Yea, here's to Sweden, and what happened in Sweden stays in Sweden all ri'?" He was already dreading his next encounter with Bridget, but he had done a lot of growing up in Stockholm, and his self-confidence was soaring after Pia, plus the adoring reaction he had gotten in the pub.

"Look what I have," says Fran, and he shows them about six cans of Delay Spray. "Skol," Everybody laughs and shouts "Skol"

Chapter 19

Missing her terribly while he was in Sweden, Billy had written and called Meg a few times. Today, he couldn't wait to see and hold her again. First thing after they get home, he visits Meg's salon. She's absolutely flying, the place is packed. She runs to him as soon as she sees him. "Hiya Billy Golden, boy have I missed you," and she hugs and kisses him. His heart stops when he sees her, his beautiful, smart, hard-working, business–savvy, funny girlfriend, and he knew without any doubt, as he sees her after a month's absence, that "she is the one for me," as he kisses her. He gives her the gift from Sweden and some flowers. She doesn't know it yet, but it's sexy lingerie from the sex shop.

Billy sees everybody is flat out busy. "Looks like business is good."

"Yea it's great, we've been like this from day one, couldn't be better. I'm even thinkin' of renting next door, for men only. There's nothin' for men in Ireland, and I think it could work. Ya know the way ye get embarrassed when we wash your hair in front of the ladies. This would be totally private."

"Wow, great idea Meg, you're flying, fair play to ya."

"Jack said he had a ball in Sweden?"

Billy smiles to himself. "He sure did."

"He told me he's going to break it off with Bridget. I can't believe she flew over there, and they had a huge fight or somethin'."

"Yea, I heard so," says Billy.
  Meg smiles in a conspiratorial sort of way, "I s'pose you know nothin' about that now do ya?"

"Nah."…. "Hey, I gotta' go," she says, "see ya tonight?"
"Can't wait, I've got somethin' for Sam."
"He missed ya."
"Really?" says Billy genuinely surprised.
"Hey, you've been a huge influence on him."
"Are ya serious?"

"Billy, you're his hero, he loves ya, all the time ya give him, you treat him like he's your son. I can never thank you enough for all you've done for him."

"Meg, if I ever have a son, I'd love him to be exactly like Sam, he makes me laugh ya know?"

Meg comes closer to Billy and hugs him. "Billy Golden, that's the nicest thing I've ever heard you say, see ya tonight," and gives him a quick kiss.

A week later, they gather for their Wednesday rehearsal at Robot's house. PJ shows up towards the end, and they take a break. "Lads, I've got good news for youse, ye're going to Germany.

"Wow, where?" says Billy all excited.
"Hamburg," says PJ, it's what they call a beer hall."
"I like it already," say Fran.

"Yea, it burned down last year. It used to be a beer hall, and they're opening it up again as a nightclub. 'Tis gonna' be harder than Sweden, as they want five forty-five minute sets, seven nights a week."

Steo, as usual, knocks it straight away. "Jaysus, PJ, we don't know that many songs."

PJ answers nonchalantly, "just repeat a few, it's a beer hall for God's sake, nobody will know the difference, and hey, I like the song. I should know if ye get in by the time ye're back. If ye're in, the skies the limit all ri?"

"All I wanna' see is Steo riding a camel," says Robot, and he gives out his typical laugh.
"I wanna' see Bethlehem, float in the dead sea, and say a prayer at the Wailing Wall," says Billy.
"Jaysus, ye think we won the feckin' thing already," says you know who.
"Steo, go way ya bollix ya," says Fran. "Tis a good song and ya know it."

The next two weeks are filled with playing some terrible dancehalls and then, finally, the boys are on their way to Hamburg. It's a different ferry, not as nice as the one from Dun Laoghaire. As usual, they're enjoying themselves at the bar.

Robot tells his latest joke... "Mary Murphy went to the local plastic surgeon in Cork and said, 'Doctor McCarthy I've been flat chested all me life, an' I'm sick of it. I want those sillycone things.' The doctor said, "oh Mary, no, no, no, they're not safe at all at all." "I don't care if they're safe or not, I just want to look like them Hollywood actresses, they look fabulous." "No, no, no Mary, sure they leak and everything, I couldn't in all conscience, but hang on a second, I was just reading where a colleague of mine in Galway has developed a brand new technique, and he's looking for his first patient. You'd be perfect Mary, I'll give him a call right away.

I'll tell you now what he does, Mary, in simple terms. He makes two tiny little incisions, puts in what look like two tiny balloons, and once he has them hooked up, all you have to do is flap your arms like this, and out they come." Robot flaps his arms wildly. "And Mary, the more you flap, the bigger they get."

She's all excited and says, "God I'll try that." So off she goes up to Galway on the train, and has the surgery. She comes home the next day, and goes right up to the bathroom for her big test, and starts flapping her arms like a mad woman. Sure enough, out they come. She has a chest at last, and she's thrilled. She can't wait to go down to the pub on Saturday night, as there's a fella' she fancies, but he never even gives her a look.

Well she's sittin' at the counter waitin' for him to come in that Saturday. Finally he comes in, gets his beer and gives a quick look over in her direction. Just then she starts flapping her arms like crazy, and her chest comes out like dat," as Robot does a visual of Mary's chest coming out, "The guys eyes come out like dat, and with great newfound confidence, chest high, she goes over to the guy and says, 'Hi, do I know you?' 'No,' he says, 'but I think we have the same doctor,' as Robot flaps his legs wildly. The lads are in fits.

After a few beers, they go down to their bunks. There are no rooms, just dormitory-style bunks with their ticket number beside the bunk. They're all snoring in minutes.

They arrive in Germany about ten hours later, and have no problem driving on the "wrong" side of the road after Sweden. They can't believe how fast everybody is driving on the German Autobahn. Compared to the BMW's and Mercedes' flying by, it feels like they're in a funeral procession, even tho' they're going flat out.

After a few hours, they arrive at the club in Hamburg. The manager, Helmut is a real prick, totally different to Sven, back in Stockholm. He is the first person they meet, no welcome at all, just orders: "bring your equipment thru' here," as he points to the kitchen door, "Then I vill show you ze apartment."

The lads bring in their gear thru' the already smelly kitchen, and arrive into the beer hall, about twice the size of the pub. It doesn't have much ambience at all, just a large banquet-like look about it. They follow him to the apartment. "You start at nine o' clock sharp tomorrow night. You come to kitchen, and we feed you before that." The lads remember when they sat in the dining room in Sweden, able to order off the menu.

"I miss Stockholm," says Mel.
"I miss Kerstin," says Robot.

Next night the lads take to the huge stage, with pretty good stage lights. There are round tables with about ten people sitting at many of them. There isn't any character or atmosphere to the place, even at nighttime. They notice the crowd is older than Stockholm, in their late thirties and early forties. They start off with their exciting Celtic Rock, expecting the same reaction they got a few weeks ago back in Stockholm. There's absolutely no reaction at all, cold unfriendly faces looking up at them, no applause after any song. It was a total shock to the system.

After about three songs, someone shouts up in a heavy German accent: "You play *Green Green Grass Of Home*." Billy knows it and says, "Okay lads in G," and the band do their best to play along. The whole place suddenly gets up to dance…. relief. At the end of the song Billy says "Thank you, any more requests?"

Another German guy shouts up, *Tie a Yellow Ribbon*.

Steo whispers, "this is shite," to the lads.

"Okay lads," says Billy a one, a two, a one two three four."….

They quickly revert back to their showband material, and have to repeat several songs during the marathon sets, but the Germans don't know the latest rock hits; it's pure torture: the dancers do not know or like the rock music the band are playing, and the lads don't know the disco hits they like and want. The night finally ends, and they troop back to the apartment exhausted and totally dejected. As they're leaving, they see the owner driving off in his flashy Mercedes Benz. He scowls at the boys, and burns rubber as he peals away. The lads are beat. "It's goin' to be a long two weeks lads," says Billy.

Fran does his best to make them feel better: "those wankers are living in the last century so they are."

"Nobody told them they're dead. Jaysus, I'm glad I'm from Ballyer, not bleedin' Hamburg." says Robot.

Next night they do the five long sets again, same non-reaction, even though they had a quick rehearsal that afternoon, turning several songs from a rock beat into a disco beat, it wasn't enough. The owner comes over to them, and in his heavy German accent he screams: "YOU ARE FIRED." The lads are stunned.

"But we have two more weeks in our contract," says Billy.

The German owner goes bananas, loses the plot altogether. "You go now, if you play for two more weeks, you vill put me out of business. YOU ARE SHISE," he screams. "Look at your clothes," looking at the gravy stains on Robot's shirt, and the tear in Jack's pants. "Look at your equipment, IT IS SHISE," he screams, as he points at their banged up speakers, and the duct tape on Billy's mike stand. "I have hired a five piece disco band from ze

Philippine's. Zey start tomorrow night, look, look, look," as he takes out eight by ten glossies of five skinny Asian guys who all look alike, and are dressed in identical blue suits. "Look, zey change outfits for each set," as he flashes the five different glossies to prove his point, "Untz zey never repeat one song all night. You play ze same rock music over untz over. We vant disco untz ballads, so you get out of my apartment now before I call ze police."

Fran tries to reason with him, "Look boss, it's three o' clock in the morning."

"I don't care, get out now, or I vill call ze police."

"But we have no money to get back to Ireland, we have nothin'," says Steo.

The owner has it all worked out, and is way ahead of the lads. "I vill give you money for travel because I'm a nice guy…. You get your shit out of ze apartment now. I vill send Helmut over to check zat it ist okay. Come back here, untz I vill give you ze money."

The boys start tearing down their equipment in quiet disgust, and then get their stuff out of the apartment, as Helmut watches them like a hawk, so they don't trash it, which is exactly what they feel like doing. They walk back to the club, assuming the boss is there with their money for the two nights. He is nowhere in sight, probably cowering just inside the door. There are four heavies on the front steps, in case the lads get any ideas. Helmut has that sneaky shitty smirk on his face that they all see and instantly hate, relishing his temporary Godlike power. "You go now or ve call ze police."

"Hey what about our money," demands Steo.

"You go now," as the huge bouncers stand in behind him, "Go, f*** off."

 The boys are on their own, with no way to get money over fast from anybody back home. They've just been screwed over by a real jerk. Even tho' they're definitely the wrong band for the venue, which is probably PJ's fault for not asking enough questions, this is no way to treat anybody. The boys are all ready to kill, full of seething rage.

The band drives off, shell shocked into the night towards the ferry. They drive in silence for about a mile, and then Billy says, "Fran, stop the van." He pulls over.

"F*** them," Billy rages as he goes around to open the back of the van, and gets the emergency gas can. "I'm gonna' go back and torch his bloody Merc. Wait here all right?"

"Shit Billy, they'll call the cops and throw us all in jail," says Steo.

"Yea," says Billy, "but they'll have to prove it won't they?"

Robot loves the idea, "I'll go with ya."

"You're a mad bollix Billy Golden," says Fran and joins him. Mel and Jack follow along behind.

They walk back to the car park, and the owner's Merc and two other cars are still there. Fran walks to the back of the club in case anyone comes out. Steo watches the front door with Mel standing halfway between the front door and the car park to alert the lads if anyone moves.

Fran had taught them "the whistle:" a few notes musicians whistle when they walk into a pub or whatever. If somebody whistles the right notes back, they know they are also musicians, and they can join them if they wish. They have "the whistle" at the ready to warn each other if there's any movement from the club.

Billy and Robot run over to the Merc, and pour the gas all over the car. Robot then pours the last bit under the gas tank on the ground. Billy nods to Robot, and he torches the car with a match, and they run like mad as the car lights up. They get back to the truck, and get the hell out of there.

"Holy shit," says Billy as he takes a swig from a bottle of whiskey, and hands it around. They see a river and toss the empty container.

Fran smiles at Billy, "Jaysus Billy, I hope I never piss you off."
"Are ya sure yer not from Ballyer, ya crazy bollix ya," says Robot, full of admiration.

They head for the ferry, and get there at about five am. The place is packed with trucks waiting to board. They park the van, and walk up to the ticket office. A big thick German in a navy marine coat looks at their ticket. He reminds Billy of Col. Klink in Hogan's Heroes.

The German officer looks at their ticket, and says in his broken English, "You are here on ze wrong night."

"Yea boss," says Fran, "but we have to go home today, ya know?" trying to be the leader, his Dublin accent sounding strangely heavier talking to the German guy.

"Ze ferry ist fuell!!! Zere ist no way you can get on ze ferry tonight, come back in ten days."

The boys feel like they've been stabbed in the heart. Everything is blowing up in their faces. There are tears running down Steo's face. "Maybe sir," says Billy hopefully, "there might be a cancellation."

The German officer looks like he's about to shoot Billy for such a stupid comment. "Zere ist never a cancellation, zey book, zey go."

Billy perseveres, "well can we wait and see?"

"You can try, bit I sink you are kaput!"

He dismisses the lads without a look, and starts spoutin' away in German to the next guy in line. The band walk back to the truck absolutely dejected.

"I'm starvin'," says Mel.

"Okay you wankers," say Fran, "let's pray we get on this ferry, 'cos if we don't, we'll all be in jail tomorrow."

So there's the band, who just torched a guy's brand new Mercedes saying the Rosary. Fran begins: "Hail Mary, full of grace,".... and the lads answering: "Holy Mary, mother of God,"....

Billy gives a grunt, smiles, and shakes his head, "Y"know, we're some submarine Catholics aren't we?"
"Wha'd'ya mean?" says Robot.

Billy laughs, "we only surface when there's trouble."

The lads give a half-hearted smile, and keep praying. They're broke, in a foreign country, know no one, starving, and praying for a break.

It was like slow Chinese torture, watching truck after truck board the ferry. They feel their chances slipping away, as they watch the endless procession. They can't believe how many trucks can actually fit on a ship.

Finally there were no more trucks, and they go back to the ticket office. The German officer looks at them, and without any hint of a smile says, "you are very lucky you Irishmen, zere ist space." The lads are too drained to show any emotion. He stamps their ticket, and finally, they drive on. They go straight down to their bunks and try and sleep off the hunger.

They sleep for about twelve hours, and wake up absolutely famished. Billy pulls out every penny he has; about forty pounds. "Okay lads, what d'y'e have?" The lads cough up about another forty pounds, and he hands it all to Fran.

"Okay, we've gotta' hang onto this for petrol, I hope it's enough to get us home."

Mel is crushed, "so we're not going to eat?"

"If ya can steal it, eat it ri'," says Robot, and they head to the cafeteria, assuming they'll have no problem grabbing some food.

They look around, but everything is behind rounded glass enclosures. There's no hope of grabbing anything. You'd have to be a bloody octopus to get your hand over to the other side of the glass. Fran summed it up perfectly: "F*** German efficiency."

Twelve hours later they land on the east coast of England, and face another full day's drive across England, and into Wales to the ferry home. They fill up at a gas station. Robot grabs a few apples, and in fairness, divvies them up between the lads. They devour them in a single bite.

They are weak with hunger as day turns into night, mostly sleeping as it's pure misery being awake. They share the driving: an hour each with the music blaring to keep them awake, except Jack of course, the bastard is comatose as usual. Fran is driving with Billy in the passenger seat, making small talk just to keep them from falling asleep.

"So when did ya start singin'?" says Fran. Billy smiles as he recalls a funny memory…

When I was about twelve my first girlfriend broke it off with me, telling me she had a new boyfriend. I was crushed, so I wrote a song called *You Left Me*, definitely the worst song ever written," and for the craic, he started to sing it a la Buddy Holly.

YOU LEFT ME YOU LEFT ME,
WITHOUT A KISS OR EVEN SAYING GOODBYE
WILL YOU PUT ME OUT OF MY MISERY,
BY COMIN' BACK TO ME
WOE OH OH, I WAS HURT MORE THAN YOU DEAR,
I NEED YOU MORE THAN YOU NEED ME
WILL YOU PUT ME OUT OF MY MISERY
BY COMIN' BACK TO ME EE EE EE EE,

Billy was enjoying hamming up the Buddy Holly stutter-like effect as he continued... "Well I sang the song for my piano teacher, and she was appalled that I was into pop music, but she saw that I could stay in key, so she asked me would I be interested in entering the boys under thirteen competition that year. I was amazed, me SINGING in a competition. "I said no way, sure nobody can beat Michael Murphy, he wins every year." I didn't want to make a fool of myself. I sort of knew what I was doing in the piano competitions. I told them all at home about it, and as usual, they all laughed at the thought, except dad.

At the time I desperately wanted a pair of flippers because Cork had just built its first public swimming pool. I couldn't stay away from it, I was almost a fish. I wanted the flippers so I could swim faster, but Christmas was months away.

My dad said, 'If you win, I'll buy you the flippers.'

'But what about Michael Murphy, nobody can beat him,' I said.

Billy smiles at the memory of how his dad always knew how to motivate him, and always the teacher said, 'You know those cowboy and Indian films you like?'

'Yea.'
'Well there's always a faster gunfighter comes along, usually the hero right?'
'Right.'

Dad comes in for the kill: 'Well try and see can you beat him. He's good, but nobody can win all the time. Go back and tell Ms.'O Leary you'll do it. Learn the piano part, and practice singing it yourself. Get used to it, and see what happens. If you win, I promise, I'll buy you a pair of flippers."

As Billy was recalling the old days, it revives him a bit, and he gets on a roll… "Well, that's all the incentive I needed. I quickly learned the song, it was called, *Come to the Fair*." He sings the first line in a mock soprano voice. "*THE SUN IS A*

SHINING TO WELCOME THE DAY, HEY HO, COME TO THE FAIR. I knew the way the adjudicators worked from all the piano competitions I had been in. The poor bastards have to sit there and listen to sixty or seventy kids playing the same old piece on the piano, over and over and over, and then pick three winners. I remember first prize was a silver medal, second a bronze medal, and third got a certificate of merit. They couldn't afford gold medals at the time. Then the adjudicator had to sit through another bunch a year older playing something a little more difficult and do the same thing. I sneaked in to hear his comments about the under twelve competition, to see if I could learn anything. I was determined to win those flippers.

The adjudicator was usually from the London Guild of Music, and sure enough there he was giving his adjudication in his posh English accent: 'all I want is plenty of volume and personality,' says Billy, taking off his fancy accent. "Hey, I thought to myself, no better man to blast it out, I might have a chance after all.

At the time, all the mothers would go and hear their children perform. Man, t'was like they were all on safari, medal hunting or somethin'. If you made a mistake, you got a wallop, or an earful or both from your mother when you got home.

Unfortunately for Mum, I was number fifty-six, and she had to go home and get dinner for everyone, so she didn't get to hear me, but she heard Michael Murphy sing like a bird as always, and assumed he'd win it. She and Michael's mother were friends at the time. Anyway, my turn came, and I belted it out, smiled my ass off, and went back to my seat.

Finally, all seventy or so did their thing, and up he comes and announces the winners: 'In third place, number forty two.' When he came up on stage, he asked his name and we'd all clap. 'In second place number twenty four,' and up goes Michael Murphy. You could see the shock on his face that he didn't win.

'And this year's Feis Mathew winner, boys under thirteen singing competition is number fifty six.' I had forgotten what my number was, and nobody came up on stage. 'Is number fifty six here?' he said. The kid next to me looked at my number and he said, 'C'm'ere boyeee, you're number fifty six, look ya won it." I looked at my number, and sure enough I did.

I grabbed the medal and adjudication slip from him, and ran over to the school of music to tell Ms. O'Leary. It was like giving her a million bucks. I ran all the way home, and they were just finishing up dessert. I sat down as Mum fixed me dinner, and since I'm such a good Irish son, I said nothing. I didn't want to show off by bursting out the news. I knew dad would keep his word about the flippers, and that was all that mattered to me.

Mum served me dinner and said, "Well, how did you get on?'

'I won it.' They all burst out laughing as usual, except dad, who was probably trying not to laugh too.

"What about Michael Murphy," she asked?
'He came second,' says I.

'Mother of Mercy, show me the medal,' she says suspiciously, and I took it out of my pocket. Mum immediately searches her apron pocket for her rosary beads in order to plead for my sinning soul.

'That's the piano medal you won last year,' says my sister.
'No no, I won it.'
'Show me the certificate Billy,' says dad. I showed it to him.
Mum leans over his shoulders and sees 'First place.'
'Did you change that?' she says.
'I think he really won it Nora, well done Billy. We'll buy you the flippers on Saturday.' That 'well done' from my dad was priceless to me at the time….

"So, that's why and when I started singin', and ya know, I don't think Mrs. Murphy has ever talked to my mother since then."

Around five a.m., just about an hour from the ferry, the van starts sputtering. Fran was driving. "Were screwed lads, we're out o' petrol." The band slowly wakes up, and sees a gas station up ahead. It's closed of course, but they pull in. It's a Mom and Pop station with living quarters up above the shop.

"We should'a saved that petrol," says Steo, in the back seat.

Fran cuts him right off, "shut the hell up Steo."

Billy explodes and jumps into the back seat, and grabs Steo by the neck, and starts banging his head against the back of the seat. "You little shite ya, ya useless skinny weaseley little prick, get the hell out o' this van, ya gutless pain in the ass."

Fran pulls him off, "come on Billy, we're all knackered, let it go, all right." Billy calms down, takes his hands off Steo's neck, gets out of the truck, and kicks the hell out of the front tires.

"Maybe he'll give us some petrol," says Mel. He starts throwing pebbles at the upstairs window. Suddenly the silence is broken by the sound of a dog barking. He sounds huge and vicious, savagely breaking the stillness of the night. The light comes on, an upstairs window opens, the owner sticks his head out the window and screams, "Get the hell out of here, or I'll call the cops."

Mel shouts back, "Sir, we're trying to catch the eight o' clock ferry, and we're outa' petrol. Could we buy some from ya?"

"I don't give a shit mate, you've woken up the whole bloody house. If you want some petrol, come back at seven," and he slams the window shut.

The dog is still barking as they try to start the van, but it's dead to the world. They push it off his property as he watches from the bedroom window. They park it on the side of the road, and fall asleep exhausted.

They're woken up by a huge eighteen-wheeler passing them, probably heading for the ferry. It wakes them up violently, as the driver lays on his horn, and the van shakes like crazy and almost tips over. It's probably the closest thing to a tornado they'll ever experience. They see how they parked; the van is sticking half way out onto the road. They're all amazed he didn't cream them. Fatigue and hunger are causing them to make dangerous mistakes.

They push the van back to the shop, and in total silence the prick gives them twenty pounds worth of petrol, their last pennies. It's seven fifteen, and they race off to the ferry and thankfully, just make it, this time having no problem with their tickets.

It's been three and a half days since they've eaten anything, apart from the apples, and once again, they head down to the bunks to sleep off the final four-hour ferry to Dublin. They're in serious trouble, weak and totally dejected. None of them have ever felt such excruciating pain before. Oh, what each of the lads would give for a real home cooked meal around their family table right now.

As they're heading towards their bunks, Billy sees a familiar face wearing a chef's white outfit walking towards them in the corridor. "My God, Pat, hello boyee," he says, in his Cork accent.

Pat recognizes him immediately, "Billyeeee, what are you doing here boyeeee?"

Its Hopeless Pat, who joined the choir in Cork a few years ago thanks to Billy. "Hey Billy, ya look terrible boyeee."

"We haven't eaten in four days."

Without any hesitation whatsoever, Pat says, "come on, follow me," and leads them down to the staff cafeteria, where they gorge on burgers, chips, bread and tea. The lads can't believe their luck. Billy tells them the story about the night Pat came for the audition to join the choir.

Pat looks in on them after a while, "Are ye all right lads?"

"Yea, hey man, thanks a million, we're all right now, thanks to you, you saved our lives," says Billy.

Pat gets serious, "No Billy, you saved mine. Remember that night, you could have told me to piss off, but you didn't, and ya let me join the choir, even tho' I couldn't sing?"

"Well, I eh,…"

"Well you could've been a right langer, [jerk] but you weren't. D'ya remember Mary McCarthy, she was an alto in the choir?"

"Yea, I do."

"Well we got married, and have a two year old daughter, so YOU saved MY life boyeee."

"Wow, good for you, I'm happy for ya." Billy shakes his hand, and thanks Pat again. As Pat heads back to his post, Billy thinks to himself… "Thanks

Ma, you must have been praying really hard on yer rosary beads tonight…" The lads head to the van, home at last.

Chapter 20

As usual, they're at Robot's house for Wednesday's rehearsal. After a while PJ arrives, taking no blame for Germany whatsoever, no apologies forthcoming, and casually says, "well lads, Germany wasn't the best huh?"

"We didn't know all they wanted was Disco and Tom Jones," says Steo.

"Well piss on 'em lads, I got a bit o' good news for youse, ye're in the song contest."

It's exactly the boost they need, fantastic news after their recent nightmare, which nearly caused the band to break up. The murmurings were definitely there on the long, painful journey home from Germany, but they are quickly forgotten with PJ's brilliant news. "Wow, holy shite, are ya serious, we're really in?" is about all they can say, still exhausted after Germany.

PJ is loving the moment, almost as if he wrote the song himself, and then gives them a huge and unusual compliment. "Well done lads, fair play to ye, it's a great song, and I think it has a good chance."

"The way our luck's been goin' lately, that would be too much to hope for," says Steo, being his usual pessimistic self.

Billy is already in high gear ready to go, "speak for yerself boyeee, what happens next PJ?"

"Well there's a reception on Friday night in RTE to announce the eight songs and singers, so there's ye're first bit o' publicity right there. They'll be record guys, promotional fellas, and all sorts of shite, so don't promise anything to anyone all ri'?" "Ri'," they all said.

"We'll need to find a really good girl singer," says Billy.

"I'm workin' on it right now. Now that ye're in, it'll be easy, and I've booked the best guy in Ireland to arrange the song," says PJ. Billy is ecstatic, "Holy shit lads, we'll be playing with a fifty piece orchestra." PJ gets up to leave, "so, practice, practice, practice."

"RI'," they all say enthusiastically.

" Hey, PJ, I'd like to co arrange it with whoever does it okay?" says Billy.

"Ri'," he says. They continue rehearsing, and run the song a few times, tightening up the harmonies.

At the conclusion of a run through, they would each interject "we did it," and "holy shit" followed by ecstatic screams and roars. Pops is like a kid in a candy store, "if only yer mother was alive for this Robot huh?" as he chokes back a tear.

On Friday night the lads arrive at the press reception in RTE. The press and cameras are out in force, booze, models, and hangers on everywhere. This is where it's at in Ireland tonight, a hot ticket, THE place to be seen.

Each singer and songwriter is introduced, and comes out for a short interview. The nearest thing to describe the feeling would be like the hype surrounding the announcements of the final teams for the Super Bowl.

The presenter announces the lads, "…and now with a song called *Love is the Answer*, here are **Billy Golden and the Touch**." The lads walk out to blinding flashlights, totally excited and nervous all at the same time. They walk over to the presenter, and he shakes Robot's hand first, "Well done lads, what do you think of your chances?"

"I hope we win for me dad," says Robot, "come 'ere dad,"….. Pops shyly comes out. "He's given me everything since me mam died when I was two, so, if we win, it's for him." The crowd is touched and clap generously.

He looks at Billy and says, "So Billy, you're the only Corkman in the group?"

"Yea, up the banks," he flashes a huge smile, and raises his fist.

"So what's the song all about?" he asks.

"It's called 'Love is the Answer.' I think the world is all screwed up, we're getting further and further away from each other. We only come together when bad things happen. If we're not careful, we'll ruin it, as the Beatles said, 'all you need is love.'"

And that was it, thirty seconds of publicity on national television that you couldn't put a price on. "Thanks lads, good luck, our next song is written by Jimmy Delaney."….

They all enjoy the craic, meeting some of the bands also selected, that they had mooned over the past few months, and visa versa. Most of the bands never get a chance to really meet each other, as everybody is always working on the same nights. The exciting vibe brings them back to their heady days in Stockholm, but this could be so much bigger than anything they've done so far. If they win this, they are guaranteed a number one hit in the Irish charts, win Eurovision, and they'll be number one throughout Europe in a few weeks, and hot, hot, hot.

Pj is all business, enjoying the power ride, his biggest level so far in the band scene. "Okay lads, two weeks to go, enjoy yerselves 'til then, 'cos if ye win, be ready to work ye're arses off before Israel, all ri'?"

That night Billy arranges to meet Meg at a nice hotel in town. He arrives at the hotel room, knocks, and Meg opens the door in the lingerie he bought her in Sweden. She looks drop dead gorgeous of course, and pulls off the look in great style. "Hello' Corkman, please come in and make yerself comfortable." He does.

Next afternoon, Billy is giving a kid a piano lesson at his house, and his mother comes in with a welcome cup of tea. "So Billy, I saw ya on the telly last night."

"Yea, t'was great craic altogether."

"I suppose we'll lose ya if ya win?"

"T'would be great for us Mrs. Donnelly, but I have someone on stand by to teach Jimmy if we do," as she hands him his two pounds.

"You're a grand lad Billy, an' we wish ya the best, an' we can always say we knew ya when ya had nothin'. Me husband has put a few pounds on ya, so he has."

"Really, I didn't know you could bet on it."

"Sure ya know how they are Billy, they'd bet on two flies walkin' up the wall."

He passes a betting office as he's driving home, or a bookmaker as they're called in Ireland, and goes in. It's Billy's first time ever in a betting office, as he was never into the horses. "Are ye takin' bets on the song contest?"

"Yea we are," said the guy.

"What odds d'ya have on Billy Golden?"

"Billy who?" said the bookie.

"Billy Golden," he says nonchalantly. "He's got a song in it." The bookie bursts Billy's bubble when he says, "Never heard of him. I hear Doc Foley is favorite to win. How many songs are in it?"

"Eight."

"I'll give ya seven to one," he says, knocking Billy's faith again with such huge odds. He quickly

226

replays the song in his head, to reassure himself, and goes for it, win or bust.

"All right, here's forty pounds to win."

"Ri', Billy Golden is it?"

"Yea, Billy Golden and the Touch." He hands Billy his receipt. If he wins he knows he'll need cash for new outfits and stage lights, and two hundred and eighty pounds would go a long way. He can't wait …. Meanwhile, it's back to piano lessons for four more days…

The night before the song contest, Billy and Meg go to a hot new Dublin nightclub. They know if the lads win tomorrow night, all hell will break loose, so they're enjoying themselves on the dance floor, being anonymous, having a laugh. The only drag was the cost of the bottle of wine, a fortune to Billy in those days.

Suddenly Meg's face drops. "Ah shite."

"What is it?" says Billy.

"It's him, Sam's father, over there, arguing with his lawyer." Billy glances over, and it looks like the lawyer is trying to calm Ronan down. He looks over at Billy as if he wants to kill him. Standing well over six-feet tall and well built, he probably could.

"D'ya wanna' leave?" she asks.

"No, I wanna' dance, screw him." They walk to the dance floor, and as Billy passes him, he brushes up against Ronan, daring him to do something in front of everybody. All he can hear him saying is "shit shit shit," as his lawyer tries to stop him from doing something stupid.

It's a slow dance and she holds him tightly, and says, "Billy Golden, my hero, whenever he tried that shite on other guys, they ran."

"Hey," says Billy, "I spent all day teaching for that bottle of wine, and we're going to finish it."

"And I thought you were being brave." She laughs, hoping he was joking....

The following night, they're back in RTE for their big night, the National Song Contest. Each of the lads is only allowed one guest, so Billy asks his dad, who is overjoyed at the opportunity to visit Dublin for the contest. Nora stayed in her favorite comfort-zone, her own home, with her rosary beads in hand, getting quite the workout.

Thankfully Meg has no problem with Finbar being Billy's guest at the contest. Billy had shared tales of all the crap he had pulled on his parents, as a youth in Cork. Pops was too nervous to go, so he joined Meg and all the lad's families in a local bar.

Billy and the lads drew number five on the order-of-play list. All the acts are in the green room after the sound checks, dress rehearsals and dinner. All the singers are wearing really gaudy seventies stage clothes, frilly shirts, permed hair, and high platform shoes. Everybody is being friendly, but hoping it's their night. They can see and hear the other acts on the telly.

The compere announces each song as the singers take to the stage: "Song three is by **Joey and the Good Times** from Limerick, written by John Connolly, called *Danny*. The band are giving it their all as they belt out the catchy chorus:

'HOW COULD YOU LOOK AT ME WITH A SMILE WHEN ALL THE TIME I CAN SEE, I'M NOT BLIND'.....

"Song number four, written by Pat McDermott is called, *You Are the Only One*,' performed by **Gina and the Countrymen**,....

They sound good. Steo's nerves get to him, "Ah shite lads, they're good songs...shite."

PJ nips it in the bud immediately. "Take it easy lads, just go out there and do it, relax, I believe in ye lads, ye'll be fine."

Then it's their turn. As they're getting into position, the orchestra puts their music up on their music stands, and the compere brings them on….

This is it: Everything Billy has dreamed of for years… "Song number five, written and performed by **Billy Golden and the Touch**, Billy is a Corkman, and the band all hail from Dublin, here they are with *Love is the Answer*."

Billy comes in first with the haunting eight bar piano intro, then eight bars singing and playing the verse. The orchestra comes in slowly but surely building to the chorus, and it sounds even better than they could have imagined, lifting the lads to give it all they've got. PJ did a great job finding the perfect girl for the song. She's a beautiful looking soprano called Tina, who gives it the perfect operatic feel nailing the high note, but without overdoing the classical aspect to it, thus possibly turning off the pop juries all over the country.

LOVE IS THE ANSWER

'IT'S ALWAYS DARK BEFORE THE DAWN,
WHEN FAITH IS AT ITS WEAKEST
OUR PRAYERS CAN SEEM UNNOTICED,
BUT WE MUST CARRY ON,
AND THO' I SEE YOUR WORRIED EYES,
YOUR TRUST FOREVER SHAKEN,
WALK WITH ME AND WITNESS,

THE BEAUTY OF THIS WORLD

CHORUS
AND STILL BELIEVE, LOVE IS THE ANSWER,
THE ROAD TO FOLLOW,
OUR STRONGEST NEED, LOVE IS THE ANSWER,
TRY AND UNDERSTAND EACH OTHER,
AND SHARE OUR FUTURE,
LOVE IS THE ANSWER, IT'S NOT TOO LATE

YOU GIVE ME HOPE THAT WE'LL GET BY,
YOUR KIND HANDS ALWAYS CARING,
ORDINARY HERO, ANGEL IN DISGUISE

REPEAT CHORUS
AND THO' I SEE YOUR WORRIED EYES
YOUR TRUST FOREVER SHAKEN
WALK WITH ME AND WITNESS
THE BEAUTY OF THIS WORLD'
WALK WITH ME AND WITNESS,
THE BEAUTY OF THIS WORLD.'

The audience seems to like it judging by their applause. The compere introduces the last three songs, as the lads wait nervously in the green room.

The compere appears back on the television screen as the last song finishes. "Ladies and gentlemen, boys and girls, those are the eight songs for this year's National Song Contest, now after a break we'll call in the votes from ten locations around Ireland."

While Billy and the lads are waiting for all the phone lines to be hooked into the TV station, as per tradition, the winner of the previous year, and one of Billy's all-time favorite singers in the world, Dublin's own Colm Wilkinson, sings last year's winning song, then sings his latest release. After the longest seven minutes of the lads lives, all the phones are now linked up to the studio in Dublin. The moment of truth nears....

After the usual advertisements, the orchestra plays a quick bar or two, and the compere says: "Welcome back everyone, our first call tonight is Mayo. Hello Mayo, are you there?" The spokesman for the Mayo vote comes in loud and clear in his fine Mayo accent. "Hello Dublin, this is Mick Lavelle from beautiful Castlebar with the Mayo vote:
Song #3, *Danny*, 2 votes,
Song #4, *You are the Only One*, 2 votes,
Song #5, *Love is the Answer*, 6 votes, and that concludes the Mayo vote, good night." The band can't believe it, what a fantastic start...

Billy remembers fondly that great night in Mayo a few years ago, when he won the Castlebar Song Contest. He couldn't afford to stay in a hotel, so he stayed in a bed and breakfast. His girlfriend Karen was with him, and before they went over for the final sound check and dress rehearsal, he had a bath.

There were no showers in the B&B's back then. People charged extra if you took a bath, as it would use up all their expensive hot water. There was a meter in the bathroom where you inserted fifty pence. You actually had to pay to get hot water! God be with the good ol' bad ol' days!

Karen was a brilliant violinist whom Billy had met in college, and was great fun. For a bit o' craic, she stood outside the bathroom door, and serenaded Billy taking his bath, to relax him for the night. He would have loved to be a fly on the wall the next day in that B&B, after Billy had won the contest: "that hussy, playin' her fiddle outside the bathroom door as he took a bath, what's the world comin' to at all."….

Billy's thoughts are interrupted when he hears the compere asking his hometown for their vote. "Hello, this is Denis McCarthy," with his heavy Cork accent, "from the banks of my own lovely Lee. Here is the Cork vote:
Song #6, *Sweet Woman Of Mine*, 1 vote,
Song #3, *Danny*, 2 votes,
Song #7, *Shalom*, 2 votes
Song #5 *Love is the Answer*, 5 votes, and that concludes the Cork vote." The lads are getting to feel like they have it.

"Hello the Dublin jury, please come in," said the compere.

"Dublin here from the banks of the Liffey:
Song #3, *Danny*, 2 votes,
Song #5, *Love is the Answer*, 8 votes, and that
concludes the Dublin vote."

The band wants to jump up from their seats, but
have to show amazing self-control, to not appear
big headed. They all want to explode and scream
their hearts out. By now it was becoming clear that
they were going to win the song contest, even Steo
was smiling. The camera crews are focusing on
them, as the build-up continues…. Just a few more
counties…. Surely it's ours… Doc Foley comes
over, and gives Billy a congratulary hug. The TV
production people begin hovering around the band,
and signal them to the edge of studio one. Sure
enough, the other juries come in with the same
beautiful score, giving the lads the majority of their
votes. There's no contest, they're winning by a
mile.

Finally the compere announces, "Well, we have a
clear winner tonight ladies and gentlemen, boys and
girls." The orchestra does a quick bit followed by a
drum roll. "And the winner of this year's National
Song Contest is, …. **Billy Golden and the Touch**."

Everybody cheers as the band comes onto the stage,
the orchestra plays suitable fill in music. The

compere shakes their hands. "Well lads, how does it feel?"

Billy is closest to him. "Thanks Mike, and thanks to everybody who voted for us, please come on out and see us now okay?" as he raises his hands in victory.

"Well lads," said the compere, "let's hear this year's winning song again." So, Billy, with a huge smile on his face, plays that haunting piano intro followed by the orchestra.

Watching in a pub nearby, everybody is ecstatic, except Meg. A friend asks, "What's the matter Meg, they won."

She chokes a little, "Yea, but will he still want me now?" They all reassure her, and she starts to feel a bit better. As far as Sam is concerned, Billy is the biggest pop star in the world right now.

Meanwhile Robot's dad is crying his eyes out, "They did it, Holy Mother of God, janey, we're going to Israel." The girls console him, someone hands him a glass of whiskey, and he downs it in one gulp, as the lads are singing the song above on the telly.

After the song, press reporters and cameras galore mob them. Finbar proudly holds his son tightly, shoulder to shoulder. The whole emotion of it all: not being the most diligent student, not being a great sportsman like his uncle, are washed away forever in that great moment for both of them. Back home in Cork, Nora silently replaces her rosary beads into her apron pocket. A very wide smile fills her face as her blue eyes glisten with tears of pride.

Suddenly the suits in RTE make a flurry over to Billy, and literally pull him away from his dad and all the excitement. One of them hands him a phone. "It's the Taoiseach." [Prime Minister]

"Hello Uncle Frank, how are you?"

He proudly speaks in Irish; "Billy, congratulations, Norma and I are delighted for you, and very proud of you and the lads. We wish you well in Eurovision next month." Then in English, putting on a strong Cork accent, teased, "I never knew you were such a good piano player, fair play to ya boyeee."

"Wow," thought Billy, "fair play to him. He knew I couldn't hit a football or hurley to save my life, but he liked what I did on the piano, and was genuinely happy for me." Billy could understand why people loved this man.

Meanwhile, PJ is talking feverishly to record executives and publishers, loving the whole power trip. He pulls the boys aside. "Fantastic lads, well done. Okay, here's the deal: we're recording the song next week. I've got a ten grand recording advance, and a five grand publishing advance, and that's just the start of it." PJ is in his glory. Every band manager in Ireland would love to be in his position right now.

"Wow, it's really bleedin' happenin' isn't it," says Robot.
Billy, wrapped around his dad once again said, "Jeez lads, I can go house huntin'."
"I'm gonna' buy a new car," says Mel.

"Lads," says PJ, "ye won't have time to scratch ye're arse for the next few weeks the way it's lookin' right now, you'll be too busy makin' money."

Fran was enjoying the scene, even tho' his brother didn't win. "Lads, get a new bleedin' truck will yez, my one is knackered. Ye gotta' look the part now, start throwing the ould shapes ya know."

Billy excuses himself. "I'm gonna' call Meg," and he finds a phone box outside in the foyer, all emptied out at this stage, as the action was all inside the studio. The barman answers the call, and hands the phone to Meg. "Hello?"

"Hiya Meg, how's it goin' like?"

"Billy, congratulations," as she holds back her tears amazed that he was calling her so soon.

"It's crazy here, even Steo is smiling his ass off. We did it Meg, we won the bloody thing."

"I know Billy, it's fantastic, we were all sweatin' buckets in the bar, it's great, I'm happy for ye all."

"Hey, I was thinkin', if you could get your extension ready before we go to Israel, we could open it for ya, you said it was nearly ready right?"

Meg is stunned that he's thinking about her, after he's just achieved what he's been dreaming of all his life. "Billy, I don't know what to say."

"Don't say anything, we'll do it, it'll be even bigger than the last time, so it should be a bit o' craic. They're having a dinner for us after this, I think it's the record company, so I'll see ya tomorrow, all right?" The band get langers mouldy drunk at the party, letting off a bit of steam they've been holding in for weeks.

Chapter 21

The next day, they are the lead stories on all the morning papers:

BILLY HAS THE GOLDEN TOUCH
The Irish Standard
THE TOUCH ARE GOLDEN
The Irish World
THE TOUCH HEAD FOR EUROVISION
The Evening Globe
IS 'LOVE THE ANSWER' FOR THE RECESSION?

And on and on, all of it huge, priceless publicity.

Billy wakes up with a massive headache as the paparazzi bang on his window. "Billy, can ya give us a few minutes?"

"Yea yea," he says, "can ya put the ould kettle on, I have to go to the toilet."

He forgot about all the madness that would happen the following day, as they were all celebrating their win, way too much last night. His whole body felt like he had barely gotten into bed. He reached for the aspirin, and swallowed about six of them. It's mayhem in the little flat, as the neighbors come by with good wishes. One of the reporters catches Billy totally off guard when he says, "...we received an anonymous call that you were living with a married woman, is that true?"

"Ronan, you bastard," thought Billy.

"Do you see any married woman here," says Billy. "If you can see a pair of panties hanging around here, or anything else belonging to a woman, write your story. Shit, I don't believe it, we just won the song contest last night, and they're already trying to tear us down."

"Sorry, Billy," says the reporter, "that was real shitty all right, I'm sorry. I was just following up on a tip."

"Look at this place, it's a dump, right? Even my father stayed at a hotel last night rather than stay here with me. I've been dreaming about winning this all my life, and even after seeing where I live, you ask me this, man that's really low." Billy is seething at the nerve of this reporter. Just then, his dad appears in the doorway, ready to head home to Cork.

Billy cools down, as he and Finbar drive over to Dun Laoghaire pier for a live interview. The microphones are shoved close to his face as the camera pans around the harbor and back around Monkstown and Dun Laoghaire. To Billy this absolutely breathtaking scenery is one of the best views in Ireland. He loved jogging down to the pier and back as often as he could. Perhaps now he really might be able to buy one of the houses he's looking at from the pier?

Billy and his dad have a few minutes alone to say their good byes. Billy thanks his dad for everything he has done to get him where he is today. They hug warmly and Billy whispers, "Thank ma for me, please. I know her rosary got a real workout yesterday!"

Billy arranges for the lads to be fitted with new clothes for stage. Fran was right on: "Youse gotta' look the part now, ya know." But first of all, he stops at the bookies to pick up his winnings. He walks in, and the guy recognizes him straight away. With a huge smile on his face, he gives him the usual Dublin tease: "Go 'way ya bollix ya." Billy modestly shrugs, and hands him his ticket.

"Fair play to ya Billy, 'tis a great song, and you believed in yerself and the lads," as he counts out nearly three hundred pounds.

"Hey Billy, autograph the ticket for me will ya, I told me mates about what ya did, and they got a great laugh out of it." Billy signed the stub and shook his hand. Now he can pay for new clothes, and put a down payment on his dream piano, a new

Yamaha electric grand, and finally, some stage lights.

He picks up the lads, as he knows where the tailor is, and if he doesn't collect them, and drive them there, there's every chance they'll be late. They're just getting to O'Connell Street Bridge, crammed into his tiny car, when the brakes go. "Oh shit, the brakes are gone." He uses the gears to slow down as fast as he can, and slowly continues across the bridge. Soon, there's a back up of cars crawling behind them. A police car pulls up beside them and gives Billy the sign to pull down his window and screams over, "Why are ya goin' so slow?" Before he can talk his way out of it, Jack sticks his head out the window and shouts back at the policeman, "the brakes are gone."

"Thanks Jack, "says Billy, "now we're screwed."

"The one bleedin' time you're awake," says Robot.

The policeman, or guard, as they are known in Ireland, tells them to pull over by the quays, with the famous Ha'penny Bridge just down the street. He pulls in behind them, gets out, and suddenly recognizes the boys. "Chrisht lads, where are ye goin' without brakes?" in his fine thick Kerry accent.

"We're going to get our outfits for Eurovision officer," says Billy.

The guard points to a building down the road. "Look, there's a garage down there, follow me, and don't crash into me, or ye won't be going to Eurovision if ye know what I mean."

Billy slowly follows the guard down to the garage who does the talking. "Okay lads, he'll fix it for ye, hop in. I'll drive ye over, we gotta' have ye lookin' good for Eurovision now don't we?" They all get into the police car, and with lights flashing, the cruiser tears down the streets of Dublin to the tailor..... Only in Ireland.

About a week later, it's opening day for Meg's new hair salon for men. With great fanfare, the lads do a quick concert on the street outside the salon. The boys are the hottest thing in Ireland, so the place is absolutely mobbed with screaming teenage girls, women, reporters, and cameramen everywhere. The Moore Street ladies, who are the funniest and warmest people in Ireland, are there, loving all the fuss, always up for the craic.

The ladies have been selling their fruit and flowers just off the main yuppie street of Grafton Street forever, through good times and bad. They could sell ice to the Eskimos. They're slagging all the lads: "...touch me Billy, janey, you're a hunk,"

Another woman slags Robot: "…hey Robot, hit me with your rhythm stick." Everybody gets a good-hearted slagging. "…hey Mel, yuse can fiddle with me anytime." Dublin at its best. The press capture it all, with the colorful flowers in the women stalls adding to the scene. Another great start for Meg.

The band go to "The Call," the next day, and Fran drives up in a brand new luxury wagon, with Billy Golden and the Touch written all over it. "Whadd'ya think of this ye shower of wankers?" he smiles proudly. He had worked like crazy to pull it all off: buying the truck; customizing it; and getting the logo paint-job organized in a few days. They check it out and are very impressed. There's room to actually spread out, and it flies along silently, compared to Fran's noisy old banger of a van.

That night they play at one of the top venues in the country. What a difference to the old days: decent lighting, even a dressing room around the back of the stage. But the best part of all is a full house with people just watching rather than dancing.

Robot goes beserk on his drums, now that they finally have "respect." Jack as always was totally into his bass guitar. Steo was actually looking hot in his new outfit, new glasses, and new guitar, compliments of Sweden, and was killing each solo. Mel doubled on guitar and fiddle, even trying a few numbers they did in Stockholm, and actually getting the same reaction as they did there.

When Billy starts with the chords of the big one, *Love is the Answer*, the crowd sings along knowing every word; the ultimate feeling of euphoria for songwriters. Yes, finally, this is it, and knowing they were getting a fair shake, as Fran was in the tiny kiosk with the manager, counting the people coming in. What a difference a hit makes.

As they ride home that night, Fran flies through a village, when suddenly the radar detector goes off for the first time. He looks at it flashing and beeping like crazy. "Holy shit lads, it's working," completely forgetting to take his foot off the throttle. Suddenly they see a huge cop a couple of hundred feet in front of them, standing with his hands in the air, gesturing them to stop. Fran screams to a halt, barely stopping before he creamed him. All the gear comes crashing down onto the floor in the back making an awful racket.

"Chrisht lads, who d'ye think ye are, the feckin' concord?"

"Sorry officer," says Fran. Billy leans over from the passenger seat and salutes the cop.

He immediately recognizes him. "Ah, 'tis yerself, sure what can I do to you?" Billy realizes he's thinking about his uncle the Prime Minister, and all Billy will have to do is call his uncle, and get the ticket squashed. He smiles to himself.

His mother and all of Frank's brothers and sisters were told in no uncertain terms, never ever to ask Frank for any favors. Billy's mom repeated it over and over to her kids. He was known as "Honest Frank." He bought his first and only house in Dublin, and unlike other politicians of his time, he lived there all his life, never taking any of the trappings that could be available to him, if he bent the law. He did his duty to serve the ordinary Joe, as best he could, and not the big shots.

"Hello sir, how are you?"

"Will ye slow down for feck's sake or ye'll never get to Israel."

"Yes sir," says Fran, grateful that he didn't give them a ticket.
The guard softens his attitude: "by the way, my daughter is mad about ye."
"What's her name?" asks Billy.

"Fiona." Billy takes out a photo of the band, and they all sign it, and he hands it to the cop. "Thank you, go on now, get outta' here, and take it easy all right?"

"Thank you officer," says Fran, as he pulls away. "Only in Ireland lads, sure isn't it a grand country all the same?"

They all know that if they win Eurovision, they will rocket to Number One in almost every country in Europe. PJ is already talking to the publishing companies to acquire top songwriters to prepare good lyrics in French, German, Spanish and Italian. Lyricists were also on standby in other Eurovision countries, should the lads win the big prize. They could quickly record the song in all these European languages, and have an even bigger hit.

In Europe, Eurovision is the biggest break anyone could hope to achieve in Billy's time.   **Abba**, of Sweden, rocketed to fame and fortune when they won with their hit *Waterloo*. **Celine Dion** blasted to international fame after she won in 1988 for Switzerland.

Two days later they're in the studio recording the song.   The record requires a B-side. Billy wrote *Because You're Beautiful* completely on his own. He stands to make a fortune in royalties if they win. The success of this recording is imperative.

The rapport between the lads and the orchestra is good, and everybody is hoping that they are part of history, playing on the Eurovision winning record. "Okay," says the conductor, "let's try a take. The studio quietens down, " 'Love is the Answer', take one." The conductor quietly counts, "One two three four...."

Billy starts that haunting eight bar intro, then eight bars solo voice and piano, then in come three accoustic guitars and the string section. He is nervous, but he has practiced this for so long, it's second nature to him. Once he relaxes, he's in Heaven, it's the ultimate turn on for him.

Robot joins lightly in the second verse, building to a great drum-fill leading into the chorus. Tina comes in in the minor chorus part, but just as a guide vocal, so the orchestra gets a feel for the melody. She's in a soundproof glass cage, so her voice doesn't bleed into the orchestral mikes, which are too numerous to count.

Many of the same musicians were in the orchestra the night of the contest, so they are familiar with the song. They are pretty comfortable with their parts already, making the finished recording all the better.

The arranger has added more brass to the chorus which sounds stronger and deeper than the night of their winning performance. They finish their first run and the conductor says, "Let's do another take, and Jack, get a bit more funky in the chorus will ya." No better boy to get funky, and Jack gives it just the right feel without overpowering the arrangement.

The conductor added, "Okay everybody, that high note in bar twenty eight, hold it for two beats, that will add to the kettle drum crescendo and create more drama I think, and everybody keep building 'til then, and don't stop 'til the end of the chorus all right."

They make a note on their music, try it and it works, and once again the magic of the studio happens. A song is born. It's sounding better and better, and the boys are thrilled. Finally the conductor is happy and he releases the orchestra after recording the B-side.

Next up are vocals. Billy has been singing his heart out since they won, and his voice sounds a bit raspy, but it actually adds to the song, sort of giving it a Rod Stewart husky sound. Tina nails her part, and they start adding harmony. They bring in session singers, along with Tina and the lads. They triple track the harmony, and it sounds like a choir, a perfectly in tune choir…. They break for lunch, come back and spend the entire afternoon mixing it.

PJ allows the cameras in, and they are on the news a few nights later, giving the Irish a close up view of how a song is recorded. They get fifteen minutes of fame in a thirty-minute news segment. Again, priceless publicity as people get to know the lads, and start picking their favorites among them.

 PJ opens up to the lads as they relax in a pub after the day's marathon recording session. "Lads, I never told youse, my sister is in a home for the mentally challenged in Dublin. D'ya think we could launch the record there as they love music, and I think the song suits a scene like that?"

"If ya think it's a good idea, I s'pose it's okay, hah lads?" says Mel.
"Ri'," they answer, almost in unison.
"Thanks lads. I'll work with the nuns at the home and make sure everything is ready to go."

Two weeks later, after some sellout dancehall shows, they launch their Eurovision record in the home which the nuns oversee. PJ has let the paparazzi know, so they're all there. The nuns are loving all the excitement, and are drooling over the band, like giddy teenage girls.

All the reporters, cameramen, family members of residents living in the home, and Fran's brother are mixing and dancing with the patients. Some have Down syndrome, but most are older men and women with severe mental retardation, loving all the fuss, totally different from the usual daily monotony.

One obnoxious reporter approaches Billy, and in a very cynical voice she says: "Don't you think you're exploiting these people launching your record here?"

Billy can't believe his ears; he loses his cool. "You stupid bitch, look around you for God's sake.".... Just then Robot flies past them in a wheelchair, on his lap is an ecstatic resident who screams with joy as all the nuns clap in approval.

Billy glares at the reporter, emphatically states, "*Love is the Answer*," and walks away.

Wednesday, following the launch party, brings rehearsal at Robot's. PJ comes in furious, and waves the morning paper in front of Billy's face. "Billy, what the hell is this?" The headline reads:

BILLY GOLDEN CURSES NEWS REPORTER AT EURO LAUNCH

.....*Billy and The Touch, released their winning National Song Contest recording of Love Is The Answer at St. Patrick's Home yesterday. The Mercy nuns direct this home-care for mentally handicapped adults. Considering this small, private home to be an unusual venue for such a huge release, this reporter asked "Why here?" Previous reports of Billy's tendency toward bursts of uncontrollable anger were quite surprisingly verified almost immediately. Billy's undignified response: "You stupid bitch." This reporter has indeed validated a skulking rumor to be more true than not...."*

Billy grabs the paper and reads the story. "This is bullshit, this isn't what she said, she's lying PJ."

"Okay, so what's the story then?"

"Look, she came up to me and said we were exploiting these people, launching the song there. She says here that she asked me "Why here?" Then she says I snapped and called her a stupid bitch. I did call her a stupid bitch, but that's not what she said to me, she's lying."

"You know Billy, you and your bloody temper, this is the last thing we need right now."

PJ goes into damage control mode. "All right,... look,.... I'm gonna' call Joe O'Leary from <u>The Irish Standard</u>, and ask him to give you a call. I'll run in right now and give him some photos of the evening, and see if he can have it in tomorrow. Look Billy, you know this country by now, everybody wants to pull you down once ya get there, so watch that temper of yours all ri?"

"Yea, I'm sorry PJ, sorry lads, I must've been dropped on my head when I was a kid or somethin', I just sort o' snap ya know?"

"All ri," says PJ, "hopefully he'll get it in tonight, and we can sort it out. Now lads, Israel is exactly a month away. I got ye workin' every night 'til then, some cabarets, dances and concerts, that's what ye said ye wanted, ri'?"

"Ri'."

Then he gives them a tough love reality check. "Ye're gonna' make some decent bread for a while, [money] but if ye don't win Eurovision, I don't know, ... ye'll get a few more months out of it, but ye won't be as hot as ye are now. But if ye do win, I'd say ye'll get at least a year's good work out of it. They'll all be glued to it on the night all over Europe, and they'll all want to see the winner. Record a good follow up to it, and the sky's the limit, even America could open up with that Irish rock stuff ye did in Sweden."

"Well at least I'll get to ride me camel," says Steo. The boys are amazed, Steo actually saying something funny.

The next day, the boys read the morning paper, and the headline reads:

BILLY GOLDEN CALLS REPORTER'S STORY INACURATE

It details Billy's side of the story, who admits to calling her a stupid bitch, quotes her question verbatim to him, tells the story that he couldn't understand how the reporter could be so cynical amidst all the excitement for the residents. There were a few photos of everybody beaming. The nuns told the reporter how grateful they were that the lads would give up their valuable time to come and entertain the residents. Billy weathered the storm.

The dance hall is full that night, but other headlines on the newspapers are grim:

MORTGAGE RATES AT HISTORIC HIGHS... PETROL SHORTAGES THROUGHOUT COUNTRY DISRUPTS THE ECONOMY... DANCE HALLS CLOSE DUE TO LACK OF BUSINESS....

Billy decides to go house hunting; he's making decent money for the first time in his life, and ever the optimist, he dives in headfirst. He goes into one real estate office after another, and depressingly, finds nothing for sale in his price range nearby.

One realtor said there was a cottage for sale amongst the Wicklow Hills that he thought would be ideal for Billy: "private, with a rock star's view right out to the Atlantic Ocean, perfect for a songwriter like yerself," he said. The salesman was good, playing up to Billy's ego, so Meg, Sam and himself head down to have a look. They head out past Bray, and after a few minutes get to Newtownmountkennedy. "It has to be the longest name for a village in Ireland," Billy thinks. They follow the written directions, up a meandering hill, climbing all the time, through beautiful forests, with the coastline dramatically visible way off in the distance. They turn a sharp corner, and are in awe at the beautiful vista stretching for miles right out in front of them; a post card view of the rolling forty shades of green descending gently to the ocean.

Sadly, Wicklow is almost unknown to the foreign tourists apart from two very scenic spots: Glendalough, an old monastic settlement, founded by St. Kevin, with its famous round tower, and forests coming right down to a beautiful lake, and Powerscourt, previously an English owned mansion with its exquisite gardens, now owned by the Irish State. The popular mini series *Ballykissangel* was also shot in Avoca, a charming little Wicklow town.

They drive up a steep dirt road as directed, and arrive at the house on the very top of the hill; a little lonely bungalow, badly needing a bit o' TLC. Billy could see the finished picture though, as he looked at this sad old bungalow overlooking a million dollar view: gut the house, add another wing, even add a sunroom to maximize the view, and then landscape the heck out of it.

The realtor isn't there yet, so they just sit in the car and admire the view: straight out is the ocean about three miles away, with sailboats passing by. Billy is hooked, even tho' the cottage has seen better days. Meg is impressed, "Billy, it's lovely."

"Yea, but its miles from you and Sam."
"I'm sure Sam would like to visit ya in the country, wouldn't ya Sam?"
"Yea Billy, I like it."

There's a small rocky hill behind the cottage, begging to be explored, and after a short climb, Billy and Sam get to the top. On their left they see a magnificent dark green hill gently descending to the narrow road. It's a huge ranch-like field, full of sheep. On their side it climbs more steeply, and is much rockier.

They see a collie, tearing around bringing the sheep down from the hill, and hear a farmer shouting directions. Even tho' he's pretty far away, his voice carries across the valley, and they can hear every word. They see him at the bottom of the field, screaming and whistling a mile a minute: "get up there ya ould bollix ya, get 'em down here, ya good for nothin' excuse for a dog." He whistles more instructions, and curses the dog again..... Billy and

Sam look at each other and smile, Sam giving him the "big eye" look that he's heard something he shouldn't have. They are amazed at how good the dog can control the sheep, despite the farmer's opinion.

They see the realtor driving up the dirt road, and walk back to meet her. Billy introduces himself. "Hello there, Billy Golden, this is Meg and Sam."

The realtor is shocked when she recognizes Billy. "Wow, Billy Golden, I can't believe it, nice to meet ya"
"You too, thanks for coming, so how much is it going for?"
"They're asking fifty thousand." Billy's dreams are deflated.

"Well, I can't afford that," says Billy. "That's that then I suppose," waiting to see if she'll budge on the fifty thousand, as Billy's realtor said they probably would, as it wasn't selling. Sure enough she sees Billy is interested, and says, "well I'm sure the owners would consider any offers."

Billy was thinking maybe they might go for forty thousand pounds or even lower, as it had definitely seen better days. He had about seven thousand saved up at this point. "What do I need to put down, ten percent?"

"Well Billy, as you're a first time buyer, they'll probably want twenty percent."

"Shit," he thinks to himself, "if I buy it, all my cash will be gone once I've paid for the down payment, and I'll have to fix it up as I go along." He was always in a hurry. "Well, we better win Eurovision then.".....

"I hope so," says the realtor, "I like the song, good luck in Israel."

They slowly meander home, exploring the back roads of the Wicklow Hills, and Billy's mind is made up. The scenery is simply stunning. Wicklow truly deserves its reputation of being known as the Garden of Ireland. Yep, if they win Eurovision, he'll buy it.

Chapter 22

As is the custom every year, they're on the **Late Late Show**, the night before they fly out to Israel. The compere introduces them, and out they come, to huge applause, and take their seats.

"Well lads, you're on your way, you're number one in the charts, how are ye feeling?"

"It's the best feeling in the world," says Robot, "we'll do our best for Ireland, we hope we win." The audience applauds.

Then the compere gets a bit serious. "Do you think Eurovision is a bit of fluff, irrelevant really, with the country in the state it's in?"

"Yea, it's not the most important thing in the world for sure," says Billy, "but it's a bit of a distraction for people with all that's happening lately. It certainly gave us lads a break we couldn't have dreamed of."

"But basically it's just a pop contest?" he persisted.

Billy's blood pressure began to boil. "Cool it," he said to himself, "say something serious, if that's what he wants." "Look, we're flying out tomorrow representing our country. Twenty-one other countries are doing the same thing, all hoping to win. We hope people will visit Ireland because we're in it, and if we win, Ireland will be on the map for a while, so what's so bad about that?" The crowd roars in approval.

The compere smiles, "Okay lads, good luck to you, would ye sing it one last time for us?" They take their positions and sing it as the audience joins in knowing every word.

Billy is just getting home from the television station around eleven, hoping for a good night's sleep, when a white construction van pulls in front of him and cuts him off just like you'd see in the movies. Billy slams his brakes on and just avoids hitting the van. A big dude jumps out of the van. "Shit, it's Ronan, what the hell does he want?"

"Get outta' the car ya bollix ya," he shouts.

Billy realized it wasn't that hard to find him, as everybody knew he lived somewhere in Monkstown. Was it the **Late Late Show** that made him snap, or was it his intention to send him to hospital, not Israel? There was no lawyer this time cooling him down.

Billy gets out, his first mistake, and Ronan pushes him back against the car. Ronan takes a wild swing, misses Billy completely, but hits the side mirror of Billy's car. It crashes to the ground. Billy looks at this impossible to replace, very costly mirror shattered in pieces, and he loses it. "Ya big ugly bollix, ya broke my mirror, ya bloddy eejit ya."

Ronan was jumping all around the place screaming in pain, holding his right hand. "Shite, shite, my feckin' hand, I'm going to kick the shite out o' you for interfering with my son." Billy realizes the man is smashed, scuttered drunk, and if Ronan lays a hand on him, Billy will not be going to Israel.

It was an open secret that the television people always had another singer on emergency standby, who knew the song, and was ready to travel if anything happened to the first singer, laryngitis or whatever. So if he gets beaten up, he's screwed. But he wasn't going to back down after what Ronan had done to his mirror. Ronan didn't know about Billy's temper.

Billy starts off as nicely as he can be under such circumstances. "What the hell do ya mean 'interfering?' I'm just his friend, you're his father. You deserted him, broke his heart man. Why don't ya call him and take him somewhere? He's a great kid, and if ya don't do it soon, he's gonna' tell ya to go screw yerself." "Shite, shite," is all Ronan can utter, as he pumps his fist in the air.

"If you beat me up, I'm done all right, I'm not going to Israel. Is that what ya want? Well let me tell ya somethin' I'm not gonna' run away from a prick like you, so if ya hit me, ya better make sure I stay down, 'cos if I get up, I promise ya I'll bloody well kill ya."

Ronan seems to have an epiphany, or at least the wind is taken out of his sails, as he shifts around. His mood suddenly changes. "Hey, … ah shite, d'ya wanna' go for a drink?"
Billy is astonished and relieved.

As only two Irishmen could, they head over to Goggin's pub, and Billy orders two pints. Recognized immediately, Billy starts signing autographs on napkins and beer mats, whatever people hand him. They back slap him and wish him luck in Israel.

Ronan calms down, and is sort of enjoying being with a celebrity. Billy gives him an opening to make him feel important.

"So what d'ya think of the song?"

"I think it's all right, but you won't win it."
"Why not?"
"'Tis a good chorus, but the verse isn't strong enough."
"Fair play to ya for being so bloody honest Mr. Music Professor, I hope you're wrong."

"I don't think so," says Ronan the music critic, delighted with himself.

Billy figures he's got to face this guy sometime, so, nothing like the present: "Look, "he says, "what'rya doin' man? You left her. She told me they had to drag you out of one of your girlfriend's bed to come and see your newborn son in hospital? Why can't ya let her be happy? You can mess around as much as you like, but she can't, is that it?"

"She's my feckin' property."

"What?" says Billy stunned. "What bloody century d'ya think you're living in boyeee?"

"We're not divorced, so under Irish law, she's still my property. I can take you to court for trespassing on my property, my lawyer told me that."

"Hey man you need help, d'ya know that. You've lost the plot altogether. You were following me from RTE weren't ya? This is crazy shit man. You left her remember? You can be happy, but she can't?"

Billy sees the funny side to this bizarre scene. "Okay, take me to court, and you'll be the laughing stock of Ireland. The papers will have a field day. Your girlfriend will probably leave ya, and you'll never score again, once they hear this shite comin' from you. They say any publicity is good publicity, so go ahead, you'll be doing me a huge favor. Just leave her alone will ya, you don't want her. Look, I love her, why don't you let her be happy. Just let her go for God's sake will ya." Ronan just looks into his pint.

"Hey man, I gotta' get a bit o' sleep. I'll send ya the bill for the mirror. Why don't ya give Sam a call? He'd love it" Billy walks home, and shakes his head at what just happened.

The next day they leave for Israel, via London, where they board an Israeli jumbo jet. They're not first class, but it doesn't matter, as it's the first time most of them flew except for Billy and Fran.

Security is tight in London, as the IRA are carrying out a bombing campaign in England,. Being Irish, they're questioned a lot more than the English travelers. Billy feels sorry for all the Irish people living and working in England during this time. Whenever a bomb goes off, they are treated with a lot of hostility.

The average English citizen never knew the true story about the brutal occupation of Ireland. The true historical extent and scandal of the Irish famine was more of an English state secret. Ireland produced multitudes of food through much of the 19th century, plenty for everybody. The English kings awarded lands to their lords. The Irish lived on and worked the properties but had no right to the lands. The English landlords consumed the crops as their own, received all of the receipts from sales and exports of all that was raised on the lands. The Irish farmers lived on the land through permission of the lords. The farmers were required to pay taxes to the English throne before they were granted permission to consume any of the herds and harvests themselves. The Irish farmers were poor and suffered a great hunger which was caused by this unrealistic cost of food. After years of deprivation, with vegetables growing plentifully in the fields, thousands of Irish men, women and children emigrated to America. The 1840's was catastrophic for the remaining Irish in the form of the potato blight. Starvation was rampant and over a million penniless but proud countrymen and their families fled their homes in search of a better life in America and Canada. Much of the world was led to believe that an indiscriminate calamity caused the hunger of these proud people rather than an overbearing policy of English kings and politicians.

The English were taught in school that they civilized the savages throughout the world. The English perspective was that even tho' their policies might have been somewhat cruel, the colonized people were the better for it overall, and should be grateful for what had been done for them. As is usually the case, ignorance led to arrogance and intolerance, and a heavy dose of superiority.

The lads step on board the jumbo jet, and can't help but notice the drop dead gorgeous Israeli flight attendants. "Pretty nice scenery huh?" says Robot. They also notice several male cabin crewmembers, who look more like marines. The 70's was the era of plane hijackings, and Billy presumes they're probably armed guards.

Billy remembers a story someone told him about an attempted hijacking of an Israeli plane... The plane had armed security on board. They overpowered the hijackers, ordered the passengers in first class to move back to the "peasant" section. Plastic bags were placed on the carpeted floor and the hijackers throats were slit. When the plane arrived in Israel, the hijackers' next of kin were called, and told to come collect the bodies. Israeli airlines were never hijacked again.

The boys can't believe that the booze is free. Everything... top of the range whiskey, brandy, vodka, and of course they generously help themselves.

Steo is truly plastered after an hour or so, and every time he sees a particularly gorgeous flight attendant walk by, with an ass to die for, he gets more and more obnoxious. "Hey miss, I'd love to get into yer knickers."

Being the professional that she is, she ignores him. He was getting more and more smashed. She goes by again. "Ah Jaysus miss, I'd eat chips outa' yer knickers." Again, she ignores him. A few minutes later she passes again, and Steo screams after her, "hey miss, I'd really like to get into yer knickers." She turns around, and sticks her head right down to Steo's ear and says; "sir, one asshole at a time in my knickers is enough right now thank you." She straightens up, and walks away. Steo is speechless, the lads are loving it; another great story for posterity.

After a long boozy sleepy flight the lads finally arrive at Ben Gurion airport in Jerusalem. The security is totally intimidating. Soldiers everywhere with machine guns, patrolling the airport with magnificent looking German Shephard dogs. They are patted down thoroughly, and every piece of their luggage is carefully checked.

Finally, they get to the King David Hotel, one of the finest hotels anyone had ever stayed in. The Eurovision greeters, television cameras, and the entire European press crew meet them. They are given the necessary passes to rehearsals, invitations to several functions, tee shirts, and a carry on bag, with all sorts of goodies - heady stuff for the band.

They have the next day to acclimatize themselves before rehearsals begin, so the RTE team decides to go to Bethlehem and visit Jesus' birthplace. The orthodox priests allow only a few visitors in at a time. They enter through a tiny door, and once inside, it was truly moving to be where Jesus was born. The atmosphere was one of pure reverence. At this moment, Billy more clearly understands the faith his Ma has in her rosary beads.

Their next stop is the Wailing Wall where Hasidic Jews pray with total faith. Billy remembers the Irish praying in a similar fashion at the Knock Shrine... In 1879, there was a silent apparition of the Virgin Mary in Knock, a small village in Co. Mayo. It was a manifestation of Mary, Joseph, St. John the Evangelist, and the lamb of God. Since then, there have been reports of many cures and miracles after people visited the Knock church, blessed themselves with the holy water, and prayed for help... As he watched the Jews praying and putting their requests into tiny cracks in the wall, he envied their total faith, exactly like the people at Knock.

At an orchestral rehearsal on the stage the next morning, each country gets fifteen minutes to introduce the song to the orchestra. Cameras shots are planned and the hosts learn a little about each singer and songwriter. No audience or outside reporters are allowed in. The orchestra is magnificent, and they have state of the art sound and monitors, so the band's confidence soars, knowing everybody knows their stuff. Thankfully, the stage crew is also terrific, very friendly and accommodating. That's one thing Billy noticed over the years; the bigger the venue, the easier everything became.

That afternoon, the RTE team hires a minibus, and they all head out to the Dead Sea. They're amazed at how easily they can float. It's actually impossible to drown. Once you wade out and get up to your knees, you were sort of flipped over, and you started floating. Off in the hazy distance is Jordan, pretty amazing stuff for the lads from Ballyer and Cork. Later on, Steo gets to ride his camel. The filthy beast was making all sorts of disgusting noises. Mel gets some hilarious pictures as Steo haggles over the outrageous price the camel owner is demanding.

There's a full dress rehearsal the following day, and the press are allowed in. Some of the songs are more show than substance, and everybody is eyeing up their competition.

Billy remembers… a few years earlier when he was in Bulgaria, there was an absolutely stunning Italian girl with a fabulous voice, and a winning song, the complete package. She wore a body-hugging full-length blue dress at the final dress rehearsal, and it was odds-on that she was going to win.

There was a break for dinner and final make up, and when she came out to sing her song, she wore another very ordinary dress, forgot her words, and didn't have the sparkle that she had at the dress rehearsal, and didn't win.

Billy learned later that someone had slipped into her dressing room, and ripped her dress to shreds. She couldn't pull herself together in time, and she blew it. This was how seriously singers, songwriters and managers, take song contests. There was an awful lot at stake for the winner, especially at Eurovision.
The boys of course were listening to all the songs intently, and figured the French and Israeli songs were their strongest competition. They do several radio and TV interviews for various countries. Billy had learned a few Swedish words, and says hi to all their friends in Stockholm, and does an interview in Irish by the lavish hotel swimming pool, surrounded by palm trees and endless sunshine, a million miles from Ireland.

Everybody back home watching this believe the lads have made it to the big leagues, and have to be millionaires by now. If they only knew....

Next day, there's one final fully-dressed run through. All the singers are introduced, as they will be that night. Final camera shots are worked out.

They break for dinner, and PJ comes in all excited. "Well lads, this is it, five hundred million people watching on the telly all over the world, and look at these lads, twelve invites to appear on all the top European pop shows even Top of the Pops in London next Tuesday, …. IF ye win …. so go out there and do yer best."

Virtually everybody in each country is glued to the telly cheering their own singer on. In Dublin, Meg, Pops and all the lads' parents and friends gather in one pub. Nora and Finbar and their friends are watching in their tiny living room in Cork, Nora, as always, holding her rosary beads, … tremendous excitement and pride.

"Dia is Muire dhibh a chairde gael, Michael O Shea annseo san Isreal," are the first words out of the Irish compere reporting from Jerusalem. Hearing the Irish language spoken, albeit a few words from so far away, was a tremendous source of pride to the Irish. Even tho' most people could only speak a few words themselves, it still mattered to the Irish psych, especially in circumstances like this.

"Hello everybody," he continued, "greetings from sunny Israel, where roughly half a billion people are watching all over Europe and the Middle East tonight. This is the biggest night of their lives for all the singers and songwriters. If Ireland wins tonight, it will be huge for the lads. You've probably heard that Ireland and Israel are the two hot favorites in the contest. Ireland picked number seven in the draw for the running list. They say singing earlier than later is a good thing, so hopefully, a little luck o' the Irish is with them so far.

First up is Sweden, where the lads are very popular, so they're hoping for a good vote from them tonight." The Swedish group sings their song, and the other countries go through their songs one by one. The Israeli group goes out, and sings it perfectly. The home crowd cheers wildly.

Suddenly, Steo is paralyzed with nerves. "Shite, I can't go out there, I just bleedin' can't, me hands are shaking, an' I can't remember the harmonies, we're bollixed lads."

PJ jumps in immediately, and saves the day. "Steo, if you screw up, and don't get yer shit together, I swear to God I'll leave ya here in Israel. You can join the Israeli army for all I care. We're all in this together. You might be five minutes away from millions. Ya love money don't ya, so the only way you'll ever make any is to go out there and do yer best. So wash yer bleedin' face, and don't let the lads down now. Just imagine you're playing in some shitty dance hall in the middle of nowhere in Ireland. Forget about the cameras, just play. Here, drink this." PJ gives him a shot of brandy, he gulps it down, and seems to pull himself together, just before they're announced.

Out they go, everybody holding their breath in Ireland, wishing them the best, and for many who gambled a few pounds on them, hoping that they will pull it off. If they win, they can brag about it the next day.

Billy once again starts on his own, a daunting thing for him, knowing so many people are watching, and God help him if he makes a mistake now, he'll never live it down. They are actually lifted by the occasion, and do their very best, tho' they're terribly nervous, which makes it hard for them to smile. Thankfully the lyrics are serious, so they get away with it. The Irish compere comes in during the applause. "Well done Billy Golden and the Touch, you did Ireland proud tonight."

The other contestants present their songs, and then that long seven-minute interval happens once again, as they line up the phone connections to all the countries competing. It feels like seven hours to everybody involved, all packed into the green room as usual.

Finally the votes start coming in. The Israeli compere, in perfect French asks the French for their vote. "Bonsoir Israel, here is the French vote:
Spain, 2 votes,
Ireland, 4 votes,
Israel, 2 votes,"…so far so good. Votes are immediately posted on the scoreboard.

Again the compere asks, "Come in England:

"Good evening Israel," in his perfect English accent, "here is the English vote:
Austria 1 vote,
France, 2 votes,
Ireland, 3 votes,
Israel, 4 votes."

The vote results continue. Ireland and Israel are neck and neck. One country pushes Ireland up a vote or two, then Israel gets a big vote next, and they are tied again. The tension is enormous. The cameras swing onto the lads, and the Israeli group, building the visual drama for everybody watching. With Israel up two votes, the lads fate comes down to the Spanish vote. Here it comes:
"Portugal, 1 vote,
France, 2 votes,
Ireland, 3 votes,
Israel, 3 votes."

The place erupts. The home team has won. The scene goes into a sort of slow motion for the lads, as they take in the enormity of what just happened, and what this will mean to them: all those TV offers gone up in smoke in five minutes, their big chance just incinerated by just two votes, having to face everybody back home, the future of the band now that they have lost…..

They are devastated, but try to put on their best faces, 'til they are off camera. PJ tries to console them, "Well lads, ye did yer best, no fault at all." Jack hits the nail on the head, "yea, but nobody remembers who came second." "Except us," says the bould Steo.

Billy goes off by himself, finds a restroom, and falls apart. He cries bitterly, and loudly. All this work for nothing, he thinks. The band are probably finished in Ireland, and he feels he's just barely getting started. He knows the lads are more easygoing about their futures. They are not as obsessed with making it as he is. Shit, what about Meg and himself, what now? His thoughts are flying through his brain like volcanic explosions.

He joins the others as they get a taxi back to the hotel. Robot, in fairness, tries to put the best face on it. "Well Steo, at least ya got to ride your bleedin' camel, and I s'pose we'll get a few more months out of it, hah PJ?"

"Ri'," says PJ, "piss on it lads, so close, I'm sorry for youse." There's nothing else to say, and they all wish they were back home with their families and friends right now.

Chapter 23

The band finally arrives home to Dublin airport around three am in the morning. They get through customs, come out to the main foyer, and are knocked out when they see a few hundred people waiting patiently to welcome them home, even tho' they're three hours late. They see them all with their homemade posters:

YOU TOUCHED US LADS.....

YOU ARE STILL GOLDEN TO US.....

WE LOVE YOUR TOUCH....

The lads are very moved, even tho' they're absolutely exhausted. They shake hands with every single person, and sign autographs.

A week later, after five nights of road shows, and not one night yet in their own beds, they are driving home at the end of a long day. The old excitement is clearly not there, and the crowds are down, in every hall. Numbers aren't as bad as their original gigs, but it's much less than they thought they'd have.

On the way home in the truck, Mel sums up how all the lads are feeling. "Lads, it's been a great two years, I don't know about youse, but I'd rather quit now than slowly die, and that's exactly what'll happen, with the country goin' the way it is. I'm going to talk to Jim, and ask him to take me on full time as a carpenter, and do this partime. I might start a band doing the Irish rock we did in Sweden, but not night after flippin' night, all over the bleedin' country. I've no life, no time for meself, ya know, I feel like I'm just existing"

"Yea, Mel's ri'," says Robot, "I'm not into it as much as I used to be. The way the ould scene is now, t'would put years on ya, ya know, whadd'ya think Billy?"

"Yea,… it's a bitch. Three lousy votes and we'd be number one all over Europe now. I think we could survive if we had about ten hits behind us, but we've barely gotten started. The record company will probably drop us now, so there goes any chance of a follow up. We'll have to surrender the truck back to the bank, so there goes four grand down the toilet just like that. We still owe money on the gear and lights. Shit, I'm glad I didn't buy the house, I'd really be screwed. I was thinkin' about tryin' America. I wanna' keep goin','…. don't just wanna' settle for second best….. Bloody hell," he laughs," I'm gonna' go to America OWING money, that must be a first."

Jack immediately thinks about Meg. "And what about Meg?"

"Yea,… three lousy votes, …ain't life a bitch, ….
I'm going to ask her would she come to America
with me."

Jack shakes his head, "Shite Billy, I know my sister,
she'll never go man, I'm sorry."

"Yea, you're probably right, three lousy votes, ….
what a bitch."…

Fran offers his twenty cents, "look lads, why don't
we do another month or two, we've got the
bookings, and the bread is still good. It'll give us all
a bit o' time to figure things out."

"Yea," says Steo, "who's going to break the news to
PJ?"

So they wander through the next month, and make
no public announcement about the upcoming
breakup of the band. They tell PJ, and he's pissed.
He shouts and roars about all he's done for them,
"and you just walk away like this, after all the work
I've done, gettin' ye this far ." Finally he cools
down, and agrees to hang in for the two months, and
take no further bookings, no matter how good they
are.

He tells them how much they still owe him, and
they agree to allow him to deduct it from future
gigs, until he's fully paid off. They figure out what
they owe on their PA system, pay it off and Mel and
Steo buy it for a song. They divide it among

themselves, as they won't need all the gear for what they want to do.

They're all broke again, so Fran's idea to do the extra two months was great. The money from the next two months is all they'll have after two hard years of hustling.

Billy hardly sees Meg at all, as the lads are busy playing nearly every night. PJ landed them a summer season in Killarney, the premier gig for a band in those days, five nights a week. They also worked the other two nights, sometimes driving to Donegal, and back to Killarney the following night. Once again, Billy's admiration for the old showband members was enormous.

They try and save as much as they can, when they are still reasonably hot, but they all know they're yesterday's news. It was galling to hear the Eurovision winner on the radio.

Finally things slow down, and Billy picks up Meg, and they go to dinner. She's looking gorgeous of course, and all excited about how the new salon is going. Billy knows in his heart he hasn't a hope, but he feels he has to give it a try.

After some small talk, he starts to get serious. "Hey Meg love, I can't stay here, there's nothin' happenin'. I was wonderin', I know this is a lot to ask, but would you and Sam come with me to America?"

Meg's reaction was exactly as he expected. "Jaysus Billy, I couldn't, the shops are flyin', Sam is happy at school, and t'would break mam and dad's heart if they lost Sam."

Billy gives it his best shot, "I know I know, but I think Sam would have a better chance in America the way the country is going Meg."

"Billy, you're asking an awful lot of me, business is great, even tho' everybody's broke, they still want to look well."

"I know,… I love you Meg. I don't want to lose you because of this shit."

"Billy, I dunno,' I don't know anything anymore,"… she starts to cry. "You made me feel…. alive again, and you're a huge influence on Sam."

"Dya think you could teach me to be a hairdresser?" asks Billy. She laughs thru' her tears…. "I don't want to go back teaching after all this Meg, t'would kill me, and what am I going to do here, weddings with the band?"

"You'd have me and Sam."

Billy realizes how selfish he must sound. "Look I know, I'm sorry, I sound like a selfish bastard, but I wrote most of that song, and I know if I stay here, I'll get into a crappy old rut feelin' sorry for myself, and probably never write anything decent again. You know me by now Meg, if I don't have a project to aim for, I'll piss you off so much you'll probably break it off with me anyway down the road."

Neither of them feel like staying, so he gets the check. Outside, they hold each other for a long time, not wanting to let go, and then head back to her place. This must be how a soldier feels before he goes off to war, Billy thought, not knowing what lay ahead for either of them. He is sick to his stomach.

Next morning Sam comes into the bedroom, and sits on the bed. Seamus starts licking Billy's face and wakes him up. "Hiya Sam, how'r'ya?"

"Mam says yer goin' to America?" Billy realizes how sad he is.
"Yea Sam, I can't make any money here anymore."
"But me mam is makin' loads of money, you could stay here with us."
Billy pulls himself up. "Sam, I'd love to stay with you and your mother, but I have to make my own money ya know?"

Sam looks like he's going to cry. "Hey, I'll be back in a few months, and I'll see ya, and ye can come over for a visit. We can all go to Disneyland. I heard they have a track over there where you can race go-karts. I wanna' see can I beat Ireland's champion racing driver," as he tosses Sam's hair and gives him a hug.

Meg comes in with tea and toast. "Okay Sam, bring Seamus out."
"Hi, good morning,…. man, that was tough."
"Are ya sure ya don't want to go back teaching, you'll have yer pension in forty years?" she says jokingly.

He laughs, "God you sound like my mother. I'm not sure of anything anymore. All I know is I don't want to lose you and Sam."
"Billy, if ya don't like it, come home, the recession can't last forever. People will come out and see ya again. For God's sake Billy, ye sang for Ireland. Everybody loves you and the boys." She sits beside him on the bed.

"I dunno' Meg, people have short memories. I think once I go, it'll be just holidays here, and I couldn't stand people saying 'There's Billy Golden, he didn't make it.'" They sit in silence, not knowing what to say.

The band has one last piss up in their local bar. Everyone's there, even Helen. She's in great form. "How'rya Billy, ya ould bollix ya? Steo Robot and I are teaming up again to do weddings. I told them they couldn't do without me, remember? Hey for what it's worth, good luck in America."

"Thanks, I appreciate that.... ya know,... you should have just screwed that culchie AFTER the dance.".... They both laugh and have one last hug.

Everybody has a good time, trying not to dwell too much on the future. Mel puts on a slide show of the lads from day one, bittersweet laughs and tears all around, realizing they came so close to achieving their dream, and knowing this was it, it's all over.

Suddenly, Billy feel's he's almost back to square one, knowing he's going to America, but hasn't a clue how to go about it. He has one cousin on his dad's side in Cleveland whom he never met, and Cleveland wasn't on his agenda as a first destination.

He figured he'd just fly to New York and network once he was there. He felt he could survive for about three months before his savings ran out, and surely he could do what he was doing in Dublin, playing in some pubs just to get a feel of the place.

All the "stuff" he took for granted came into play, and it all felt way more daunting than just moving up to Dublin: find a place to stay, get some wheels to get around, find places to play. It wasn't a very appealing future, but he knew he had to take the plunge, and the sooner the better, as he knew more and more musicians would be facing the same fate, so get in now before the avalanche.

A few days later, Valerie, his ex choir director in Dublin, calls to invite him to a party. He wasn't much in the mood, but Valerie's description of the host and where he lived intrigued him. "He's a sort of a James Bond type, who lives in a semi-detached Castle in Killiney."

So that night, off he goes with Valerie and her husband Noel. The house was exactly how Valerie described it, a fortress-like duplex castle, with turrets, and concrete second floor balconies overlooking the beach. Dublin's harbor was right there in all its glory, in one of the suburbs most prestigious areas.

Tom and Ann Shevlin, the hosts, warmly greeted them at the door. Tom was a handsome Irishman, over six feet tall, with that black Irish hair that had just a touch of the silver strands, and piercing blue eyes. Ann was an equally attractive American lady with her long blonde hair framing an angular face, and green eyes speckled with gold, which pierced your soul.

Tom wasn't bashful in the least as he described for his guests that he managed to leave Iraq before an unknown 'they' shot him. His business was selling heavy equipment to both Iran and Iraq, apparently being one of the few salesmen who had the balls to go into a very hostile situation, and sell tractors and bulldozers to both regimes at the same time, thus, doing very well for himself.

Tom set up a scenario whereby after the war broke out, he was caught in the middle of it all. His company hadn't been paid for the recent deliveries, and it was Tom's job to collect the money. He felt the Iraqis would never pay up, and were tying up loose ends. He got the strong feeling that he would simply "disappear," so luckily, he managed to bribe his way out.

The debonair Irishman appeared seemingly blessed with the nine lives of a cat. After his escapades in Iraq, he cooled his heels back in Dublin for a while 'til he got bored again, and when Billy met him, he had just come back from a supposedly successful gold mining adventure in Canada.

Tom's from Co. Down, and still has his marvelous Northern Irish accent, after years of travelling. His first entrepreneurial job was building up a successful fashion industry in Northern Ireland. He combined world class Northern Irish linen with expensive silk materials, and made clothes for the likes of Debbie Reynolds, and other high profile Hollywood stars.

His business was going gangbusters until his factory was bombed to smithereens one night. Being Catholic and successful, apparently didn't go down too well at the time, in Northern Ireland. As his wife was American, he had dual citizenship, and was well used to travelling and selling in America.

Billy originally thought Tom to be a total bullshitter, but later on he discovered it was all true. Inevitably, he was asked to play at the party, which he did in great style. He was working on a boogie-woogie version of Tchaikovsky's piano concerto, and played it for the first time at the party. It turned out to be a showstopper thankfully. Tom was very impressed and had a chat with Billy about his future plans.

About two weeks later, Billy got a call from America. It was Tom. "Hey Billy, I'm over here in America. My brother owns a golf club in Michigan, and he's had a heart attack, so I'm runnin' it 'til he's okay again." Tom the salesman kicks into gear; the guy could sell sand to the Arabs…. "Billy, this place is a potential goldmine. There's a clubhouse here that's totally unused. I've hired the best local band I could find. They're prison guards in the jail nearby, but they play at weekends, and they are terrific. I poached them from the best restaurant in Jackson, and they have a fantastic following. They're packin' the place every Friday and Saturday night. Billy, with you here we could do five nights a week. We need the money as there's no golf right now, so what d'ya think?"

"When are ya talkin' about?" asks Billy.

"Yesterday, the sooner the better."

"But I,...." as Billy stutters, "I wasn't planning to go for another bit."

Tom comes in for the kill: "Billy, do yerself a favor, Ireland is finished, you know it, I know it. The sooner ya get yer arse over here the better. I'll pay for yer ticket, I'll pay ya a thousand bucks a week, and I'll meet ya at the airport."

He hadn't really decided when he was actually going to leave, and wanted to spend as much time as possible with Meg after all the madness of Eurovision, before making any move. "Call me back same time tomorrow, and let me think about it okay?" "Billy, there's nothin' to think about. Do somethin' for yerself, and come over as fast as ya can. I'll talk to ya tomorrow."

Billy sat down, his head spinning. He thought about his cousin in Cleveland. Most Irish people have a cousin in the Bronx or Boston or Chicago, who were good for a few weeks lodging 'til you found your feet, but not Billy. All his crowd had done well in Ireland, probably because they came from big cities, and not the country, where jobs were few and far between, so they didn't have to emigrate. But Michigan? A golf club in the middle of winter? Leaving and trusting someone Billy still wasn't sure about?

Over the phone with Meg, Billy outlines for her the guts of what Tom said. She came right over, stopping along the way to buy him a decent suitcase, and plonks it down right in front of him. "I 'spose I'm going then?"

"I 'spose you are. Look, here's a guy who knows America, and seems like a real hustler from what you told me about him. You need a hustler in America Billy. It's probably way worse than here, dog eat dog, survival of the fittest, so go, see what it's all about all ri'?" They had been back and forth about this for weeks, so it was time to shit or get off the pot.

Tom calls the following night, and Billy agrees to come out immediately on one condition: that Tom find him more work than just the golf club. Tom quickly and exuberantly agrees. Billy parks his beloved car in Meg's garage, and stays in her place for the last few days, and amidst a mixture of passion and worry there rose, in all fairness, great anticipation for Billy's future..

She couldn't drive him to the airport that morning, as she had to work, so their goodbyes are hurried, muddled and tearful. The tears ran down Sam's face. Billy is gutted knowing Sam probably thinks that another father figure, whom he loves, is deserting him. It all made for a very lonely trip in the taxi to the airport, and an even longer, lonelier flight to New York.

As quickly as he leaves the cocoon of the airplane and steps foot upon the floor of a frenetic JFK concourse, the first thing Billy notices is the total contrast in attitudes – Ireland's negativity versus America's positivity. The amazing vibe and upbeat buzz all around him, everybody hustling for the almighty dollar, blue skies, quick smiles. The contrast is stark and Billy realizes it has to come from America's story of immigration and hope, compared to Ireland's 800 years of British rule with all of its brutal suppression, and the total lack of hope.

As he waits another four hours for the flight to Detroit, this obvious contrast, makes him recall a memory of his early years, when he was five years old or so back in Cork. Mrs. Green, an old neighbor of his mother's, had emigrated to America many years ago, and came back for a visit. When she walked in the door and saw, at the time, the three Golden kids she said, "Oh Nora, your kids are beautiful."

Immediately touching her rosary beads in humble solemnity, his mother said, "God I dunno,' I think they're all very plain lookin'." She was cursed with the old Irish affliction of not being able to take a compliment. So Billy's self-esteem was challenged from the very start. He assumed he had a face only a mother could love.

As the old joke goes "I was so ugly, the priest slapped my mother."

After agonizing years of acknowledging and appreciating their self worth, Irish mothers today would say "Thank you," so, we've come a long way in thirty years.

He smiles when he thinks of his mother, a very petite, pretty lady. She could make small talk 'til the cows came home. If you took her up on her offer of a cup of tea, good luck trying to extricate yourself from her clutches.

Of course all the other mothers on the street seemed to have the same gift of the gab, so she was in her element chatting away by the fireside, as she and her friends enjoyed her famous pastries: chocolate éclairs, which were so light they would nearly rise up from the table, huge colorful sherry trifles, perfect apple and rhubarb tarts and delicious cup cakes. He buys a donut, and it's like a concrete block compared to her pastries. "Ma could make a fortune over here," he ponders, "but what would she think of this crazy mass of humanity all around him?" Nah, there aren't enough rosary beads in the world to pull her away from her beloved Cork for any of this.

Sadly, Nora carries the scars of her own mother dying when she was only thirteen, a very frightening and confusing time for a daughter to lose her mother, as she enters puberty. Her father, according to the old stories from people who knew him, was a weak individual. Everybody knew they had lost the stronger parent, so the entire family, her dad and five kids, went to live with their cousins, a family of eight kids and a husband and wife. They offered them this amazingly generous and compassionate opportunity of keeping the family together, thus not risking foster care or worse.

Both families were very bright. One of Nora's brothers came first in the country in his Leaving Certificate exams, [GED] and was offered scholarships in all the four universities of Ireland at the time. He surprised everybody when he decided to become a priest. He spent all the WWII Years in his London parish, going around blessing body parts after the nightly Luftwaffe bombings. Billy's mum said her brother was never the same after that. He obviously suffered from "shell shock," or PTSD as they call it today, and who wouldn't after that experience.

When Billy was eleven or so, he told his mother he wanted to be a priest when he grew up. With his vivid imagination, he was convinced he saw Jesus with His arms stretched out on the altar one Sunday at Mass, calling Billy to join Him. After hearing several foreign missionary priests giving their sermons on Sundays about the awful conditions of the people in Africa, he thought it would be great to become a priest, and spend his life helping "the black babies," as they were called.

Despite her deep faith and reliance on her rosary, when faced with this vocational revelation, she gave Billy a smack and squashed his dreams when she said, "No son of mine will ever be a priest." Her brother's experiences had soured her towards the priesthood. He secretly harbored that dream until he was about twelve, when he discovered girls, and that was the end of Billy's religious vocation.

Another of Nora's brothers, Frank, was a gifted athlete in Gaelic football and hurling, and went on to become one of the country's top politicians. So, with all that former and present glory, her kids couldn't possibly come up to those heady achievements, in her opinion, and depressingly, everyone else's as well.

Billy remembers a great story, now one of legendary proportions, of how Frank saved his team from losing an important football match in the 1940's. His team was losing by two points with minutes to go. Frank's team was threatening and looked likely to score, so the other team kicked the ball, the only ball, into the river, across the road from the football pitch. If they didn't get the ball back, the game would be over, and they would have lost.

Frank ran out of the field, dived into the river, and swam after it, as it was being taken down river by the current. He got it, and swam back to shore, ran into the field, told one of his teammates to kick the ball to him. He did, and Frank ran in and scored the winning three-point goal, with seconds to go.

As a child, Billy felt Nora's unspoken pressure to perform well in the athletic realm of competition. He always tried his best, usually playing against huge guys much older than himself. In Billy's time, there was no under-eleven, under-twelve leagues. The trainers had no problem in toughening up the lads by getting them creamed by fellas much older and tougher than the younger guys.

Billy chased after the ball like a kid playing his first soccer match, and then he'd end up in bed for a week with joint pains. The diagnosis of rheumatic fever complicated by a murmur in his heart, reared its ugly head. The doctor tried to explain to Billy that if he kept running around like that he could die. But what does an eleven year-old kid know about dying?

However, his parents knew, and they kept him under house arrest for an entire summer of his eleventh year. Television hadn't come yet, so he had nothing to do but play the piano for hours. Thankfully, that was the turning point for Billy's future musical direction. Nothing else, except girls, got him as focused through the years, much to the dismay of his teachers and parents.

Those sky-high athletic expectations were crushed to the ground for Billy. Unfortunately, he was useless. Couldn't kick a ball straight to save his life, couldn't run by doctor's orders and probably was a major disappointment to his uncle at the time.

Unfortunately, whatever youthful aspirations Nora held for herself, as a girl, were dealt another blow when she finished high school. In those days, the girls got any ould job 'til they got married and then stayed home with the kids, for the rest of their lives. College was mostly for the boys, and then only for the very lucky few whose parents had the vision and the wherewithal to send their sons to university.

Nora was very smart, and was obsessed that all five of her kids get the best education possible, both girls and boys. She hit it right on the button when she called a degree "your passport." "Get your piece of paper and you can travel the world." She drilled this into all her kids ad nauseam, continuously beseeching through rosary prayer that they would listen.

She always felt inferior to anybody who had a posh accent, and this sort of followed down to her kids, making them feel less than people who were better off, whether they got it through being born into old family wealth, marriage, or hard work. But she could also see through some of those same people's bullshit. "That one, suffers from notions of 'upperosity', who does she think she is?" was one of her classic comments as she took them off perfectly.

Through it all Billy's Mum kept her sense of humor, and always put her best face forward, never bringing her own dreams to fruition: "Who am I? I'm Finbar's wife, the kids' mother, but who am I, what have I done?" Her family took precedence over everything.

Nora encouraged all of her children to do their best. Billy's "best" was writing songs. Rather than considering the positive aspects of his songwriting, she put up with it. Compliments were not shared, it's not the Irish way. Billy's music kept him from getting into too much trouble, so Nora didn't interfere. She could never imagine her Billy and his creations making it into an actual song contest, much less one in Japan.

When Billy learned of a song contest in Tokyo, sponsored by Yamaha music, he just went ahead and got himself an entry form. He submitted his latest song, and within a month, he was informed that he had qualified. The qualification brought with it an all expenses paid trip to Japan. During the competition, he sang to eighteen thousand people in the great Budokken Hall in Tokyo. His singing and piano playing was accompanied by a fifty-piece orchestra which played his arrangement of a song he wrote himself. Upon returning home, Nora would greet him with her Irish smile but never a "Well done," or "We're proud of you." Of course, she worried while he travelled so far from home, she maintained constant contact with her rosary beads in his absences, but as each day passed, Billy dreamed all his big dreams alone.

Billy mused again that he was so glad he invited his dad to be his guest at the National Song Contest. Finbar loved all the excitement, and when he went back to Cork after Billy and the lads had won, as principal of his school, he gave everybody a "half day" in honor of his son winning the song contest. This was huge for all the students, as they could go home at lunch, and not come back. This was indeed a non-spoken form of 'Well done, son' that the Irish could offer and accept while not being boastful of Billy's accomplishments.

Billy sips his coffee waiting for the plane to Detroit, and thinks more seriously about his dad, and how much he gave him.

Finbar inherited his mother's piano; Billy was three at that time, and when his dad sat down and played "Peg of My Heart," Billy was hooked. He couldn't believe a piece of furniture could produce such magical sounds, and he played and played it after that. There was a black stain on the high "G" note and he began to play his first song, "*I Love To Go A wandering*," by starting on that note and plonking out the tune. Within a few months Billy was playing with two hands, so they sent him down to the school of music. Luckily it was just around the corner from where he went to school, The Model School. This was an all-Irish speaking school just across from the City Hall, right smack in the middle of Cork City.

Billy was casual at best about his piano lessons, preferring by far to play by ear, tho' he always passed his grades and won loads of medals in the local piano competitions. He liked to play every now and then, but it would be another few years before he got really serious about playing the piano, during his "house arrest" that fateful summer.

His dad was a teacher both at school and at home. The kids respected him, and felt secure. He was the man of the house. But it was his mother who laid down all the rules. If they screwed up, she would chase Billy and Noellie around the house with a rolling pin, and as they hid under the bed, she'd lash out and whack their legs or whatever was in her range.

His dad used words which were much more effective in making the boys feel guilty about their latest mischief. Billy can't remember a single time when he hit any of them, which was remarkable for the times. Each child was just one of the five kids, three daughters and two sons, no favoritism was ever shown or given to any of them.

Finbar was totally immersed in all of his educational activities except for two glorious weeks every summer where the kids had him all to themselves.

Every summer for six long weeks his dad corrected the Leaving Certificate papers in Math. This is the test to assess students' aptitude for college in Ireland. Billy remembers papers strewn all over the living room table, and his mother serving endless cups of tea to him as he patiently went through hundreds of papers, only coming out to eat and sleep.

Billy didn't know it at the time, but that extra money his dad earned gave everybody a two week family vacation in a town called Youghal, a scenic seaside town which separates the counties of Waterford and Cork.

They had great times swimming in the freezing Atlantic every day. Nobody told them that ocean water actually heated up in other countries in the summer, lips didn't turn blue, nor did one shiver to death coming out of the water, they just loved it all. Ignorance was bliss.

He remembers how his dad, and all the other dads would sit on the beach in their three-piece suits. The old pictures he has, shows his mum and dad dressed to the nines with just their shoes and socks off smiling at the camera. Billy and his brother and sisters were also fully dressed except for their shoes, as they made sandcastles on the beach - so much for remembering the good old days always being sunny.

Later on in the afternoon, his dad took the kids into the countryside and pointed out the wildlife, and the complex eco-system in every hedge, with their little nests and insects. He'd have them listening for the sound of the cuckoo, and he knew the names of all the different trees. The kids thought he knew everything. In the evening they went down to "the merries" as it was called, a tiny amusement park, but at the time, it was as magical as Disneyworld to every young kid in Ireland.

It was a given, even during their holidays at the beach, that every Sunday without fail they would go to Mass. Billy must have missed the "God loves you sermon," as they were drilled constantly that God was watching them, and if they strayed in any way, it was eternal flames awaiting everybody. They lived their young lives in the fear of God rather than believing in the loving, forgiving Father. After a while all Billy heard was "blah blah blah."…..

One sermon did strike a chord with Billy when he was around twelve years old. It grabbed his attention because there was a great story to it. It was different from the usual boring, "and he was begat of this person, and she was begat of that person." The parish priest gave a sermon telling women it was all right to stand up to their husband if he was abusing them. This was revolutionary at the time, as "spouse abuse" was a private matter between families. The poor women had to take this mental and physical abuse, and keep it to themselves because there was no one to turn to, and nowhere to go.

The priest told the congregation about this guy Pat, who abused his wife very badly. He beat her up when he came home drunk every Saturday night, and she died young as a result. He, of course, got off scot-free as there was no formal investigation into how she died.

Pat was shunned so much after that by her family, his kids, and his wife's friends, that he went to England. He rented digs [lodgings] from an attractive widow there, and started wooing and courting her, on his best behavior of course.

Well they married shortly thereafter. The first Saturday night after the wedding, he reverts back to his old ways, comes home legless and beats the crap out of her. The next Saturday night he wakes up in hospital, his head all bandaged up with a fractured skull. "What happened?" he asks. "I hit you with the poker dear, and every time you come home drunk I'll hit you again." Pat became a model husband and they lived happily ever after.

This is the only sermon Billy can remember apart from the usual fear of God and the "begat" lectures. They had everybody convinced that you had to go through them to get into Heaven. Pray, pay, obey. Nearly everybody believed it, and the priest's authority was never questioned.

Billy's daydreaming was rudely interrupted by the announcement that boarding had now begun for the flight to Detroit.

Tom meets him as promised at Detroit airport, and drives him to the golf course in Jackson, Michigan. It's the middle of November, and Billy has never seen so much snow, and definitely, isn't dressed for the cold. He couldn't believe how cold, cold could actually be. It's a total shock to his Irish system.

They arrive at the clubhouse. Well, it was a golf course with a small non-descript unimpressive looking building which Tom called the clubhouse. People were coming in for dinner, and Tom immediately morphed into the greeter extraordinaire. He chatted to them all as if they were his long lost friends, danced with all the ladies, old, and not so old, making them feel like they were the only person in the world. There was no one Billy's age in sight for miles... Tom was the first and last to leave. He charmed them totally. He was the place, period.

Billy was still awake when Tom came into the small room with two small beds. "Goodnight Billy, sleep well, every bone in my body hurts, see ya in the mornin'." He had spent that day knocking out a wall to increase the kitchen, and then drove to the airport and back, greeted everybody, danced with all the ladies, several times, and then tidied up. He was exhausted.

Tom is gone already when Billy wakes up next morning. He goes down to the kitchen for some breakfast, and he hears all sorts of banging going on in the restaurant. "Mornin' Billy, I'm just knockin' this wall down. 'T'will open up the bar and the restaurant, and it'll make the place look bigger, hand me that hammer there would ya? By the way, the boys are coming over this afternoon to rehearse with you. I figure if we feature you for an hour's cabaret after dinner, it will go down well, then the lads can play a few hours dancin'. You can do Wednesday and Thursday on your own okay?" Tom was one of the most amazing and dynamic people he had ever met so far, and he was true to his word about finding work for Billy.

Every Sunday, he would take off with Billy in search of more work for him. They went to all the Irish pubs in Detroit, Flint, Toledo and Kalamazoo, but nobody was interested in hiring an Irish singer/piano player who didn't know all the rebel songs everybody wanted to hear in an Irish pub.

Finally, they get to Chicago one Sunday night, and once again, go to an Irish pub, on the north side of the city. There's a terrific entertainer on stage from Clare called George Casey. He recognizes Billy from all the publicity he got in the Irish papers in America from Eurovision, and suggests they go to a more sophisticated place out in the southern suburbs called Dooley's.

They take the long drive out to the Southside, and luckily, Pat Dooley, the owner, is there. Tom lays on the blarney about how big a star Billy is back home, and he's going to break any minute into the big time here in America, so he'd be doing himself a huge favor, if he hired Billy now before he gets too big, and then he couldn't possibly afford him. Pat asked the barman to get the piano out of the coatroom, and Billy and a few people wheel it right up to the stage.

The entertainer that night happened to be another terrific character from Galway called Norman Payne. He helps Billy get set up, and then asks the crowd to give it up for Billy Golden, from Cork, who is just over from Ireland. Nearly every Irish born person in the bar that night was from County Mayo, so they weren't that excited about Billy. Apart from the Celtic rock songs, he only knew two Irish songs; *Danny Boy*, and *It's a Long Long Way from Clare to Here*, which wasn't known in America at the time. He sang them and then belted out the *Piano Man*, and a few Elton John songs, followed by the Tchaikovsky piece. Unfortunately, he needed the band to pull off the Irish rock songs, so that was it. The crowd was kind, and gives him a decent applause.

Tom's sales pitch saves the day, and Pat Dooley hires Billy for a two month run beginning in

January. Tom negotiated $1500 a week, plus a trailer Pat used for his musicians, plus fifty percent off anything he ate at the restaurant. Once again, he was on his way.

Norman Payne came up to him during a break. "How'r'ya, Billy from Cork, how many Irish songs d'ya know?"
"I just sang 'em."

"Oh Billy, sure that won't do at all at all. You'll be booed off the stage, if ya don't know the songs they want. Here, you're going to need these." Norman takes a bunch of tiny song books out of his guitar case, with about twenty songs in each book, such as, *Four Green Fields*, *The Wild Colonial Boy*, *The Black Velvet Band*, *Galway Bay*, *Kevin Barry*, *Take Me Home To Mayo* and many more. "When ya come back in January, you'd better know every song, in those books, okay Billeen."

Those song books were one of the greatest gifts Billy ever got, as he was now just about covered when somebody would shout up a request or write it on a piece of paper with a dollar or two tip. Billy learned ten songs a day. He knew most of the melodies, so all he had to do was learn the words. It was a world away from the showband scene, or the Celtic Rock music in Sweden.

Meanwhile back in Jackson Michigan, he was learning to talk to people from the stage. In Ireland all he had to say was "next dance please." Now he introduced the song, say, the *Rose of Tralee*, and he told the story about what the song was all about. This, luckily, was also in the song-books, so his confidence was growing.

Tom's introduction every night made him feel like a million bucks, so by the time he took to the stage, Tom had them all in a trance, with his powerful charisma.

Tom knew that Jackson was too small for Billy to keep playing to the same people every night, and luckily the timing was right to go: Christmas week. Everything dies down entertainment wise, as everybody frantically prepares for Christmas.

Billy happily flew home, and stayed with Meg for one gloriously happy week. The passion flared again, tho' nothing had changed, she was staying, he wasn't. He told her he'd be back in March, as he had nothing planned after the two months in Chicago.

He started in **Dooleys** in early January 1983, and was reasonably ready with all the Irish songs he had learned thanks to Norman. He loved it when the audience was split fifty-fifty: fifty percent American, and fifty percent Irish, as he could do a wide selection of music, form Irish to Country, Broadway to Classical, and he was learning some funny songs that went down well, like *The Oldest Swinger In Town*, and *Whatever You Say Say Nothin'*. Pat appreciated the fact that Billy spent his entire break talking to all the customers, instead of disappearing for his fifteen-minute break. He started writing again after a long time, as he had hustled an old piano from a customer in the restaurant, who was glad to get rid of it, and had it moved into the trailer.

About the third night or so, Pat Dooley came over to Billy when he was taking a break and said, "You know kid, you're doomed for this country okay. You like people, they like you okay. We've gotta' get you legal okay? I'm gonna' make a few calls for you, so be ready when I call you to go downtown okay?" He always followed up his sentences with an "okay," as if he had just declared an order, and you had better jump to attention immediately, or face his wrath. He was the big man, and don't you forget it.

Pat Dooley was a short stocky man, married with kids, who together with his hard working wife, had built up a mini-empire of three successful restaurants in the suburbs of South West Chicago. He could be obnoxious and belittling to customers and staff alike, probably to mask his small man's complex, but his heart was in the right place as

Billy soon discovered. Some people loved him, others loathed him, but he was willing to give new Irish immigrants a break, at a time when there was still a bias against Irish Catholics in Chicago, especially the new ones.

Billy got the call from Pat one morning to get his ass in gear, take $600 with him, and meet him at the restaurant in an hour, as they were going downtown to get his green card. They take the long drive into the city, and go into a fancy law office, where a tiny female Chinese immigration lawyer meets them. She obviously had some cosmetic surgery done to her eyes, as they were all bandaged up, puffy, and almost closed. She's in a lousy mood. Billy thought the surgery mustn't have gone too well, so he kept his mouth shut. As his mother said: "when in doubt, do nothing."

Pat had told Billy to hand over the money as soon as they meet, so he does. He hands over the entire $600. She quickly counts it. "Have you got a high school education?" No "thank you, how are you," or "Welcome to Chicago."

"Yes," say Billy.
"College?"
"Yes."
"What degree?"
"Music."

"Is it equivalent to a bachelor's of music degree here?"

"I don't know," say Billy.

"Okay," she says, "we find out," in her clipped Chinese accent. "Who was your Professor? What is his address? She is writing away furiously. "Mr. Dooley, are you willing to give him three years work?"

"Yes," says Pat.

"Okay," she said, "once we learn that your degree is equivalent to the music degree here, we will have to prove that you are not putting an American out of a job. How do we prove that Mr. Dooley?"

Pat was brilliant. "Well, I need an Irish guy who knows the Gaelic language okay. I need an Irish guy who knows musicians in Ireland who can fit into what we're doing here okay: Irish Pageants and musicals and suchlike okay, and Billy here is the man I need okay?" Billy smiles to himself. The thought of actually having Irish Pageants in **Dooley's**, was a huge stretch, but once again, he keeps his mouth shout

"Very good," she says. "The next thing we must do is put an ad in the paper, advertising this job, and if other people answer the ad, and are equally qualified, are you willing to interview them too?"

"Yes," says Pat.

"Once we start filing, you will not be allowed to leave the country, do you understand Billy?"

He was taken aback. "How long will it take?"

"Six to nine months."

Billy had to make a huge decision right there and then. He figured the sooner he got his green card, he could come and go as he pleased, and not run the gauntlet, entering several times a year illegally, raising suspicions that he was working here, and then possibly not be allowed re-enter America. "Yes," he answered.

He also figured he might get back to Ireland in March before everything was ready to be filed, but he was astonished at how quickly she moved after getting the letter from Billy's Professor telling her the basic Irish bachelor's of music degree was actually only a few credits short of a master's here. She wrote him a letter in February saying she had filed for the green card, and under no circumstances was he to leave the country until he got it.

Chapter 24

Billy hates making this call to Meg, telling her he won't be home for at least another six months. It's made all the worse by the fact that he has to use a public phone box, as he doesn't know anybody well enough to ask them if he could use their phone.

Calling Ireland isn't exactly a local call. Add to the challenge the fact that a six-hour time difference exists, Billy is forced to seriously plan each attempted call. He gathers seven dollars and fifty cents in quarters, makes the call, waits for the operator to say, "Please insert seven dollars and fifty cents." Now he waits and prays that he gets through. Ecstasy fills his heart when he hears her voice. He tells her how much he misses her and Sam, and all the news about the green card, which he feels she doesn't quite understood, and all too soon his three minutes were up.

He treasures her letters, giving him all her news, and the new salon she's opening, her third. He calls her the next week and tries to be as upbeat as he can. "I've met other people who are willing to hire me once I finish in **Dooley's**, but once I've got the green card, I can come and go as I please, and maybe PJ can get me some gigs back home."…

Once again, the fastest three minutes of his life are up. He curses the fact that he can't just sit down and chat to her for an hour. He might just as well be on the moon, as standing out in the freezing cold at a phone booth, in the strip mall near the trailer park. He also senses her frustration, as he knows she's busy, busy, busy.

The months go by very very slowly for Billy. He misses Meg like he's never missed anyone before.

For the first time in his life, he feels he's not in control, and he hates the feeling. He's getting better and better on stage, as he becomes a decent solo entertainer, and people are very kind and generous. But he feels he's caught between a rock and a hard place, knowing his future is here, but his heart is in Ireland. Living alone in the trailer sharpens his loneliness. The frustrating phone calls become more of a hassle: the call doesn't get through, or she's not there, probably at meetings about her new shop.

Suddenly, he receives the news he is waiting for, his lawyer calls to tell him his green card is approved. He reaches Meg, tells her about his great news. He got his green card, and as soon as he has it in his hands, he'll be home to see her and Sam. He notices a change in her voice, just a tiny change, but she was more businesslike than she ever was before to him, kinda' like he was bothering her with his call.

Days turn to weeks and the weeks turn into a month, he has not received his green card. He calls the Immigration Office in Chicago, and they said they had sent it out. If he leaves the country without it, he'll lose all the prep work he has done for the last six months, and he will have to start the process all over again. He's stuck.

Using his best logic, he attempts to explain what was happening via those damned public phone calls to Meg, but they were always way too short, and

Meg was nearly always interrupted by other people while she was talking.

The months fly by and Billy gets more and more work. One evening an audience member approaches him, and tells him about his friend who owns a popular restaurant in Pittsburgh, and would Billy like to do a few shows there? Of course he accepts, and the manager likes what he hears, and asks him to stay. Billy's next two-month Chicago gig was several months away. He didn't have any other option so he moves to Pittsburgh and starts yet another chapter of his American adventure.

The owner of the restaurant was a great man from Listowel in County Kerry, called Tom O' Donoghue, who had made a good life for himself and his family in Pittsburgh. He owned a very established restaurant there called **The Blarney Stone**.

He took a liking to Billy, and thankfully, he booked all the top acts from Ireland at the time at his dinner shows in Pittsburgh; **The Wolfe Tones**, **Hal Roach**, **Frank Patterson** and many others, so he knew all their agents, who in turn hire Billy throughout the east Coast of America.

Pittsburgh was nearer the East Coast than Chicago, for work up and down the huge "Irish/ American corridor." Eventually Billy decides to permanently relocate there. He also likes the city and its people very much. It has hills and valleys just like home, so he doesn't feel as homesick. The only thing missing is the ocean.

Billy never met his cousin in Cleveland who might offer some company. He had made a few friends along the way, but he didn't want to bore the pants off of them with his love troubles by pouring his heart out to them. He remains faithful to Meg all this time, even tho' there had been several tempting situations that he could have had a bit of company and craic with. By now, he has an old station wagon, equipment and a few cassettes for sale. Business was getting better and better. People hear him and start to book him for concerts instead of the much longer, harder, pub scene he was doing up until then. He has his work, but that's only a few hours each day. He travels a lot of miles to his gigs. A spurious idea had come to him, Pittsburgh is home; he went out on a limb and bought a house. He finally has time to write music again. He spends hours each day playing on his new baby-grand piano, writing new songs. Through the darkness of his solitude, a light shone: it was clear more than ever, that his future lay right here in America.

One evening, while on break he tells a friend about his green card mess. The fellow knew someone in immigration in Washington. He called on Billy's behalf the next day, and it transpired that they had posted the card to Billy's address in Chicago. Because Billy moved on to Pittsburgh by then, it had been returned as undeliverable. It was lying in a lost and found green card box in Texas. Within days, Billy has it in his hands, and as soon as the gig is finished in Pittsburgh, he'd be home after a long year's absence.

The longest, most interminable month passes and he flies home. He lands at Dublin airport, hires a car, heads straight to the Burlington Hotel, and checks in. After a quick shower, he eats some breakfast, grabs a bunch of flowers from the hotel shop, and with his heart beating faster than it ever did before, drives over to Meg's shop.

She is shocked to see him, as he didn't tell her when he was coming. She looks as beautiful as ever, tho' a little tired. She is distant and depressingly cold. "Hi Meg, how are ya?"

"Billy, what are you doing here?"

"Well, I finally got my green card, and wanted to see ya."

She seems aggravated and not happy to see him at all. She fusses with some paperwork, as she gathers her thoughts, "Listen, eh,…I've got a meeting that I've gotta' be at, could I meet ya later?"

"Yea sure, I'm staying at the Burlo."
"All right, I'll call ya later."

Billy awkwardly gave her the flowers and he leaves. Uncertainty filled his heart; he's gutted. It was like talking to a stranger. This is it, he felt. It's been over a year since they last met, due to that damned green card screw up, and she's changed. He heard it in her voice and saw it in her body language. It was ages since she wrote her last letter. He had them off by heart. It kept him going through all those lonely months when he first came over.

Meg calls later, and they meet for a coffee in the hotel bar. She gets straight to the point.

"Look Billy, I've had to get on with my life. Sam and I missed you like mad when you left. I understand why you had to leave and all that, but now, that you have your green card, you're not coming back, so even tho' it was hard for both of us, we had to get on with it, and look eh,... I've met somebody, and I like him, and he's here, and you're making a new life for yerself over there."

Billy's whole life explodes. It's like a battering ram has just hit his stomach. He's feels shaky, like all of the blood streaming through his body has just stopped dead in his veins. His heart has just broken in two. He's sure he is dying. He makes every human attempt to hear what her lips are now saying.

"Look Billy, I'm sorry, but you've gotta' get on with your life in America. I will never forget our times together, and what you did for Sam and me, but that was a long time ago, it's in the past. I brought your car over, it's parked behind the hotel, and I packed all your stuff into it." She hands him the keys.

Billy is devastated, hearing his worst fears coming true. He has a house in Pittsburgh. The house could be a home, if she would reconsider and come to America. This was to be their home, Meg, Sam and Billy, together as a family. Meg could expand her business far beyond the circumference of one Dublin neighborhood. Sam could have the best of educational opportunities at his fingertips. If only she would reconsider; if only she would come with him to America. Haunting words pass through his brain "Shite Billy, I know my sister and she'll never go man, I'm sorry." Jack knew, had tried to tell him, but Billy wouldn't, no, couldn't accept that decision so long ago.

He had been focused so much on his work, and his hustle to make sure he had bookings six months down the road, he never thought of being with anybody other than Meg for the rest of his life, but the long absence had killed such a beautiful love story. He loved her more that moment than he ever did, and he had lost her. Now he is faced with the reality of Meg's words…he was alone in his adventure.

They hug awkwardly like strangers, and she leaves. Billy orders a pint, and a shot of whiskey, and shortly after stumbles back to his room exhausted from the flight, and numbed from what just happened.

Chapter 25

Waking from a lousy night's sleep, he tries his best to accept his new reality. First, he returns the rental car to the airport and gets a taxi back to the hotel. He then drives his beloved car down to Cork to visit his parents. The route to his hometown brings him past several of the venues where he and the lads played. Most of them were sadly boarded up, some had been converted into supermarkets. The villages along the way appear sad, tired, and almost as lonely as he is.

He doesn't feel like he belongs here anymore, a stranger in his own land as they say. He has changed in the last eighteen months. It wasn't noticeable at first, but now he realizes he was becoming Americanized. His tastes, work ethic, his comfort level over there, just the way America works. Simple things effected these changes; he could have breakfast at three in the morning if he wanted; he always has a few dollars in his pocket; and, unlike Ireland, he knows there will be more opportunities tomorrow.

The lashing rain added to his gloom; it was probably beautiful back home. Wow, he quickly realizes, I said 'back home.' America is truly my home from now on.

As he parks the car, Nora comes to the doorway. "Oh Mary, mother of God," she utters, rosary beads clasped in her hand as she hugs him tightly. "You're a sight for your ma's old eyes."

She tells him that Finbar is due home for the mid-day meal within minutes. And then she hustles him inside, out of the pouring rain. The family gathers around the table, everyone talking at once, "What's it like in America?" "How much money do ya make?" "How could ya afford to buy a house already, son?" The questions are coming faster than Billy can respond. He eventually regains order at the table and updates all of them on the where, when, why and how of his new life in America. Throughout the boisterous gathering, he can't help but notice that his ma is praying intently on her rosary beads—at once thankful for his return and in full trepidation that he will leave again, all to soon.

He stays a few days in Cork, catches up with his parents, brother and sisters, visits Sean O' Se and Peter in Crosshaven. His old choir invites him to a show in the Opera House, and afterwards he has a great night with them in the backstage bar.

The craic was mighty as always. This is the greatest thing he misses about Ireland, apart from Meg. It's impossible to explain what craic is exactly, to an American, but it's just different, and unique to Irish people. "It's the way we tell it," as one famous comedian put it. But it's also the way we answer "it" as well. Nobody can pull it off like the Irish. When you have to explain the joke, or the harmless slag, it ruins it, so you don't even bother. You start to lose your edge.

It takes him years to "get" the American humor. He couldn't stand Johnny Carson at first. He thought he was way too dry and obtuse. Now he appreciates his comic genius, and all the late night talk show hosts who followed.

Noellie is beside himself as Billy signs over his car to him, 'as repayment for all those years ya had to deal with me as your bunkmate.' Billy changes his ticket, and returns "home" sooner than planned. He enjoys the family gathering and the local craic, but realizes that it's time to get cracking on the remodeling of his new house. It's good therapy for him, and he spends hours playing his new piano, just doodling, and every now and then, wallowing in self-pity. Once again, he buys his pots and pans, and resumes his love of cooking, inviting all his neighbors over for dinner. There were a few people from Ireland living in Pittsburgh who become friends, so he gets his 'Irish fix' every now and then.

In retrospect, Billy considers himself lucky, blessed and honored. His parents brought music into his life. Music is his gift. Talent ignited the gift into a windstorm of adventure. Without his talent and gift, he was enroute to becoming a full-time teacher. This would have been a very difficult route for both Billy and his students. Billy's patience would not have lasted long with young people who now tell their teachers to go f*** themselves in Ireland. With little support from administrators and few alternatives to change behaviors, Billy witnessed friends and relatives burn out in the world of teaching. His personality would have been crushed in this environment.

Curiously, he becomes more Irish the farther and longer he's away from Ireland. Searching through Irish history and the writings of Irish essayists and poets for the first time in his life becomes an obsession. All the great poets and writers that were forced on him back then in school that he hated, now are a joy to read, and make him more and more proud of being Irish. So long ago, yet so near.

In what seems to be the blink of an eye, he realizes that seven years have passed. He is working, organizing gigs, writing and recording new CD's, and travelling about forty thousand miles each year to all the concerts. After a while, all the hotels and restaurants begin to look and taste the same. His house is completely remodeled and is appropriately called home during his infrequent spurts of time spent there.

He misses his mother's home cooked meals terribly. He tries his best to cook a meal exactly like hers, using the exact same ingredients, cooked the exact same way, but try as he may, he can never match that wonderful taste and smell of his mother's gourmet dishes that they all took for granted growing up in Cork.

He misses the song contests, as it was exciting to find out if you qualified or not to get the freebie to another country. There was always something to look forward to. In America, it's profitable, but repetitive. He's very much aware of the worsening economic state of Ireland, so he's very grateful for what he has, but man, he misses the craic.

He starts dating again, nice girls, but he continues to compare them to Meg. And Meg, they are not. This wasn't fair to them, but he couldn't help it.

One special night in Cape May, New Jersey changes his life forever. The gig-of-the-day is a piano bar on the beachfront, where a reasonable group of tourists come and go as he plays his music. A beautiful blonde approaches and asks him to play an Irish song for her mother. This vision of natural beauty is sophisticated, but has no superior vibe at all. She places two dollars in his tip jar. He hates this tradition of tip jars, he feels sort of cheap taking tips, but sometimes he makes over $100 a night. Ireland knew not the practice of tipping. You have a job; you do your job; you get paid. Americans are a different breed of humans. You have a job; you get paid, and if you perform well, you get a tip of extra cash. So what's wrong with that? It pays for his gas money.

He reads the request immediately, hoping to impress her if he knows it. Unfortunately, it's some God-awful song about someone's mother who died, drowned in a lake behind her cottage back in Ireland a few hundred years ago, or something along those lines. He obviously doesn't know the song, but his eyes follow this attractive girl back to her seat. She is about five foot eight, athletic and slim, and looks just as good from the back as she does from the front.

At the break, he approaches her table and returns her two dollars, "Hi, I'm sorry, but I don't know the song." It was a lousy opening line, but it gave him an in. "I'm Billy."

"Hi, I'm Kate and this is my mother Julia." He makes some small talk with her, asks is she Irish?

"I'm Irish, French Canadian, and American Indian," she says. "Well it worked," says Billy.

She smiles her beautiful warm smile, and Billy for once in his life is speechless. He doesn't know what to say, except he has to go back, and do his final set, and excuses himself. During his final set, the crowd starts thinning out, but he notices that Kate and her mother have moved to the bar, and are still there when he finishes.

"May I join you?" he asks, and she smiles. "What brings you to Cape May on a Monday night?"

"Well, I used to come here with my boyfriend. I remembered an Irish guy used to play here, I thought it would be nice for my mother. But when we came in it wasn't him, it was you."

"Well sorry about that," he deadpanned. "I do Mondays and Tuesdays and Ken does the other nights, and I guarantee ya, Ken doesn't know that song either. So,... what's a pretty girl like you doing out with yer mother?"

"Well we live about two hours from here, and I'm giving my mother a little break from looking after my brother."

"Is he sick or somethin'?"

Julia explains in her soft-spoken way: "well he got into a fight at a wedding when he was nineteen, and he's paralyzed from the neck down."

Billy tries to wrap his head around this, "Wow, I'm sorry, when did this happen?"

"Eleven years ago," says Julia.

Billy is astonished. "And you've been looking after him for the last eleven years?"

"Yes she has," says Kate, "in a tiny one bedroom condo, so she deserves a break. My sister is looking after him for a few days."

Billy is very touched. "Wow, what a story, how sad for your brother, and fair play to ya Julia, you're some mother I'll tell ya that. Hey, would ye like to join me here for dinner tomorrow night before I start?"

Kate smiled, "That would be nice thanks."

"So, I'll see ye around seven then." Billy returns to his room, excited about a date for the first time in ages.

The hours of the day pass way too slowly for his liking. Finally, it's time to head to dinner. They meet, as arranged, in Carney's. Kate looks fabulous, tanned and fit. He figures she might be a fitness trainer or somethin'. "So what d'ya do for a few shillings?"

"I beg your pardon?" she says.

"What d'ya do for a living?"

"Oh, I own a hair-dressing shop in Haddon Heights in New Jersey." Billy nearly fell off his chair. Then he nearly had a heart attack when she said, "I'm divorced and have a twelve year old son."

Billy is gobsmacked; déjà vu all over again. Meg and Sam come roaring back into his head. He feels his heart pumping and tries to compose himself. He takes a few deep breaths, looks at Kate, sweet lovely Kate, and suddenly a breath of beautiful sunshine fills his lungs. It's a sensation thankfully opposite to that awful morning so long ago. He's getting to like her more and more. He likes her bluntness, sort of challenging Billy to make the next move…. He asks her if she would like to go for a walk on the beach after his show, and she agrees.

They walk Julia back to her hotel room, after packing away his gear. Not very romantic, but it had to be done, as he was leaving for Pittsburgh first thing next morning. He had to do it then, or wait for the restaurant to open again at midday. They walk out to the rear of the restaurant to put it in his station wagon, his battered old beaten up brown station wagon. The restaurant owner's brand new Jaguar is parked beside it. Kate told him years later, that she was hoping he owned the Jaguar. "Please let it be the Jaguar."….. It wasn't.

They go for a walk on the beach. They walk and talk hand in hand. She is straight up with Billy, which he admires. "I sort of feel funny being here with you, I'm sort of on the outs with my boyfriend, but I'm still with him…"

"Well ya don't strike me as the sort to two-time someone, so I dunno', maybe you are finished with him, except he doesn't know it yet."

She lightens up and starts teasing him, "You know, you're the skinniest, shortest guy I was ever out with."

What the hell, he thinks to himself, she's here with me, so I must be doin' somethin' right, not put off by the slag. "Who do you go out with, football players or somethin'?"

"Well yea, sort of, but you're cute," and she laughs her throaty laugh that Billy loves already. "Well then I s'pose I'd better be nice to ya then."

"Well you scored some brownie points by including my mother for dinner."

He stops, faces her, almost eye to eye, wishing he were six foot thirteen, and kisses her. It's nice, she doesn't pull away…. Suddenly a cop shines his flashlight on them from the boardwalk. "Hey you guys, you can't be on the beach after eleven, all right?"

They walk to the local WaWa store and have a cup of tea, and eventually, he walks her back to her hotel. She gets something out of her car before she goes in. It's a snazzy Nissan 300 Z, Fire Engine Red sports car. Billy casually remarks, "Nice car, my other car is a Z 300 too."…. She was thinkin', "yea right."

He kisses her passionately for what seems like an eternity. "Wow, Billy Golden, what just happened?" He thinks to himself, "you didn't think of Meg the entire time you were with Kate, apart from the shock at dinner." He walks back to his room giddy as a teenager after his first kiss.

A few days later, he sends her a bunch of flowers with a card saying: "See you sometime in Pittsburgh, stranger things have happened, love Billy." She smiles reading the card.

Even tho' he couldn't wait to call her, he waits for about a week. He figures, give her a few days, don't seem too eager. "Hey Kate, it's Billy the Irish leprechaun, remember me?"

"Hi Billy," laughing at his touché about him being the smallest guy she was ever out with, "thanks for the flowers, they're beautiful."

"Ah sure, you're more than welcome, t'was a great night."

"Yeah it was.,... eh,.. I've eh broken up with my boyfriend.".... Billy took the hint, and decided to play all his chips.

"Wow,.... so eh,... look 'em, I'm playing at the Pittsburgh Irish Festival in two weeks time, would ya like to come as my guest?"

"Eh, that sounds good, I've never been there."

"It's a great city, I think you'll like it. Your mother won't be coming with ya now will she?"

She laughs, "Okay, I'll see you then."

Billy is back in Cape May the following Monday, August 31st, 1994. He enjoys breakfast at a particular diner, as most of the service staff are Irish college kids. They're over from Ireland on work visas, and there's always a bit o' craic in the place. As he sits down, a Galway girl blurts out the fabulous news: "The IRA have declared a ceasefire! Isn't it fantastic?" She is nearly gasping for breath, tears welling in her sparkling green eyes.

"My God," thinks Billy, "this could be it; peace in our lifetime, in Northern Ireland. Something we thought could never happen." He is overcome with emotion as the possibilities swirl in his brain: what this might mean for everybody up there, for their kids, for the whole of Ireland. How will the Protestant equivalent react? Will they follow through with their own ceasefire? How will England react?

Obviously he reckons, there had to be a lot of back channels going back and forth with solid commitments offered, before the IRA would do anything like this, so Billy is inclined to believe that this could actually be "it:" The start of the end of the "Troubles."

He finishes breakfast, walks out onto the rocks and sits facing Ireland. As the waves gently crash onto the beach a new, long-awaited song takes form in his head. He gets out a pen and paper:

PEACE IN MY LAND

GREEN IS MY LAND,
WHERE A NEW DAY IS DAWNING
PEACE IN OUR TIME IS A MIRACLE UNFOLDING
GONE ARE THE DAYS OF THE
TEARS OF MY COUNTRY,
PEACE IN MY LAND.

GREEN IS MY LAND,
WHERE THERE'S HOPE FOR TOMORROW
TIME'S HEALING HANDS
WILL END HATRED AND SORROW

GIVE PEACE A CHANCE,
IS THE WORLD'S PRAYER FOR IRELAND
GREEN IS MY LAND

CHORUS
AND WE CAN LIVE TOGETHER, IN PEACE,
LET'S JOIN HAND IN HAND
ONE FOR THE SAKE OF OUR CHILDREN,
ONE FOR THE LOVE OF OUR LAND

SWEET IS THE AIR ROUND
THE GREEN GLENS OF ANTRIM
WILD AND UNTOUCHED IS MY COUNTRY
NOW TRANQUIL
TRUE ARE MY FRIENDS FROM BANTRY TO BELFAST,
GREEN IS MY LAND

CHORUS

WARM ARE THE SMILES OF THE PEOPLE OF DERRY
THE BROAD STREETS OF BELFAST
ARE PEACEFUL AND MERRY
GOD SHED HIS GRACE ON MY HOMELAND
OF IRELAND,
GREEN IS MY LAND, PEACE IN MY LAND

The melody begins to come together in his head, plus he has a seven-hour drive back to Pittsburgh to work on it.

During the ongoing peace talks of the 1990's, England couldn't turn their backs on all their British citizens in Northern Ireland. It was an incredible mix of people from all persuasions trying to find a peaceful, equitable solution.

333

Thankfully with the help of President Clinton, and his tireless and brilliant ambassador, Senator George Mitchell movement began. The tremendous and powerful goodwill of Irish America provided momentum during a very long process. English and Irish Prime Ministers Bertie Ahern, and Tony Blair, as well as Nobel Peace Prize winner John Hume, Fr. Alec Reid, and Jerry Adams, the leader of Sinn Fein were all critical players during this process.

84 years, the majority of the 20th century, had passed since that Easter Rising in Dublin. Finally, in April of 1998, almost four years after the first ceasefire, England, Northern and Southern Ireland signed the peace deal known as the Good Friday Agreement. Thankfully it has lasted.

Holding true to her promise, Kate arrives at the festival as Billy and his band are playing their final set. He spots her, looking as good as he remembered, with her gorgeous friendly open smile. He finishes the song, and announces over the microphone: "Ladies and gentlemen, we have a huge Philadelphia Eagles fan here with us tonight,".... friendly boos from the audience. He looks straight at her and says, "but we hope someday she'll be a fanatical Steelers' fan,".... cheers from the crowd. "So here's a song I just wrote for her," and proceeds to sing a song he wrote a few days after coming home from Cape May.

IF YOU COULD SEE YOURSELF
THRU' MY EYES

OH YOU'D NEVER WANT TO CRY, NEVER DOUBT
YOURSELF INSIDE,
YEA YOU'D NEVER THINK I WOULD EVER GO AWAY
IN A MOMENT ALL YOUR FEARS,
THEY WOULD ALL JUST DISAPPEAR
AND YOU'D REALIZE MY LOVE WILL NEVER
CHANGE

AND YOU'D UNDERSTAND
JUST HOW BEAUTIFUL YOU ARE TONIGHT
IF YOU COULD SEE YOURSELF THRU' MY EYES

YOU WOULD LEARN TO TRUST YOURSELF,
THROW A PENNY IN A WISHING WELL
YOU'D KNOW THAT I'LL BE THERE IF YOU SHOULD
FALL
ALL THE DREAMS THAT YOU STILL KEEP,
YOU'D BEAR THEM ALL TO ME
AND YOU KNOW THAT I WOULD HELP YOU CHASE
THEM ALL
AND YOU'D UNDERSTAND,
JUST HOW BEAUTIFUL YOU ARE TONIGHT
IF YOU COULD SEE YOURSELF THRU' MY EYES

'COS YOU ARE THE ONLY ONE,
WHO SET MY HEART ON FIRE
YOU ARE THE ONLY ONE I WOULD GIVE
MY WHOLE LIFE FOR
AND I'VE NEVER WANTED MORE

AND YOU'D UNDERSTAND,
JUST HOW BEAUTIFUL YOU ARE TONIGHT

IF YOU COULD SEE YOURSELF THRU' MY EYES
IF ONLY YOU COULD SEE YOURSELF THRU' MY
EYES

At the conclusion of the set, he brings her up the famous Pittsburgh Incline, kissing her as they climb. The small antique looking cable cars have been there for what seems like forever. The Fire Engine Red cars served as a quick convenient way for the people who lived on top of the bluffs, known as Mt. Washington, to reach their work along the river valley below. Travelling up and down the steep four hundred feet high hill on train tracks, the iconic cable cars are now a major tourist attraction. They bring people from the happening riverside, shopping, concert tourist attraction known as Station Square in Pittsburgh, up to the top of the hill to enjoy the view.

They walk along Mt. Washington, and he proudly shows her what he thinks is America's finest skyline: Pittsburgh sparkling in all its glory beneath them, with the famous three rivers reflecting all the skyscrapers lights.

They walk to his favorite restaurant overlooking the city. There aren't too many places more romantic in the world than the view stretching out for miles beneath them, and the ambience of the restaurant completes the mood.

They talk about everything and anything. Billy is delighted to see that she's not afraid to express her opinion, and is very capable of arguing her corner. From that very first walk on the beach, she doesn't see Billy as a performer, or any of the star stuff that goes with it. In her eyes, he's an ordinary person with an unusual job. He likes everything about her, and if it were possible, he falls more in love with her during their fabulous first weekend.

The drive back to his home just outside the city takes about a half an hour. Kate follows him home in her car. He turns into the driveway of an old farmhouse he has lovingly restored over the years. Sure enough, she pulls up right beside Billy's fire-engine red 300Z sports car. She smiles to herself. The property is nicely secluded with a creek running thru' it, glistening in the moonlight. Inside, he lights the fireplace, in case the evening should turn cool. They enjoy a glass of wine on the deck, as the soft trickle of the stream below them fills the night. Without a cue, they go upstairs. Opening the door, "This is your room my dear," he escorts her into the master bedroom.

"But I don't want to put you out of your bedroom," she says.

Billy smiles, "no no you're not."

"Oh....."

EPILOGUE

Billy is belting out a Celtic Rock classic at his stepson Johnny's wedding. Everybody is having a ball: bridesmaids, groomsmen, aunts, uncles, and friends, all enjoying the craic at this very Irish-American wedding. Billy is in rare form, singing with his favorite Celtic Rock band he's hired for the wedding. Even tho' he's in his mid-fifties, he can still belt it out with the best of 'em.

He goes over to the bar and orders a pint. A trio of young men, all friends of his son, see him and join him. Joe screams over the music, "Hey Mr. Golden, how are you?"

"Hiya Joe, how'rya doin'? Are ya finished college yet?"

"One more year to go, this is Josh and Brad, they're friend's of Liam. Hey guys, Mr. Golden had a band in Ireland."

Brad shakes his hand, "What sort of stuff did you play?"

Billy points to the band, "That stuff..... BEFORE they called it Paddy Rock, or Celtic Rock or whatever."

"You played that stuff back then? I thought that was new"

"Nah," says Billy proudly, "we were doing it in 1978,…. God it feels like 1878,"….

Billy sees Brad getting a text and smiles, "Yea, way way before texting, cell phones, the internet, credit cards,…. a long time ago."

"So what brought you to America?" asks Josh. Billy smiles wistfully…..

"Have ya got a few hours?"

Just then Billy and Kate's son comes over. "Hey dad, they're coming in, mum wants you to come over."

"Okay Liam, thanks."

He walks over to Kate, putting on his tux jacket, and fumbling with his bow tie, she helps him straighten up.

The band stops and announces: "And now ladies and gentlemen, for the first time, it gives me great pleasure to announce the new Mr. and Mrs. John Jordan." Everybody looks to the door of the function room as Billy's stepson, Johnny and Brook, his beautiful bride, enter to a standing ovation, and are mobbed by their friends.

Kate grabs Billy. "Come on, Mr. Golden, we haven't danced in ages," as she takes him by the hand and gently pulls him towards the dance floor.

"Ah come on Kate, you know how much I hate dancin'."

"Now now Mr. Golden, our first son is married, and I think I deserve at least one dance for all those years." They slow dance, and smile at each other. He looks over at Johnny and Brook. Liam is with them, and they're all having a laugh.

This is, and has been Billy's life for the past sixteen years. He is married to the greatest lady he ever met. Kate says she fell in love with him on the turnpike, having a laugh, arguing about the politics of the day, and hustling the gear in and out of countless places.

Everybody had to get used to their new life: Kate and Johnny moving up to Pittsburgh when they got married; Kate selling her business, and becoming a mom again; Johnny leaving all his high school friends behind in New Jersey, and doing his best to fit into his new life; Billy's crazy lifestyle, away half the year travelling to his shows, and then, the greatest high he ever experienced: being there for the birth of their son Liam, Billy's name in Irish, and the name of his grandfather.

Billy is very moved and whispers, "You know Kate, you did a great job with them."

"No Billy," says Kate lovingly, "WE did a great job with them."

He cups her face in his hands and gently kisses her. "And ya know Kate, I wouldn't change a thing."

Through the years, Billy has done his very best to relieve his dear mother of the stress she experiences with him being so far away. At the close of each phone conversation, as farewells are shared, after visits on either side of 'The Pond,' and in letters which he, Kate and the boys send frequently, the conclusion is always the same: Put Yer Rosary Beads Away Ma, everything is fine!

THE END

Author's Note

The adventures of Billy Golden reflect the era in which I was raised in Ireland. Without a few breaks coming my way over the years, I would most definitely have been a rather unhappy veteran teacher by now. I'm very grateful instead, to have had a lifetime of entertaining, which I still enjoy more than ever to this very day.

We are the music makers,
We are the dreamers of dreams,
Wandering by lonely sea breakers,
And sitting by desolate streams.
World-losers, and world-forsakers,
Upon whom the pale moon gleams;
Yet we are the movers and shakers,
Of the world forever, it seems.

Edgar O' Shaughnessy   1844 - 1881